KT-174-679

The Contract

MELANIE MORELAND

The Contract
Copyright © 2016 Melanie Moreland
Registration # 1129457
ISBN # 978-0-9936198-6-1
All rights reserved

Published by Enchanted Publications

PUBLICATIONS

Edited by:
D. Beck

Interior design & formatting by:
Christine Borgford, Perfectly Publishable

Cover design by:
Melissa Ringuette, Monark Design Services

All rights reserved. No part of this book may be reproduced or transmitted in any form or by any means, electronic or mechanical, including photocopying, recording, or by any information storage and retrieval system, without permission in writing from the copyright owner.

This book is a work of fiction. The characters, events, and places portrayed in this book are products of the author's imagination and are either fictitious or are used fictitiously. Any similarity to real persons, living or dead, is purely coincidental and not intended by the author.

Deborah Beck, my friend and editor.
This one is for you.
Thank you.

And, as always,
To my Matthew—my reason for everything.

One

RICHARD

I BENT OVER the table, the din of the busy restaurant fading into the background as I struggled to contain my anger. Repressing the urge to yell, I kept my voice low, fury dripping from the words. "What did you say? I'm sure I didn't hear you correctly."

David relaxed back in his chair, not at all concerned by my ire. "I said, Tyler is being promoted to partner."

My hand tightened around my glass so hard, I was surprised it didn't shatter. "That was supposed to be my promotion."

He shrugged. "Things changed."

"I worked my ass off. I brought in over nine million. You told me if I surpassed last year, I'd be made partner."

He waved his hand. "And Tyler brought in twelve million."

I slammed my hand on the table, not giving a shit if it drew attention to us. "That's because the bastard went behind my back and stole the client. The campaign idea was mine. He fucking ripped me off!"

"Your word against his, Richard."

"Bullshit. This is all *bullshit*."

"The decision is made, and the offer has been extended. Put in the effort, and maybe next year will be your year."

"That's it?"

"That's it. You'll get a generous bonus."

A bonus.

I didn't want another fucking bonus. I wanted that promotion. It should have been mine.

I stood up so fast my chair toppled back, hitting the floor with a loud thud. I drew myself up to my full 6'4" height and scowled down at him. Given the fact that David didn't break the 5'8" mark, sitting, he looked rather small.

David raised his eyebrow. "Careful, Richard. Remember, at Anderson Inc., we're all about teamwork. You're still part of the team—an important one."

I regarded him steadily, tamping down the desire to tell him to go fuck himself. "The team. *Right*."

Shaking my head, I walked away.

I STRODE INTO my office, slamming the door behind me. My assistant looked up, startled, a half-eaten sandwich in her hand.

"What did I fucking tell you about eating at your desk?" I snapped.

She scrambled to her feet. "Y–you were out," she stuttered. "I was working on your expenses. I thought . . ."

"Well, whatever you thought was fucking wrong." Reaching across her desk, I plucked the offending sandwich from her hand, grimacing at the concoction. "Peanut butter and jam? Is that the best you can do on what they pay you?" I cursed as the jam dripped on the edge of my jacket. "Goddamnit!"

Her already pale face blanched further as she looked at the red smear on my gray suit. "Mr. VanRyan, I'm so sorry. I'll take it to the cleaners right away."

"Damn right you will. Get me a sandwich while you're out."

She blinked. "I–I thought you went to lunch?"

"Once again, your thought process is incorrect. Get me a sandwich, and a latte—extra foam—no fat. I want Brian Maxwell on the phone—*now*." Impatiently, I yanked off my jacket, making sure the pockets were empty. "Take this to the cleaners—I want it back this afternoon."

She sat stock-still, gawking at me.

"Are you deaf?"

"Which would you like done first?"

I flung down my jacket. "That's your fucking job. Figure it out and get it done!"

I slammed my office door.

FIFTEEN MINUTES LATER, I had my sandwich and latte. My intercom buzzed. "I have Mr. Maxwell on line two for you."

"Fine." I picked up the phone. "Brian. I need to meet with you. Today."

"I'm fine. Thanks for asking, Richard."

"Not in the mood. When are you available?"

"I'm booked all afternoon."

"Cancel."

"I'm not even in the city. The earliest I can be there is seven."

"Fine. Meet me at Finlay's. My usual table." I hung up, punching the intercom. "Get in here."

The door opened, and she tripped in—literally. I didn't even bother to hide the fact I rolled my eyes in disgust. I had never met anyone as clumsy as her—she tripped over air. I swore she spent more time on her knees than most of the women I dated. I waited until she struggled to her feet, picked up her notebook, and found her pen. Her face was flushed, and her hand shook.

"Yes, Mr. VanRyan?"

"My table at Finlay's. Seven o'clock. Book it. My jacket better be back on time."

"I asked for rush service. It, ah, there was an extra charge."

I raised my eyebrows. "I'm sure you were happy to pay it, considering it was your fault."

Her face darkened even more, but she didn't argue with me. "I'll pick it up in an hour."

I waved my hand; I didn't care when she retrieved it, as long as it was in my possession before I left.

"Mr. VanRyan?"

"What?"

"I have to leave today at four. I have an appointment. I sent you an email about it last week?"

I tapped my fingers on my desk as I observed her. My assistant—Katharine Elliott—the bane of my existence. I'd done everything I could to get rid of her, but I'd never had any luck. No matter what task I gave her, she completed it. Every demeaning chore she handled without complaint. Pick up my dry cleaning? Done. Make sure my private washroom was stocked with my favorite brands of toiletries and condoms? Without fail. Alphabetize and clean my massive CD collection after I decided to bring them into the office? Completed—she even boxed up every CD when I "changed my mind" and had them delivered back home, spotless and in order. Not a word passed her lips. Send flowers and a brush off message to whomever I had dumped that month or week? Yep.

She was at the office every day without fail—never late. She rarely left the office unless it was to do an errand for me or scuttle to the break room to eat one of her ridiculous brought-from-home sandwiches since I forbade her to eat at her desk. She kept my calendar and contacts in precise order, my files done in the exact color-coding I liked, and screened my calls, making sure my many exes didn't bother me. Through the grapevine, I knew everyone liked her, she never forgot anyone's birthday, and made the most delicious cookies, which she shared on occasion. She was fucking perfection.

I couldn't stand her.

She was everything I despised in a woman. Small and delicate, with dark hair and blue eyes, she dressed in simple suits and skirts—neat, tidy, and completely dowdy. Her hair was always twisted into a knot, she wore no jewelry, and from what I observed, no makeup. She had zero appeal and not enough self-respect to do anything about it. Meek and timid, she was easy to roll over. She never stuck up for herself, took whatever I dished out at her, and never responded negatively. I liked my women strong and vibrant—not a doormat like Miss Elliott.

However, I was stuck with her.

"Fine. Don't make it a habit, Miss Elliott."

For a second, I thought I saw her eyes flare, but she simply nodded. "I'll pick up your jacket and leave it in your closet. Your two o'clock teleconference is set and you have a three-thirty in the boardroom." She indicated the files on the corner of my desk. "Your notes are all there."

"My expenses?"

"I'll finish them and leave for your signature."

"All right. You can go."

She paused at the door. "Have a good evening, Mr. VanRyan."

I didn't bother to reply.

Two

RICHARD

BRIAN SIPPED HIS rye, regarding me over the edge of the glass. "I agree that must burn, Richard. But what do you want me to do about it?"

"I want another job. That's what you do. Find me one."

He laughed dryly, setting down his glass. "We've had this discussion already. With your credentials, I can get you any job you want—except here. There're two major players in Victoria, and you work for one of them. If you're finally ready to move, give me the word. I'll have offers for you in any major city you want to consider. Toronto is booming."

I huffed in annoyance. "I don't want to move. I like Victoria."

"Is there something holding you here?"

I drummed my fingers on the table as I pondered his question. I had no idea why I refused to move. I liked the city. I liked its proximity to the water, the restaurants and theatres, the bustle of a big town in a small city and especially the climate. There was something else—something I couldn't put my finger on that held me here. I knew I could relocate; in fact, it was undoubtedly the best thing to do, but that wasn't what I wanted.

"No, nothing tangible. I want to stay here. Why can't I get a job at The Gavin Group? They'd be fucking lucky to have me. My portfolio speaks for itself."

Brian cleared his throat, tapping his glass with his manicured fingernail. "As does your personality."

"Blunt and in charge works in the advertising industry, Brian."

"That's not exactly what I'm referring to, Richard."

"What exactly are you fucking referring to then?"

Brian signaled for more drinks, and sat back, adjusting his tie before he spoke. "Your reputation and name speak for themselves. You know you're known as 'The Dick' in many circles." He lifted one shoulder. "For obvious reasons."

I shrugged. I didn't care what people called me.

"The Gavin Group is a family-run company. Unlike Anderson, they operate the company on two fundamental principles: family and integrity. They're extremely particular when it comes to their client base."

I snorted. Anderson Inc. would work for anyone. As long as there was money to make, they'd create a campaign—no matter how distasteful it was to some consumers. I knew this, and I didn't care much one way or another. I knew The Gavin Group was far more discriminating in regards to clients, but I could work within those boundaries. David hated The Gavin Group—to leave Anderson Inc. and work there would piss him off so thoroughly he'd offer me a partnership to come back. He might even offer it on the spot when he discovered I was leaving. I had to make this happen.

"I can hold back and work within their parameters."

"It's not only that."

I waited until the waiter withdrew after delivering our fresh drinks. I studied Brian briefly. His bald head gleamed under the lights, and his light blue eyes twinkled. He was relaxed and at ease with himself, not at all worried over my dilemma. He stretched his long legs, leisurely crossed them, swinging one as he picked up his glass.

"What else?"

"Graham Gavin is a family man and he runs his business the same way. He only hires people of the same mindset. Your, ah, personal life isn't what he'd consider acceptable."

I waved my hand, knowing exactly to what he was referring. "I dumped Erica a few months ago."

My ex-whatever, made headlines with her drug problem when she walked off the runway in a narcotic-induced high during a fashion show. I was tired of her high-maintenance attitude, anyway. I had Miss Elliott send flowers to rehab with a note saying we were done, and then I blocked her number. Last week, when she tried to see me, I had security escort her out of the building—or, rather, I had Miss Elliott take care of that task. She actually looked sorry for Erica when she went downstairs, returning a short time later to assure me Erica would not bother me again. Good riddance.

"It's not only Erica, Richard. Your reputation is well known. You're a playboy outside business hours and a tyrant during the day. You've earned your nickname. Neither sits well with Graham Gavin."

"Consider me a changed man."

Brian laughed. "Richard, you don't get it. Graham's company is family-oriented. My girlfriend, Amy, works there. I know how they operate. I've never seen a company like it."

"Tell me."

"His entire family is involved with the operation. His wife and children, even their spouses work there. They have picnics and dinners for their staff and their families. They pay well; they treat them well. Their clients love them. Getting hired there is difficult since it's rare anyone leaves."

I mulled over what he said. It wasn't a secret how important family was at The Gavin Group, or how little turnover the company had in personnel. David hated Graham Gavin and everything he stood for in the business world. To him it was a dog-eat-dog world, and that was how he played. The bloodier, the better. We had lost two major accounts to Gavin recently, and David had been furious. Heads rolled that day—many of them. I was lucky they hadn't been my accounts.

"So, I'm shit out of luck."

He hesitated, glanced at me, then looked over my shoulder. "I do know one of their top executives is leaving."

I leaned forward, interested at that piece of news. "Why?"

"His wife was ill. Her prognosis is good, but he's decided to make a change for their family, and stay home."

"It's a temporary position?"

Brian shook his head. "This is the sort of man Graham Gavin is. He's giving him early retirement with full pension and benefits. He told him once his wife recovers, he'll send them on a cruise to celebrate."

"How do you know this?"

"Amy is his assistant."

"He needs replacing, then. Get me an interview."

"Richard, have you not been listening to a word I said? Graham won't hire someone like you."

"He will if I can convince him I'm not what he thinks."

"And how are you going to do that?"

"Get me the interview and I'll figure out that part." I took a long sip of my scotch. "This has to be done under the radar, Brian."

"I know. I'll see what I can do, but I'm telling you—this will be hard to sell."

"There's a generous finder's fee if you get me in."

"Is it worth it to prove to David you'll leave? You want the partnership that much?"

I ran my hand across my chin thoughtfully, scratching at the scuff. "I've changed my mind."

"What do you mean?"

"David hates Graham. Nothing would anger him more than losing me to him. I know a few of my clients would jump ship too, which would add insult to injury. I'm going to get Graham Gavin to hire me and when David tries to get me back, it'll be my turn to say 'things changed' to him."

"You're rather confident."

"I told you—that's what makes it in this business."

"I'm not sure how you plan to accomplish it, but I'll see if I can get you in." He pursed his lips. "I went to school with his son-in-law, and we still golf together. We're supposed to get together for a round next week. I'll feel him out about it."

I nodded, my mind going a thousand miles an hour.

How did one convince a stranger they weren't what they seemed?

That was the million-dollar question.

I only had to figure out the answer.

Three

RICHARD

THE NEXT MORNING, I had an idea, but I wasn't sure how to execute it. If Graham Gavin wanted a family man, he'd get one. I only had to figure out how to accomplish that small detail. I could do it—it was my field of expertise, after all—I was an idea man.

My main problem was the sort of women I typically had in my life. Female versions of myself. Beautiful to look at, but cold, calculating, and not interested in anything except what I could give them: the fancy dinners, expensive gifts, and if they lasted long enough, a trip away somewhere before I dumped them. Because I always did. I only cared about what they could give me, as well. All I wanted was something pretty to look at and a warm body to bury myself in at the end of the evening. A few hours of mindless pleasure until the stark, cold reality of my life set back in.

None of them would be the sort of woman Graham Gavin would believe I'd spend the rest of my life with. Sometimes I could barely spend an entire evening.

Miss Elliott knocked timidly, waiting until I shouted for her to come in. She entered, carefully carrying my coffee, setting it on my desk. "Mr. Anderson has called a staff meeting in the boardroom in ten minutes."

"Where's my bagel?"

"I thought you'd rather have it after the meeting since you'd be rushed. You hate eating too fast. It gives you heartburn."

I glowered at her, hating the fact she was right.

"Stop thinking, Miss Elliott. I already told you, you get it wrong more often than you get it right."

She glanced at her watch—a simple black one with a plain face, no doubt bought at Walmart or some other common store. "There're seven minutes until the meeting. Do you want me to go get your bagel? By the time it's toasted, you'll have two minutes to wolf it down."

I stood, grabbing my mug. "No. Thanks to you, I'll be hungry in the meeting. If I make a mistake, it's on you."

I stormed out of my office.

DAVID TAPPED THE glass-topped table. "Your attention. I have some good news and some bad. I'll start with the good. I'm pleased to announce the appointment of Tyler Hunter to the role of partner."

I schooled my face, keeping it blank. I could feel the sidelong glances, and I refused to let anyone know how pissed off I was with the situation. Instead, to mess with them, I rapped the glass with my knuckles. "Good on you, Tyler. Best of luck."

The room was silent. Internally, I smirked. I could act like a decent person. It didn't change the fact I loathed the deceitful bastard or resented David for doing this to me.

David cleared his throat. "So, the bad news. As of today, Alan Summers is no longer with the company."

My eyebrows shot up. Alan was one of the heavy-hitters at Anderson Inc. I couldn't keep my mouth shut. "Why?"

David shot me a look. "I beg your pardon?"

"Why is he gone? Did he leave on his own?"

"No. He . . ." David curled his lips in a twisted grimace. "It was brought to my attention he was seeing one of the assistants." He glowered. "You know there is a strict policy about dating within the company. Let this be a lesson to all of you."

Anderson Inc. was firm on their rules. You followed them, or you were gone. They'd figuratively rip off your balls, leaving you floundering. Fraternizing within the company was a stringent no-no.

David believed romance in the office clouded your mind. Anything that took your focus off work or his bottom line, he frowned upon. I assumed he was against his employees having any sort of life outside Anderson Inc. Glancing around the table; I realized every executive was either single or divorced. I had never noticed, or cared about the marital status of my co-workers.

"On a side note, Emily has left us, as well."

It didn't take a genius to know which assistant Alan had been seeing. Emily was his PA. What an idiot. You never got involved with someone at work, especially your PA. Luckily, I wasn't even remotely tempted.

David droned on a bit, and I tuned him out, going back to my own problem. When others started to stand, I jumped to my feet, leaving the boardroom, not wanting the see all the handshakes and slaps on the back Tyler would receive.

Fucker.

I strode into my office; stopping at the sight of Brian perched on the edge of Miss Elliott's desk, his wide shoulders shaking with laughter. They both looked up when I came in, two very different expressions on their faces: Brian looked amused and Miss Elliott looked guilty.

"What are you doing here?" I demanded. I turned to Miss Elliott. "Why didn't you let me know someone was waiting?"

Brian held up his hand. "I got here a few minutes ago, Richard. Katy offered me coffee, and to let you know I was here, but I was enjoying her company far more than I ever do yours, so I wasn't in a hurry." He winked at me. "She is more entertaining, not to mention prettier than you. I always like spending time with her."

Pretty and entertaining? Miss Elliott? And what was this Katy shit?

I barked out a laugh at those descriptions.

"In my office," I ordered.

He followed me in, and I shut the door. "What are you doing here? If David saw you . . ."

He shook his head. "Relax. It's not as if I've never been here before today. And what if he does see me and suspects something? Make him sweat a little."

I paused. Maybe it wasn't such a bad idea. He knew Brian was the biggest headhunter in Victoria. Maybe if he saw Brian wander around Anderson Inc. it would make him a little nervous.

"Lay off charming my assistant. It's a waste of time, and I thought you had a girlfriend."

"I do, and I wasn't charming her. She's great. I enjoy talking to Katy."

I snorted. "Yeah, she's great—if you like doormats who masquerade as emaciated scarecrows."

Brian frowned. "You don't like her? Really? What's not to like?"

"She's fucking perfect," I stated, my sarcasm thick. "She does everything I tell her. Now, drop the subject and tell me why you're here."

He lowered his voice. "I had coffee with Adrian Davis this morning."

I crossed the office and sat down at my desk. "Adrian Davis of The Gavin Group?"

He nodded. "I was visiting Amy, and I went to see him to arrange our round of golf next week. He's agreed to talk to Graham about interviewing you."

I thumped the top of the desk with my fist. "*Fucking* great news. What did you tell him?"

"I said you were leaving for personal reasons. I told him, despite the rumors, your situation had changed and you were no longer comfortable with the direction of Anderson Inc."

"My situation?"

"I told him your playboy days were behind you, and the way you conduct business had evolved. I informed him you wanted a different sort of life."

"He believed you?"

Brian smoothed the crease of his pants with his fingertips, meeting my gaze. "He did."

"Did you tell him what caused this miraculous turnabout?"

"You sort of suggested it yourself last night. I said you fell in love."

I nodded. It was exactly what I was thinking. Graham liked the family atmosphere, and I would have to fit in.

Brian regarded me shrewdly. "Given your *history*, Richard, this woman will have to be vastly different from the women you've been linked with, especially recently." He tilted his head. "Someone more down-to-earth, warm, and caring. Real."

"I know."

"Is it really worth it?"

"Yes."

"You'll lie and pretend, all because of a job?"

"It's more than a job. David screwed me over—so did Tyler. It's not the first time. I'm not taking this shit anymore." I reclined in my chair, staring out the window. "I may be hired under less than honest intentions, but Graham will get a fucking great addition to his company. I'll work my ass off for him."

"And the woman?"

"We break up. It happens."

"Any ideas who the lucky lady is going to be?"

I shook my head. "I'll figure it out."

There was a knock and Miss Elliott entered, placing a bagel and fresh coffee on my desk. "Mr. Maxwell, can I get you another cup of coffee?"

He shook his head, smiling at her. "I told you, it's Brian. Thanks, Katy, but no. I have to get going, and your boss here has a huge project to work on."

She turned to me, her eyes wide. "Is there something I need to do, Mr. VanRyan? Can I help in some way?"

"Absolutely not. There is *nothing* I need from you."

Her cheeks flushed, and her head dropped. She nodded, exiting the office, closing the door behind her.

"God, you're an ass," Brian observed. "You're so rude to her."

I shrugged, unrepentant.

He rose from his chair, buttoning his jacket. "You need to watch your attitude to have a chance for your plan to work, Richard." He indicated in the direction of the door. "That pretty girl is the exact sort of person you need to interact with Graham."

I ignored the *pretty* remark, gaping at him. "Interact?"

He smirked. "Do you really think he's going to accept a name and a brief introduction? I told you how involved he is with his staff. If he decides to hire you, he is going to want to meet your lady—more than once."

I hadn't thought that far ahead. I thought I could get someone I knew to pose for an evening, but Brian was right. I would need to keep up the façade for a while—at least until I proved my worth to Graham.

He hesitated at the door. "I assume Miss Elliott isn't married."

"That should be obvious."

He shook his head. "You're blind, Richard. Your solution is right in front of you."

"What are you talking about?"

"You're a smart man. Figure it out."

He departed, leaving the door open behind him. I heard him say something that made Miss Elliott laugh, the sound unusual coming from her area. I grabbed my bagel, tearing off a bite with more force than necessary.

What the hell was he suggesting?

A niggling thought began to grow, and I glanced at the door.

He couldn't be serious.

I groaned, dropping my bagel on my plate, my appetite gone.

He was totally serious.

Fuck my life.

Four

RICHARD

THE NOISE OF the treadmill was a steady hum under my feet as I pounded away. I had hardly slept last night, and my mood was dark. Sweat dripped down my back and face. I picked up my towel and wiped it away roughly, tossing it to the side. My iPod blared with heavy music, and still it wasn't loud enough, so I turned it up, glad the condo was soundproofed.

I kept going, almost at a frantic pace. I had gone over all my options and plans in the dark of the night, coming up with two ideas.

My first thought had been if Brian and Adrian got me in, I could try to bluff my way through an interview, telling Graham only vague details of the woman who supposedly changed my outlook and therefore, me. If I approached it right, I could manage to keep up a façade until I had proven myself to Graham, then have the unspeakable happen—this perfect woman leaves me. I could play heartbroken, and throw myself into work.

Except from what Brian had explained, my idea probably wouldn't work.

It meant I needed to produce a physical woman—one who would convince Graham I was a better man than he believed me to be. Someone, as Brian put it, "real, warm, and down-to-earth."

I didn't know many women who would fall in those categories, unless they were over sixty. I didn't think Graham would believe I could fall in love with someone twice my age. None of the women I fraternized with would be able to pass his inspection. I rolled around the idea of hiring someone—an actress perhaps—but that seemed too risky.

Brian's words kept repeating themselves in my head. *"You're blind, Richard. Your solution is right in front of you."*

Miss Elliott.

He thought I should use Miss Elliott as my girlfriend.

If I took a step back and tried to be objective—he had a point. It was the perfect cover. If Graham thought I was leaving Anderson Inc. because I was in love with my assistant and chose her—and our relationship—over my job there, it would score major points with him. She was unlike any other woman I had ever been with. Brian found her warm, bright, and engaging. Other people seemed to like her. All pluses.

Except, it was *Miss Elliott*.

With a groan, I shut off the machine, grabbing my discarded towel. In the kitchen, I got a bottle of water, chugged it down, and turned on my laptop. Signing into the company site, I scrolled through the employee files, stopping on Miss Elliott's page. I studied her photograph, trying to be unbiased.

There was nothing remarkable about her, but her bright blue eyes were wide with long lashes. I imagined her dark hair was long since I had never seen it done in any other way aside from a tight bun. Her skin was very pale; I wondered how she would look under the skillful hands of a makeup artist and dressed in some decent clothes. Squinting at the screen, I stared at her picture. Some sleep wouldn't hurt to rid her of the dark circles under her eyes and maybe eating something other than peanut butter and jam sandwiches would help. She was rail thin. I liked my women with a few more curves.

I groaned in frustration, rubbing the back of my neck.

I supposed, in this case, it didn't matter what I preferred. It was what I *needed*.

In this case, I might have to admit I needed Miss Elliott.

Goddamn my life.

My phone rang, and I glanced at the screen, surprised to see Brian's name.

"Hey."

"Sorry if I woke you up."

I glanced at the clock, seeing it was only six-thirty. I was surprised he was awake, though. I knew he was a late riser.

"I've been up a while. What's going on?"

"Graham will see you today at eleven."

I stood up, feeling a flow of nerves ripple down my spine. "Are you serious? Why so fast?"

"He's away for the remainder of the week, and I told Adrian you were considering accepting a job interview in Toronto."

I chuckled. "I owe you."

"Big. So big you'll never be able to repay me." He chortled. "You know there's a good chance this will go nowhere unless you can convince him things are different for you, right? I laid it on pretty thick with Adrian—but my word is only going to take you so far."

"I know."

"Okay. Good luck. Let me know what happens."

"I will."

Hanging up, I checked my schedule, smirking when I realized Miss Elliott had updated it last night. I had a breakfast meeting at eight, which meant I'd be back in the office by ten or so. I decided not to go into the office. I had an idea how to introduce my so-called girlfriend into my interview.

I dialed Miss Elliott's number. She answered after a few rings, mumbling her sleepy greeting.

"Mmmm . . . ello?"

"Miss Elliott."

"What?"

I sucked in a deep breath, trying to be patient. It was obvious I had woken her. I tried again.

"Miss Elliott, it's Mr. VanRyan."

Her voice was raspy and confused. "Mr. VanRyan?"

I sighed heavily. "Yes."

I could hear a lot of movement, and I had the mental image of her scrambling to a sitting position, looking rumpled.

She cleared her throat. "Is, ah, there a problem, Mr. VanRyan?"

"I won't be in the office until after lunch."

There was silence.

"I have a personal matter to take care of."

Her voice was dry when she spoke. "You could have texted me . . . sir."

"I need you to do two things for me." I kept going, ignoring the somewhat sarcastic edge to her voice. "If David comes in and asks where I am, tell him I'm on a personal matter and you have no idea where. Is that clear?"

"Crystal."

"I need you to call me at eleven-fifteen. *Exactly.*"

"Did you want me to say anything or just breathe heavily?"

I pulled the phone away from my ear, surprised at her tone. It would seem my PA wasn't pleased at being woken early. She was being far mouthier than usual, and I wasn't sure what to make of it.

"I need you to tell me my four o'clock appointment has been switched to three."

"That's it?"

"Yes. Now repeat what I just told you."

She made a strange sound, somewhat like a grumble, which made me smirk. Miss Elliott appeared to have a bit of a backbone if the circumstances were right. However, I wanted to make sure she was awake enough to remember my instructions.

"I'm to tell David you are on a personal errand and I have no idea where. I will call you at *exactly* eleven-fifteen and tell you your four o'clock has been switched to three."

"Good. Don't screw it up."

"But Mr. VanRyan, it doesn't make any sense, why would—"

Not bothering to listen anymore, I hung up.

Five

RICHARD

THE BUILDING HOUSING The Gavin Group was a polar opposite to that of Anderson Inc. Unlike the vast skyscraper of steel and glass I worked from daily, this building was brick, only four stories high, and surrounded by trees. I parked my car after checking in with the guard at the entrance, who smiled pleasantly and handed me a guest pass. Entering the building, another security guard greeted me and let me know Graham Gavin's office was located on the top floor, then wished me a good day.

Minutes later, a secretary led me to a boardroom, handed me a fresh cup of coffee, and told me Graham would be with me momentarily. I took the time to absorb the details of the room around me, again struck by the difference between the two companies.

Anderson Inc. was all about flash. The offices and boardroom were all state of the art—white and black was the predominant palette. Even the artwork was monochrome with lots of metal everywhere. Hard, modern chairs, thick glass-topped tables and desks, blond hardwood on the floor—all cold and remote. If this room was any indication, I wasn't in Kansas anymore. The walls were lined with warm oak paneling, there was an oval wood boardroom table surrounded by plush leather chairs, and deep, soft carpeting underfoot. An open area to the right housed an efficient kitchen. The walls showcased many of their successful campaigns, all framed and displayed tastefully. Various awards lined the shelves.

At one end of the room was an idea board. There were scribbles and ideas sketched out on it. I stepped closer, studying the images, quickly absorbing the structure of the campaign they were outlining for a brand of footwear. It was all wrong.

A deep voice brought me out of my musings.

"From the look on your face, I'd say you don't like the concept."

My gaze met the somewhat amused expression of Graham Gavin. We had encountered each other at industry functions a few times, always polite and distant—a professional shake of hands and brief acknowledgment being the only interaction. He was tall and confident, with a headful of silver hair that gleamed under the lights.

Up close, the warmth in his green eyes and the low timbre of his voice struck me. I wondered if the idea board had been left on purpose—a test of sorts.

I shrugged. "It's a good concept, but not new. A family using the same product? It's been done."

He perched his hip on the edge of the table, crossing his arms. "Done, but successful. The client is Kenner Shoes. They want to appeal to more than one demographic."

I nodded. "What if you did that, but only featured one person?"

"I'd like to hear more."

I pointed to the image of the family, tapping my finger on the youngest child. "Start here. Focus on him. The very first purchase of their product—shoes bought by his parents. Follow him as he grows, highlighting some pertinent points in his life wearing them—first steps, first day of school, hiking with friends, playing sports, on dates, graduation, marriage . . ." My voice trailed off.

Graham was quiet for a moment, then started to nod. "The product stays with you as you grow."

"It's a constant. You change—it doesn't. Yours for life."

"Brilliant," he praised.

For some reason, his compliment made my chest warm, and I ducked my head at the strange sensation. He pushed off the table, holding out his hand. "Graham Gavin."

I took his hand, noting the firmness of his grip. "Richard VanRyan."

"I'm impressed already."

Before I could reply, my phone buzzed. Right on time. "I'm sorry." I glanced at the screen, hoping I looked sheepish. "I need to take this. I apologize."

"No problem, Richard." He smiled. "I need coffee."

I turned away as I answered. "Katharine," I murmured, pitching my voice low.

For a moment, there was silence, then she spoke. "Mr. VanRyan?"

"Yes." I chuckled, knowing I had confused the fuck out of her. I didn't think I had ever called her anything besides Miss Elliott, and certainly never in a voice like the one I had just used.

"Um, you asked me to call and tell you your four o'clock was changed to three?"

"Three o'clock now?" I repeated.

"Yes?"

"Okay, I'll adjust. Is everything all right there?"

She sounded shocked when she replied. "Mr. VanRyan, are *you* all right?"

"Of course, I am." I couldn't resist teasing her more. "Why?"

"You sound, ah, different."

"Stop worrying," I soothed, knowing Graham was listening. "Everything is fine."

"David was looking for you."

"What did you tell him?"

"Exactly what you instructed me to say. He . . ."

"What? What happened?"

"He's on a bit of a tear this morning."

"David's always on a tear. Take an early lunch and lock the office door. I'll deal with him when I return," I instructed as I smirked into the phone, injecting a concerned tone to my voice.

Bewilderment led to bravery for her. "Lock the office and take an *early* lunch? Are you *drunk?*"

That did it. I burst out laughing at her words. "Just do it, Katharine. Stay safe, and I'll see you when I get back." I hung up, still smiling, and turned around to face Graham. "My assistant," I explained.

He regarded me with a knowing look. "I think I know why you're looking to leave Anderson Inc."

I returned his look with a small shrug.

I had him.

�✿

"TELL ME ABOUT yourself."

I grimaced at his question. "I think you know a lot about me already, Graham. At least you know *of* me."

He nodded, taking a sip of his coffee. "Your reputation does precede you."

I bent forward, hoping to appear earnest. "People change."

"And you have?"

"What I want in life and how I get it has, yes. Therefore, the person I was, no longer exists."

"Falling in love does that to a person."

"So I'm discovering."

"Anderson Inc. has a strict policy about interpersonal relationships."

I snorted. "David doesn't like his staff to have relationships inside or outside the office. It detracts from business, he thinks."

"And you disagree?"

"I think you can do both—with the right person."

"And you found that person?"

"Yes."

"Your assistant."

I swallowed hard, only able to nod.

"Tell me about her."

Shit. When it came to business, I could talk forever. Strategies, angles, concepts, visualizations—I could go on for hours. I rarely spoke on a personal level about myself, so what could I possibly say about a woman I barely knew, and didn't like. I had no idea. I swallowed again and glanced at the table, running my fingers over the smooth surface.

"She's the biggest klutz I've ever met," I blurted out—that much was at least true.

He frowned at my tone, and I was quick to cover my mistake.

"I hate it when she hurts herself," I explained in a softer voice.

"Of course." He nodded.

"She's, ah, she's perfect."

He laughed. "We all think that of the women we love."

I searched my brain, making a mental list of the things I knew about her. "Her name is Katharine. Most people call her Katy, but I like to use her whole name."

It wasn't really a lie. I called her Miss Elliott all the time.

He nodded. "Such a lovely name. I'm sure she likes to hear you say it."

I smirked, remembering her reaction earlier. "I think it confounds her."

He waited as I mulled over my next words. "She's tiny and unobtrusive. Her eyes are like the ocean—so blue they're fathomless. Everyone adores her at the office. She bakes cookies for people—they love them." I wavered, trying to think of more. "She hates to be woken any earlier than necessary. Her voice gets all growly, which makes me laugh."

He smiled encouragingly.

"She keeps me in line—she's an amazing assistant and I'd be lost without her." I sighed, unsure what else I could add. "She's undoubtedly too good for me," I admitted, knowing deep down it was true. I was certain I was the bad person in this scenario, especially given what I was doing currently.

"Do you want to bring her onboard with you?"

"No!" I exclaimed. This was my chance to get rid of her.

"I don't understand."

"She, ah, we want to start a family. I'd rather have her at home, and have someone else at work. I want her to have the chance to relax and enjoy life for a while—without working."

"She isn't enjoying it now?"

"It's difficult, given the situation, and she works too hard," I added, hoping that sounded right. "She's looked tired the past while. I want her to sleep as much as she wants."

"You want to look after her."

We were getting into dangerous territory. I had no idea how to respond; I had never wanted to take care of anyone, except myself. Nevertheless, I nodded in agreement.

"You live together, I assume? I imagine it's the only time you can relax and be a couple."

Shit. I hadn't even thought of that.

"Ah, we, yeah . . . we value our private time."

"You don't like to discuss your personal life."

I smiled ruefully. "No. I'm used to keeping it all in."

That, at least, wasn't a lie.

"We're a unique operation here at The Gavin Group—on many levels."

"Something I'm looking forward to."

He indicated to the board. "We believe in teamwork, here and in our personal lives. We work on the campaigns as a group, feeding off each other, much like you and I did a few moments ago. We share in the triumphs and the disasters." He winked. "Not that we've had many of those. I value every employee I have."

"It's an interesting way of doing things."

"It works for us."

"Obviously. Your name is well respected."

Our eyes met. I kept my expression open, level, and I hoped, sincere.

He rested back in his chair. "Tell me more about your idea."

I relaxed back, as well. That was easy—far easier than talking about Katharine Elliott.

AN HOUR LATER, Graham stood up. "I'm away until Friday. I'd like to extend an invitation to attend a barbeque my wife and I are having on Saturday. I'd like you to meet her and a few other people."

I knew what that meant. "I'd enjoy that, sir. Thank you."

"With Katharine, of course."

I kept my face impassive as I grasped his extended hand. "She'll love it."

BACK AT THE office, Miss Elliott was at her desk when I arrived. Although she was on the phone, I felt her eyes watching me as I crossed her path. No doubt, she was waiting for my wrath to descend on her for whatever infraction I chose to pick out today. Instead, I nodded and kept walking to my desk, flipping through the messages, and the small pile of documents waiting for my approval. Feeling oddly disinterested, I stood up, looking out at the skyline and the city below; its bustle and noise muted by the glass and height from the street. The view and sound would be much different at The Gavin Group.

Everything would be different.

Often, by the time I finished any sort of meeting with David, I was a mass of nerve endings, pulsating and anxious. He knew how to push the buttons of every person who worked for him; how to say and do exactly what he needed to get what he wanted—be it positive or negative. Until this very moment, I hadn't realized that. Meeting with Graham, even though I was on edge, given the premise I was meeting him under, I was still calm.

In my research of his company, and of the man himself, I had read over and again of his kindness and generosity of spirit. In fact, other than David's low opinion of Graham, I hadn't read or heard another unkind remark. Sitting with him, discussing the concepts in my mind for the footwear campaign, I had felt an enthusiasm that had been lacking for a long time. I felt creative again, energized. Graham listened, truly listened, encouraging my thought process with positive reinforcement, and adding ideas of his own. To my surprise, I liked his concept of teamwork. I wondered what it would be like not to be involved in the daily cutthroat world of Anderson Inc. How it would feel to work *with* people instead of against them. Would it make for a better life? An easier one—of that fact I was certain. Yet, I felt it would be no less challenging.

All I knew was, by the time our meeting ended, my reasons for wanting to work for him were no longer all about revenge. I wanted to feel that enthusiasm—to be proud of the campaigns I created. It was an unexpected situation, yet not unpleasant.

My door slammed and I turned, frowning, my thoughts interrupted.

"David." I regarded him pointedly. "Good thing I wasn't with a client."

"Katy told me you were free. She buzzed you, but you didn't answer."

I had been so deep in thought I hadn't heard the intercom. That was a first.

"What can I do for you?"

He drew back his shoulders, preparing for an argument. "Where were you this morning? I was looking for you, and you weren't answering your phone, or returning my messages."

"I was on a personal appointment."

"Your assistant said it was a doctor's appointment."

I knew he was lying. One thing Miss Elliott was good at was keeping my secrets. I called his bluff. "Why she would say such a thing, I have no idea. I didn't tell Miss Elliott where I would be. As I said, it was personal."

He scowled at me, but dropped it. He walked around a bit, patting his comb-over; a gesture of his I knew well. He was going in for the kill. He pivoted to face me. "Why was Brian Maxwell here the other day?"

I shrugged, moving to sit at my desk so he wouldn't see my smirk. Now, I understood what this was all about.

"Brian and I are friends. We were setting up a round of golf."

"He couldn't do that over the phone?"

"He was in the neighborhood. He likes to flirt with Miss Elliott, and he dropped by in person. Is there a problem?"

"What are you up to?"

I lifted my hands in supplication. "I'm up to nothing, David, except a round of golf and a couple hours outside the office. Dock me if you want." I picked up the stack of documents. "I think if you checked though, you'd see I have a lot of unused vacation time—take the two hours out of there."

"I'm watching you," he warned, turning on his heel, and storming out. The door slammed so hard the windows rattled.

I grinned at the door. "Watch away, David. Watch me walk away."

I stretched over the desk, and punched the intercom button.

Miss Elliott answered, sounding more cautious than usual. "Mr. VanRyan?"

"I need a coffee, Miss Elliott."

"Anything else, sir?"

"A few moments of your time."

She drew in a stuttering breath. "Right away."

I turned my chair back toward the window, and heaved a sigh. I couldn't believe what I was about to do.

I hoped I wouldn't fail. God help me—either way.

Six

KATHARINE

"I DON'T UNDERSTAND," I murmured into the phone, trying to remain calm. "I didn't receive any other notice about this increase."

"I know, Miss Elliott. We only received the instructions two days ago, which is why I'm calling to inform you of the change."

I swallowed the lump in my throat. Four hundred dollars more a month. I needed to pay four hundred dollars more.

"Did you hear me, Miss Elliott?"

"I'm sorry—could you repeat what you said?"

"I said the new fee structure begins as of the first."

I glanced at the calendar. That was two weeks away.

"Is this even legal?"

The woman on the phone sighed in understanding. "It's a privately run home, Miss Elliott. One of the best in the city, but they also make their own rules. There are other places where you could see about moving your aunt—ones that are government run with fees set in place."

"No," I insisted. "I don't want to do that. She's so well cared-for and settled."

"The staff is the best. There are other rooms, semi-private ones you could move her into."

I rubbed my head in frustration. Those rooms didn't have a garden view—or a space for Penny's easels and art books. She would be so unhappy and lost. I had to keep her in her private room, no matter what.

Mr. VanRyan walked in the office, staring at me. I hesitated before saying anything else, unsure if he would stop, but he kept walking, entered his office, and shut the door with a quiet click behind him. He didn't acknowledge me, not that he ever did, unless it was to yell or curse, so I could only assume the strange call he had me make had been acceptable.

"Miss Elliott?"

"I apologize. I'm at work, and my boss came in."

"Do you have any other questions?"

I wanted to scream at her and say, *"Yes! How the hell am I supposed to come up with another four hundred dollars to give you?"* but I knew it was useless. She worked in the accounting department; she didn't make the decisions.

"Not at the moment."

"You have our number."

"Yes, thank you." I hung up. They certainly had *my* number.

I stared at my desk, my mind going a mile a minute. They paid me well here at Anderson Inc.—I was one of the highest salaried PAs because I worked for Mr. VanRyan. He was horrible to work for—his dislike of me obvious. However, I did it because it made me extra money, which all went to care for Penny Johnson.

I traced my finger along the worn edge of the blotter I kept on my desk. I already lived in the cheapest place I could find. I cut my own hair, bought my clothes at second-hand stores, and my diet consisted of ramen noodles and a lot of cheap peanut butter and jam. I splurged on nothing, using every opportunity to save a little. Coffee was free in the office, and there were always muffins and cookies around. The company paid for my cell phone, and in the warm weather, I walked to and from work, to save the bus fare. Every so often, I used the kitchen at the home to bake cookies with the residents and brought some in to work to share. It was my silent way to make up for the goodies I snagged. If an unexpected expense arose, there were days those cookies and muffins were all I could afford to eat. I checked to see if there were any in the break room before I left at night that I could put in the small freezer in my apartment.

I blinked away the tears that were building. How was I going to come up with another four hundred dollars a month? I already lived from paycheck to paycheck. I knew I couldn't ask for a raise. I would have to get a second job, which meant I would have less time to spend with Penny.

The outer door opened and David came in, his face like thunder.

"Is he in yet?"

"Yes."

"Is he with someone?"

"No, sir." I picked up the phone, surprised when Mr. VanRyan didn't answer my buzz.

"Where was he?" he demanded.

"As I told you this morning, he didn't tell me. He said it was personal, so it wasn't my place to ask."

He scowled at me, his beady eyes almost disappearing. "This is my company, young lady. Everything that happens here is my business. Next time you ask. Understand?"

I bit my tongue so I wouldn't tell him to go fuck himself. Instead, I nodded, relieved when he marched past me and slammed into Mr. VanRyan's office.

I sighed. That door was slammed so often I had to get maintenance to rehang it almost every month. A few minutes later, David slammed back out, cursing under his breath. I watched him leave, an anxious sensation building in my stomach. If he was in a bad mood, it meant Mr. VanRyan would be in a bad mood. That meant only one thing: soon he'd be yelling at me for whatever mistake he thought I'd made today.

I hung my head. I hated my life. I hated being a PA. I especially hated being a PA for Mr. VanRyan. I had never known anyone so cruel. Nothing I did was ever enough—certainly not enough to warrant a thank you or a grudging smile. In fact, I was certain he had never smiled at me the entire year I'd worked for him. I could remember the day David summoned me to his office.

"Katy,"—he looked hard at me—*"as you know, Lee Stevens is leaving. I am going to reassign you to another account rep—Richard VanRyan."*

"Oh." *I had heard horror stories of Richard VanRyan and his temper, and I was nervous. He went through PAs quickly. However, reassignment was better than no job. I had finally found a place for Penny where she was happy, and I didn't want to take her out of it.*

"The pay rate is higher than what you're making now and that of the other PAs." *He quoted me a figure that seemed enormous, but the amount meant I could give Penny her own room.*

Surely, Mr. VanRyan couldn't be that bad.

How wrong I had been. He made my life hell, and I took it—because I had no other choice.

Not yet.

My intercom buzzed, and I steadied my nerves. "Mr. VanRyan?"

"I need a coffee, Miss Elliott."

"Anything else, sir?"

"A few moments of your time."

I shut my eyes, wondering what was about to happen. "Right away."

CARRYING HIS COFFEE, I approached his office with trepidation. I knocked, entering only when he bade me to come in. I had made that mistake once and would never do it again. His biting remarks had stung for days over that infraction.

I made sure my hand didn't shake as I placed his coffee in front of him and readied my notebook, waiting on his instructions.

"Sit down, Miss Elliott."

My heart began to hammer. Had he finally convinced David to let him fire me? I knew he'd been trying since the first week I worked for him. I tried to keep my breathing even. I couldn't lose this job. I needed it.

I sat down before my legs could give out and cleared my throat. "Is there a problem, Mr. VanRyan?"

He waved his finger in the space between us. "What we discuss in this office, I trust it remains confidential?"

"Yes, sir."

He nodded and reached for his mug, sipping the beverage in silence.

"I need to speak with you on a personal matter."

I was confused. He never spoke to me about anything unless it was to shout out his demands.

"All right?"

He glanced around, looking uncharacteristically nervous. I took a moment to study him as he gathered his thoughts. He was ridiculously handsome. Well over six feet tall, his shoulders were broad, his waist trim—he was the poster child for how to make a suit look good. He was clean-shaven most of the time; although on occasion, like today, his jaw bore a day or two's growth, which highlighted his strong profile. He kept his light brown hair short on the sides, but longer on top, and had a cowlick, causing one patch to fall over his forehead. An imperfection, which only made him more perfect. He yanked on it when he was agitated, which was how he acted at this moment. His mouth was wide, his teeth bright white, and his lips were so full I knew many women envied them. His hazel eyes lifted to mine, and he straightened his shoulders, once again in control.

"I need to ask something of you. In doing so, I will be placing a huge amount of trust in your discretion. I need to know you will honor my trust."

I blinked at him. He wanted to ask me something? He wasn't firing me? A small shudder of relief flowed through me; my body relaxed a little.

"Of course, sir. Whatever I can do."

His eyes locked on mine. I had never noticed how the colors swirled in his eyes under the lights—a mixture of gray, green, and blue. Often they were so dark with anger, I never held his gaze for more than a second or two. He seemed to study me for a moment, then nodded.

He reached for one of his cards and wrote something on the back, handing it to me.

"I need you to come to this address this evening. Can you be there at seven?"

I glanced at the card, noting the address wasn't far from the home where I would visit Penny after work. To get there by seven, however, my stay would have to be short.

"Is there a problem?" he asked, his voice void of the usual hostility.

I lifted my gaze to his and decided to be honest. "I have an appointment after work. I'm not sure I can make it for seven."

I expected his ire. For him to sweep his hand in the air, and demand I cancel whatever plans I had and be where he needed me to be at seven. I was shocked when he only shrugged.

"Seven-thirty? Eight? Can you work with that?"

"Seven-thirty would be doable."

"Fine. I'll see you at seven-thirty." He rose to his feet, indicating this strange meeting was over. "I'll make sure my doorman knows you'll be arriving. He'll send you up right away."

It was all I could do not to gasp. *His doorman?* He was asking me to his home?

I stood up, disconcerted. "Mr. VanRyan, is everything all right?"

He regarded me with a strange look on his face. "With your cooperation, it will be, Miss Elliott." He glanced at his watch. "Now, excuse me, I have a one o'clock meeting to attend."

He picked up his mug. "Thank you for the coffee and your time."

He left me staring after him, wondering if I had entered an alternate universe.

Never once in the year I worked for him had he ever said thank you to me.

What the hell was going on?

Seven

KATHARINE

I STOOD ACROSS the street from Mr. VanRyan's building, staring up at the tall structure. It was intimidating and spoke of wealth—all tinted glass and concrete looming over the city, reminding me of the man who lived within it. Cold, remote, unreachable. I shivered a little as I looked at it, wondering why I was there.

The building was about a ten-minute walk from the home, and I was on time. It hadn't been a good visit with Penny today; she had been upset and agitated, refusing to eat or talk to me, and I ended up leaving early. I was disappointed. She had been good all week, and I had hoped today would be the same; that I'd be able to talk with her as we used to, but it hadn't happened. Instead, it just added to my stressful, odd day. I left the home feeling despondent, and unsure as to why I was going to see Mr. VanRyan.

Mr. VanRyan.

He had already confused me asking me to his home this evening. His behavior the rest of the afternoon proved to be equally bizarre. When he returned from his meeting, he asked me for another coffee and a sandwich.

Asked me!

He didn't demand, he didn't sneer or slam his door. Instead, he stopped in front of my desk and politely requested lunch. He even said thank you. Again. He hadn't come out of his office the rest of the day until he left, when he stopped, asking if I had his card. At my murmured,

"Yes," he nodded his thanks and left, not slamming the door.

I was beyond puzzled, nerves taut, and my stomach in knots. I had no idea what I was doing at his home, much less why.

I inhaled a calming breath. There was only one way to find out. I straightened my shoulders, and crossed the street.

Mr. VanRyan opened his door, and I tried not to stare. I had never seen him look this casual. Gone was the tailored suit and crisp white shirt he favored. In its place, he wore a long-sleeved, thermal shirt and jeans, and his feet were bare. For some reason, I wanted to giggle at his long toes, but I tamped down the odd reaction. He indicated for me to come in, stepped back, allowing me to pass. He took my coat, and we stood staring at each other. I'd never seen him look uncomfortable. He gripped the back of his neck, clearing his throat.

"I'm eating dinner. Would you join me?"

"I'm fine," I lied. I was starving.

He grimaced. "I doubt that."

"I beg your pardon?"

"You're too skinny. You need to eat more."

Before I could say anything, he grasped my elbow and led me to the high counter separating the kitchen from the living space. "Sit," he ordered, pointing to the high, padded stools.

Knowing better than to argue with him, I did. As he moved into the kitchen, I looked around at the enormous, open space. Dark wood floors, two large, chocolate brown leather sofas, and white walls highlighted the vastness of the room. The walls were undecorated, aside from a massive TV hung over the fireplace—no personal photos or knickknacks. Even the furniture was bare—no cushions or throw blanket anywhere. Despite its grandeur, the room was cold, impersonal. Like the set of a magazine spread, it was well appointed and pristine, with nothing giving a clue about the man who lived in it. I glimpsed a long hallway and a set of elegant stairs that I assumed led to the bedrooms. I turned back to the kitchen—it was similar in style and impression, dark and light combined, and void of personal touches.

I repressed a shiver.

Mr. VanRyan set a plate in front of me, and with a smirk, opened the lid on a pizza box. I felt a smile tug on my lips.

"This is dinner?"

Somehow, it seemed too *normal* for him. I hadn't had a slice of pizza in ages; my mouth watered looking at it.

He shrugged. "I usually eat out, but I felt like pizza tonight." He lifted out a slice and slid it on my plate. "Eat."

Too hungry to argue, I ate in silence, keeping my eyes on my plate, hoping my nerves wouldn't get the best of me. He ate steadily, devouring the rest of the pizza, aside from a second slice he put on my plate. I didn't object to it or the glass of wine he pushed in my direction. Instead, I sipped it, enjoying the smoothness of the deep red merlot. It had been a long time since I had tasted such a good wine.

When we finished our strange meal, he stood, discarding the pizza box, returning fast. He picked up his wine, drained his glass, and paced for a few minutes.

Finally, he stood in front of me. "Miss Elliott, I will reiterate from earlier today. What I'm about to share with you is personal."

I nodded, unsure what to say.

He tilted his head to the side and studied me; I had no doubt he found me lacking in every way. Still, he continued.

"I'm leaving Anderson Inc."

My jaw dropped. Why would he leave the company? He was one of David's golden boys—he could do no wrong. David bragged about Mr. VanRyan's talent and what he brought to the company all the time.

"Why?"

"I was passed up for partner."

"Maybe next time . . ." I stopped talking when I realized what this meant. If he left and they chose not to reassign me, I was out of a job. Even if they did reassign me, I would be taking a pay cut. Either way, I was screwed. I could feel the blood draining from my face.

Mr. VanRyan held up his hand. "There won't be a next time. I have an opportunity I'm exploring."

"Why are you telling me this?" I managed to ask.

"I need your help with this opportunity."

I swallowed. "My help?" I was even more confused. He never

wanted my personal help.

He stepped closer. "I want to hire you, Miss Elliott."

My mind raced. I was sure, if he moved on, he would want a clean break. He didn't even like me. I cleared my throat. "As your assistant at your new opportunity?"

"No." He paused, as if thinking about his words, then spoke. "As my fiancée."

All I could do was to stare at him, unmoving.

RICHARD

MISS ELLIOTT GAPED at me, motionless. Slowly, she slid off the stool, facing me, her gaze flitting around the room. "Do you think this is funny?" she hissed, her voice shaking. "I'm not sure what kind of a prank this is, Mr. VanRyan, but I assure you, it's *not* amusing."

She marched past me, grabbing her coat and purse from the sofa, whirling back around. "Are you taping this so you can watch it later? Laugh over it?" A tear slid down her cheek and she brushed it away, the movement jerky and angry. "Isn't it enough you treat me like shit during the day, now you want to have fun after hours, as well?"

She stormed toward the door, and I recovered from the shock of her angry outburst quick enough to rush forward and prevent her from leaving. I leaned over her, pushing the door shut.

"Miss Elliott . . . *Katharine* . . . please. I assure you, it's no joke. Hear me out." She was so close I could feel her body trembling. I had thought about her reactions but hadn't considered anger. "Please," I coaxed again. "Listen to what I have to say."

Her shoulders sagged and she nodded, allowing me to draw her away from the door and over to the sofa. I sat down opposite her and indicated she should, as well. She did warily, and it took all I had not to snap at her and tell her not to look like a frightened rabbit. What did she think I was going to do to her?

Her words echoed in my head. *"Isn't it enough you treat me like shit during the day, now you want to have fun after hours, as well?"*

I shifted a little in my chair—I supposed I deserved her wariness.

I cleared my throat. "As I said, I'm planning on leaving Anderson Inc. The company I'm hoping to move on to is vastly different from the way David runs his company. They value their employees—to them family and integrity are paramount."

Her brow furrowed, but she didn't say anything.

"In order to even get my foot in the door, I had to convince them I wasn't the person they think I am."

"Which is?"

"Arrogant, selfish." I sucked in a long breath. "A tyrant at work and a playboy after hours."

She tilted her head; her voice was quiet and firm. "Pardon my bluntness, Mr. VanRyan—you are *exactly* that."

"I'm aware." I stood and paced a little. "I'm also good at my job and tired of being shit on by David." I sat back down. "I felt something talking to Graham—something I haven't felt in a long time: excitement at the thought of a new campaign. Inspired."

She gaped at me. "Graham Gavin? You want to go work for The Gavin Group?"

"Yes."

"They rarely hire."

"There is an opening. I want it."

"I still don't understand where I come in."

"Graham Gavin will not hire someone unless he feels they fit in with the image he has: family first." I leaned forward. "I had to convince him I'm not the playboy he heard about. I told him I'm leaving Anderson Inc. because I fell in love and want a different way of life."

"With who?"

I reclined against the cushions. "You."

Her eyes widened to the point of hilarity, her mouth opened and closed, with no sound coming out. Finally she spoke. "Why–why would you do that?"

"It was pointed out to me that you were the exact kind of person to convince Graham Gavin I had changed. When I thought about it, I realized that person was right."

She shook her head. "You don't even like me." She swallowed. "I'm not overly fond of you, either."

I had to chuckle at her politeness. "We can work around that issue."

"What are you proposing?"

"Simple. One way or another, I'm out of Anderson Inc. You'll have to leave, too."

Immediately, she began shaking her head furiously. "I can't afford to leave, Mr. VanRyan. So my answer is no."

I held up my hand. "Hear me out. I will pay you to do this. You will have to give up your job, as well as your apartment and come live here with me. I'll pay you a salary plus all your expenses for however long this takes."

"Why would I have to live here?"

"I may have indicated to Graham we live together."

"You did *what*?"

"It made sense when he asked. I didn't plan it—it happened. Now back to my offer."

"What would you expect me to do?"

I tapped my fingers on the arm of the sofa, contemplating. I should have thought this through more.

"Live here, appear at any function I go to as my fiancée, present yourself as such at all times." I shrugged. "I haven't thought it all through yet, Miss Elliott. We'll have to figure it out. Set some ground rules; get to know each other so we can actually pass as a couple." I shifted forward, resting my arms on my thighs. "And this has to happen fast. I'm supposed to take you to a function this weekend."

"This weekend?" she squeaked out.

"Yes. You don't have to be living here by then, but we need to get our stories straight and at least know the basics. We have to seem close—comfortable with each other."

"Maybe you should start by not calling me Miss Elliott."

I laughed dryly. "I suppose it would seem odd . . . Katharine."

She didn't say anything, dropping her gaze to her lap, her fingers playing with a loose thread on her shirt.

"I'll buy you a new wardrobe, and make sure you have spending money. You won't want for anything if you agree to this arrangement."

She lifted her chin. I had never noticed the stubborn little cleft in it until now. "What would you pay me?"

"I'll give you ten thousand dollars a month. If the charade lasts longer than six months, I'll double it." I smirked. "If we do have to get married, I'll pay you a bonus. When we can divorce, I'll make sure you get a good settlement and handle all the details. You'll be set for life."

"*Married?*"

"I have no idea how much time it will take to convince Graham so my cover isn't blown. It could be two months or three. I can't see it being more than six. If I think it's needed, I'll marry you at city hall and we'll end it when we can."

She clasped her hands, her pale face now a ghostly white. Indecision and shock etched all over her expression.

"Chances are," I spoke in a quiet voice, "even if I don't go to The Gavin Group, when I leave Anderson Inc., David will fire you anyway. If I do get the job there, he will for sure. He'll be convinced you knew of my plans somehow. I know how his mind works."

"Why can't you get someone else?"

"I don't know anyone else. The kind of women I usually date won't . . . They aren't the right fit."

"And I am? Why?"

"You want me to be honest?"

"Yes."

"You're practical, sensible . . . plain. I have to admit there's a warmth about you people seem drawn to. I don't see it myself, but it's obviously there. The fact you're my assistant is the perfect cover for me leaving. I could never date you and stay at Anderson Inc. Not that I ever would under normal circumstances."

Hurt flashed across her face, and I shrugged.

"You said to be honest."

She didn't respond to my statement, except to say, "I'm not sure how you expect to pull this off when you dislike me so much."

"Katharine, do you think I like most of the people I work with— or the clients I deal with? I don't. Most of them I can't stand. I smile and joke, shake hands and act as though I'm interested. I'll treat our *relationship* the same way. It's business. I can do that." I paused and lifted my chin. "Can you?"

She didn't speak, and I kept going.

"All of this rides on you. I've placed a great deal of trust in you right now. You could run to David tomorrow, or even Graham, and blow this entire idea for me—but I hope you won't. Think about the money and what it could do for you. A few months of your time, for what I'll pay you, is more than you'll make all year. In fact, I'll guarantee you sixty grand. Six months. Even if we part ways after three. It has to be twice what you make in a year."

"And all I have to do is . . ."

". . . is act as though you love me."

She fixed me with a look, which said everything she didn't want to express. "Do I get this in writing?"

"Yes. We'll both sign a confidentiality agreement. I'll pay you twenty grand up front. You'll get the rest at the end of each month. In addition, I'll open an account for you to use for expenses. Clothes, any incidentals; that sort of thing. I expect you to dress the part, as well as act it."

She studied me for a moment. "I need to think about this."

"You can't think long. If you agree, you need clothes for Saturday, and we need to spend some time together getting to know each other."

"If I don't agree?"

"I'll tell Graham you're ill and can't make it. Then hope he gives me a chance to prove myself and hires me regardless."

"And if not?"

"I'll leave Victoria, but I don't want to. I want to stay here, and I'm asking you to help me."

She stood up. "I have to go."

I rose to my feet, looking down—she barely reached my chest. "I need your answer soon."

"I know."

"Where are you parked?"

She blinked at me. "I don't have a car, Mr. VanRyan. I walked here."

"It's too late for you to be out on your own. I'll get Henry to call you a cab."

"I can't afford a cab."

"I'll pay for it," I huffed. "I don't want you walking. Can you drive? Do you know how?"

"Yes, I just can't afford to own a car."

"I'll get you one. If you agree to do this arrangement, I'll buy you a car. You can keep it. Think of it as a signing bonus."

She bit her lip, shaking her head. "I don't know what to think about any of this."

"Think of it as an opportunity. A lucrative one." I flashed a grin. "A deal with the devil, if you want."

She only arched her eyebrow. "Good night, Mr. VanRyan."

"Richard."

"What?"

"If I can't call you Miss Elliott, you can't call me Mr. VanRyan, either. My name is Richard. You'll have to get used to saying it."

"Maybe I'll call you something else entirely."

I could imagine what she called me to herself. I could think of several names that would be appropriate.

"We'll speak in the morning."

With a nod, she left. I called down to Henry, telling him to get her a cab and put it on my account. I got myself a scotch and sat down on the sofa, frustrated. Earlier, when I spoke, I made the snap decision to make Miss Elliott my fiancée rather than merely my girlfriend. It made my decision to leave Anderson Inc. all that more solid. It showed I was serious and ready for real commitment—something I felt Graham would value. It didn't matter to me one way or another—girlfriend or fiancée—but to someone like Graham, it would. Girlfriend said temporary, replaceable. Fiancée implied permanency and trust. I was certain he would react favorably to that title.

I yanked on my cowlick in apprehension, and downed the scotch in one swallow. I had hoped to get an answer from her right away; however, it became apparent I wasn't going to get it. So now, Miss Elliott, the woman I disliked, and from all accounts, felt the same way about me, held my future in her hands. It was an odd feeling.

I didn't like it.

I sank into the cushion of the sofa as my head fell back, my mind drifting. My phone beeping startled me, and I realized I'd nodded off. I picked up the phone, glancing at the two words on the screen.

I accept.

With a smirk, I tossed my phone on the table.

My plan was full steam ahead.

Eight

RICHARD

THE NEXT MORNING, we both acted as if nothing was different. Miss Elliott brought in my coffee and bagel, carefully placing them on my desk. She went over my schedule, confirming two meetings I had outside the office.

"I won't be back this afternoon."

She looked puzzled, checking her notebook. "You don't have anything in your schedule."

"I made the appointment myself. Personal business. I'll go straight to my two o'clock afterward. In fact, I won't be back this afternoon. Take the time off."

"Pardon me?"

I sighed. "Miss Elliott, can you not understand English? Take the afternoon off."

"But . . ."

I pinned her with a glare. "Take the afternoon off." I lowered my voice. "My place at seven, okay?"

"Okay," she breathed out.

"If you need anything—business related—text me. Otherwise, it needs to wait."

She nodded. "I understand."

It was common knowledge Anderson Inc. monitored emails. Not one to take chances, I had my own cellphone, to which only a select few had the number. I knew there was no point asking Miss Elliott if she had one, as money seemed limited. I planned to rectify that today, along with my other errands. I didn't want to take the chance David had texts and calls monitored, as well.

"You can go." I dismissed her.

She hesitated before withdrawing an envelope from her thick notepad, and placed it on the desk. She left without a word, closing the door behind her. I took a bite of my bagel, then reached for the envelope and opened it, removing the folded papers. It was a list about her. Things she thought I should know: pertinent dates, her favorite colors, music, foods, general likes and dislikes.

It was a good idea. It would save some monotonous conversation tonight. I would write up one for her, later.

I refolded the list and slid it into my jacket pocket. I'd be sitting in waiting rooms on and off all day—it would give me something to keep me busy.

MISS ELLIOTT WAS punctual, arriving at seven o'clock. I opened my door, letting her enter, took her coat, and hung it up—the whole time silent. There was such stiffness, a formality to our interactions, which I knew had to change. Problem was, I didn't know how to make it happen.

I escorted her to the counter by the kitchen and handed her a glass of wine. "I ordered Chinese."

"You didn't have to."

"Believe me, you don't want me cooking. You wouldn't survive." I chuckled. "I'm not sure the kitchen would survive."

"I like to cook," she offered, a small smile curling her lips.

That was as good a place to start as any. I sat down, dragging a file toward me. "I had a contract drawn up this afternoon. You should read it."

"Okay."

"I made you a list, much like yours. You can go over it and we need to talk about what's on it. Make sure we're both comfortable with the facts."

She nodded and took the proffered envelope.

I pushed another smaller one toward her. "Your first payment."

She waited, her fingers not touching the innocent-looking envelope.

"Take it. It's all documented."

Still, she didn't touch it.

"Miss Elliott, unless you take it, we can't go forward."

She looked at me, frowning.

I nudged the envelope. "It's a job, Katharine. This is your compensation. Simple. Take it."

Finally, she picked it up, not even looking at it.

"I want you to resign tomorrow. Effective immediately."

"Why?"

"If this happens, and I think it will, I'll give my notice fast. I want you out of there before the shit hits the fan."

She worried the inside of her cheek, jittery and silent.

"What?" I snapped, getting impatient with her demeanor.

"What if it doesn't work? Will you . . . will you give me a letter of reference? I'll have to get another job."

"I've got that covered. I spoke with some contacts, just in general, and if this doesn't work, and I leave Victoria, I have two companies I know will offer you a job. You won't have to worry about looking, if you don't want. In answer to your question, though, I will give you a glowing letter of recommendation."

"Even though you think I'm a lousy assistant?"

"I've never said you were a lousy assistant. You are, in fact, good at your job."

"You could have fooled me."

A knock at the door saved my reply. I rose to my feet. "Dinner is here. Read the contract—it's very simple. We can discuss it and other things after we eat."

When she opened her mouth to protest, I slammed my hand on the counter. "Stop arguing with me, Katharine. We're having dinner, and you're going to eat. Then we'll talk." I spun on my heel and headed to the door, exasperated. Why was she so against accepting a simple meal? She was going to have to get used to accepting many things for this to work. I slipped my hand in my pocket, encountering the small box I had hidden away. If she was unsure of dinner, she was going to hate what I had in store for her after.

DINNER WAS QUIET. She read the contract and asked a few questions, which I answered. She vacillated when I handed her a pen, but signed the documents, watching as I did the same.

"I have two copies. One for each of us. I'll keep them in the condo safe, for which I'll give you the combination."

"Does your lawyer have a copy?"

"No. This is an arrangement between us. He knows about it, but he is bound by client confidentiality. We have the only two copies. Once this is over, we can destroy them. I had them drawn up for your benefit."

"All right."

I handed her a box. "This is your new cellphone. You'll have to give yours up when you resign, so now you have one. I programmed my personal number in there so you can reach me. You can text freely on it."

She bit her lip, accepting the box. "Thank you."

"How much stuff do you have to move in?"

"Not much."

"What about breaking your lease?"

"It's month-to-month. I guess I'll lose the last one."

I waved my hand. "I'll cover it. Should I hire a moving company for you?"

She shook her head, her eyes downcast. "It's only a few boxes."

I frowned. "No furniture?"

"No. Some books, a few personal pieces, and my clothes."

I spoke without thinking. "You can donate your clothes back to Goodwill since I presume most of them came from there anyway. I'll be purchasing you a new wardrobe."

Her cheeks flushed, eyes flashed, dark and angry, but she said nothing.

"I'll pick up your boxes and bring them here when we move forward."

I handed her another envelope. "This is your new bank account and debit card. I'll make sure there are appropriate funds in it at all times."

She accepted the envelope with a shaking hand.

"I need you here as much as possible so we can get used to each other and talk. Tomorrow we can go over the lists and ask questions, fill in the blanks."

"Okay."

"Saturday morning, I want you here early. I have arranged an appointment for you to get ready for the barbeque. Do your hair and makeup. In fact, you may want to stay over Friday night, to save you the trip."

Her gaze flew to mine. "Stay over?" she repeated, a slight tremor in her voice.

I stood up. "Let me show you the place."

SHE DIDN'T SAY a word during the tour. I showed her the guest rooms, the den, and the private gym located at the other end of the condo on the main level. Upstairs, she was decidedly nervous when I showed her the master bedroom.

I indicated the guest room across the hall. "That one has a private en suite. I assume you'd like that room."

Her shoulders seemed to loosen. "You don't, ah . . ."

"I don't what?"

"You don't expect me to sleep in your room," she stated, sounding relieved.

I smirked at her uncertainty. "Miss Elliott, this is a business arrangement. Outside these walls, we will appear as a couple. We'll hold hands, stay close, do whatever other couples do who are in love." I waved my hand in the air. "In here, we are real. You have your space; I have mine. I won't bother you. I expect nothing from you." I couldn't help the dry chuckle that escaped. "You didn't really think I'd want to sleep with you, did you?"

Her head snapped up, and she glared at me. "No more than I'd want to sleep with you, Mr. VanRyan." Turning on her heel, she marched down the hall, her footsteps small thumps on the hardwood floor.

I followed her, still smirking. When we reached the living room, she whirled around, her eyes flashing.

"You asked me to do this, Mr. VanRyan. Not the other way around."

"You agreed."

She crossed her arms, anger pouring off her body. "I'm doing this, because at the moment, I have no other choice. Your decisions have directly affected my life, and I'm trying to keep up. I hate lying, and I'm not a good actress."

"What are you saying?"

"If you're not even going to attempt to be polite, or at least be a decent human being, this isn't going to work. I can't turn off my emotions that quickly."

I pulled on my stubborn cowlick in vexation. "What do you want from me, Miss Elliott?"

"Could we not at least try to get along? Surely we can find something we have in common and engage in a conversation without your veiled insults and holier-than-thou attitude."

A grin tugged at my lips. I was catching another glimpse of the backbone in Miss Elliott.

I tilted my head. "I apologize. I'll try to do better. Is there anything else you want since we're putting everything on the table?"

She hesitated, her fingers worrying the ugly shirt she wore.

"Spit it out."

"You can't, um, you can't mess around while we're doing . . . while we're *together*."

"Mess around?"

She looked everywhere but at me. "You can't sleep with other women. I won't be humiliated like that."

"So what you're saying is: I can't fuck anyone?"

Her cheeks were so red I thought her head would explode; however, she straightened her shoulders and looked right at me. "Yes."

This was too fun for me.

"Yes, I can fuck around!"

"No!"

"No *fucking*," I enunciated the last word.

"No."

"You expect me to remain celibate the whole time?" I asked, now incredulous.

"I will be, so I expect you to do the same."

I snorted. "I doubt it's anything new for you."

She threw up her hands. "That's it. You want to *fuck* someone? Go *fuck* yourself, VanRyan."

I gaped at her retreating figure as she grabbed her coat and stormed to the door.

Like the idiot I was, I chased after her—for the second time.

"Katharine!" I reached past her so she couldn't open the door. "I'm sorry. My remark was uncalled for."

She turned; her eyes were bright with tears. "Yes, it was. So many of the things you say are."

"I'm sorry," I repeated. "It's almost instinctual with you."

"That doesn't make it any better."

"I know," I conceded, then changed tactics. "I won't."

"You won't what?"

"I won't fuck around. I'll abide by your wish." I pressed harder against the door—if she left, I was *really* fucked. "I'll try not to be such an ass, as well."

"I'm not sure you can change your DNA, but good luck with trying," she mumbled.

I relaxed—crisis averted.

"I'll drive you home."

She began to shake her head, and I gave her a fierce look. "Katharine, we agreed I was going to be less of an ass. I'll drive you home. Tomorrow is going to be a long fucking day."

"Fine."

I grabbed my coat and opened the door for her, knowing my life was about to change in ways I never planned.

I only hoped it would be worth it.

Nine

RICHARD

ASIDE FROM KATHARINE'S hesitant instructions, the drive was silent. The farther away we went from my neighborhood, the darker my mood turned. When we pulled up in front of a dilapidated house, I turned to Katharine.

"This is your house?"

She shook her head. "No. I rent an apartment in the house."

I slammed the car into park, yanking off my seatbelt. "Show me."

I followed her up the uneven path, double clicking the key fob. I hoped the tires were still attached to my car when I returned. In fact, I hoped the car would be there.

I didn't try to hide my displeasure as I looked around at what I assumed was considered a studio apartment. I considered it a dump. A futon, an old chair, and a desk that also served as a table were the only pieces of furniture in the room. A short counter with a hot plate and a small refrigerator posed as a kitchen. There were a half dozen boxes piled by the wall. A wardrobe hanger held the dowdy suits and blouses Katharine wore.

I strode over to the one door in the room and threw it open. A tiny bathroom held a shower so minute I knew I would never be able to use it. I closed the door and turned to Katharine. She watched me with nervous eyes.

None of this made any sense to me.

I stepped in front of her, towering over her small stature. "Do you have a problem I should know about?"

"I beg your pardon?"

"Do you have a drug problem? Or some other addiction?"

"What?" She gasped, her hand clutched to her chest.

I flung out my arm. "Why are you living like this—like a poor church mouse? I know what you make. You can afford a decent place. What are you spending your money on?"

Her eyes narrowed, and she glared. "I do not have a *drug* problem. I have other priorities for my money. Where I sleep doesn't matter."

I glared right back. "It does to me. You aren't staying here anymore. Pack your shit. *Now.*"

She slammed her hands on her hips. "No."

I stomped forward. The room was small enough, when she retreated, her back hit the wall. I towered over her menacingly and studied her face. Her eyes, although angry, were clear. Holding her gaze, I grabbed her wrist, pushing her sleeve up. She almost snarled as she tugged her arm away, holding it up, then doing the same to her other arm.

"No needle tracks, Richard," she spat. "I don't do drugs. I don't smoke them, ingest them, or shoot them into my system. Satisfied? Or, do you want to check more? Should I pee in a jar for you?"

"No. I suppose I have to trust you. If I find out you're lying, this whole deal is off."

"I'm not lying."

I eased back. "Fine. This isn't up for discussion—you're out of here tonight. I won't risk Graham finding out you live in a place like this shithole."

"And if you aren't offered the job? What do I do then? I doubt you'll let me stay on with you."

I barked out a laugh. She was right. "With what I'm paying you, you'll be able to afford something decent." I looked around again. "You aren't bringing this furniture."

"It's not mine."

"Thank God."

"You're a snob, you know that? It's old, but it's still serviceable and clean."

I had to admit, the small space was meticulous and clean—but it was still hideous. I ignored her jibe.

"Do these boxes go?"

"Is it really necessary to do this right now?"

"Yes."

"Yes." She sighed. "The boxes go."

"Fine. I'll put those in the back seat. Your, ah, wardrobe can go in the trunk. What else do you have?"

"A few personal things."

I pushed an empty plastic laundry hamper her way. "Put them in there. Throw out any food you have."

A strange look crossed her face. "I don't have any—except a few muffins."

I snorted. "Is eating a problem, too? No wonder you're so fucking thin."

She tossed her head. "Are you going to even attempt to be polite? Or will you only save the effort for when we're in public?"

I lifted the first set of boxes. "I guess you'll find out. Now, get your stuff. You're not coming back here."

I OPENED THE guest room door, striding in and turning on the light after I set down the same boxes I had loaded up on the other side of town. Together, after we made a few trips, we brought all the contents into her room. I stepped back and assessed the situation. It wasn't much. I was tempted to demand to know why she had so little, then decided it wasn't worth the fight. I could tell from the tense set of her shoulders and the way her lips pressed together, I had pushed her enough for the night.

"Katharine, trust me. This is for the best. Now when they ask you, you can honestly say we live together."

"And if your idea fails, my life is shattered."

"If my idea fails, your life was done anyhow. David would never trust you to remain; he'd fire you and you'd have nothing. This way you'll have some money in the bank, I'll make sure you get a new job, and you can have a nicer place. One way or another, it has to be a fucking lot better than what you had."

She stared at me.

"In the meantime, you have a place that's safe and it's far more comfortable. *When* we move forward, you can decorate the room to suit your taste. You have access to the whole condo. Besides my workout room, there's a great pool and spa area downstairs, and I guarantee you, your bathroom is luxurious."

"Is there a bathtub?" she wondered, a trace of wistfulness in her voice.

I felt strangely pleased to be able to tell her yes, and I opened the door with a flourish, showing her the massive tub. For the first time, I saw a real smile on her face. It softened her expression, lighting up her eyes. They really were an incredible shade of blue.

"It's yours, Katharine. Use it whenever you like."

"I will."

I walked over to her door. "Get settled and get some sleep. Tomorrow will be long and difficult, and we need to get you ready for the weekend." I hesitated, but I knew I needed to begin *trying*. "Goodnight, Katharine."

"Goodnight, Richard."

KATHARINE

I COULDN'T SLEEP. No matter how hard I tried, I couldn't fall asleep. I was exhausted, both mentally and physically, yet I couldn't relax. The strange events of the past few days played on a constant loop in my mind. Richard's unexpected offer, my even more unexpected response, and his reaction to where I'd been living. He'd been beyond disgusted and furious, with his usual demanding demeanor in full force. Before I could blink, my few possessions were in the trunk of his large, luxury car and I was back in his condo—on a permanent basis, or until he was done with his inane plan. The inane plan I was now entrenched in as deeply as my boss.

The condo was silent. There was literally no noise. I was used to the sounds that surrounded me at night: traffic, other tenants moving around, yelling, and the constant sound of sirens and violence outside my window. They were the noises that kept me awake, sometimes fearful, yet now they were absent, I couldn't sleep. I knew I was safe. This place was a hundred, no a thousand times safer, than the terrible room I had lived in the past year. I should be able to relax and slumber peacefully.

The bed was huge—deep and plush—the sheets silky soft and rich, and the duvet felt like a warm feather floating over my body. The silence, however, was too loud.

I stole out of bed and went to my door. I opened it, wincing at the low creak as the hinges protested their use. I strained my ears, yet I couldn't hear anything. We were up too high for traffic, and the walls were well insulated, so there was no noise from anyone in the building.

I tiptoed down the hall, pausing in front of the door I knew was Richard's room. It was slightly ajar, and bravely I pushed it open wider and stuck my head in the opening. He was asleep in the middle of a gigantic bed—bigger than the one I had—bare-chested, with his hand resting on his torso. Obviously, the events of the past couple days weren't bothering him at all. His shiny hair showed up in the dim glare against the dark color of his sheets, and to my surprise, he snored. The sound was subtle but constant. In repose, and without the ever-constant sneer on his face, he looked younger, and less of a tyrant. In the muted moonlight, he appeared almost peaceful. It wasn't a word I had ever associated with him, and he wouldn't look that way if he woke up and found me in his doorway.

Nevertheless, it was the sound of his even breathing and rumbling snores I needed to hear. To know I wasn't alone in this vast, unfamiliar space. I listened for a few moments, left his door opened, and returned to my own room, leaving the door ajar, too.

I settled back into the bed and concentrated. It was low, but I could hear him. His odd wheezes offered me a small measure of comfort—a lifeline I needed desperately.

I sighed realizing if he knew he was comforting me, he would probably sit up all night in order to deny me the security it brought.

I turned my face into the pillow, and for the first time in months, cried.

HE WAS SUBDUED in the morning when I walked into the kitchen. He sipped from a large mug and indicated I could help myself to the Keurig machine on the counter.

In awkward silence, I made a coffee, unsure what to say.

"I hadn't expected company. I don't have cream."

"It's fine."

He pushed a piece of paper my way. "I wrote your resignation letter."

I frowned as I picked it up and read it. It was simple and straightforward.

"You didn't think I could write this myself?"

"I wanted to make sure it was plain. I didn't want you detailing your reasons for leaving."

I shook my head. "I don't understand."

"*What?* What don't you understand now?" He ran a hand along the back of his neck.

"If you don't trust me enough to write a simple resignation letter, how do you expect to trust me enough to act like we're—" the word stuck in my throat "—lovers?"

"One thing I do know about you, Katharine, is you work hard. You'll do a good job because it's what you do. You're a pleaser. You'll act exactly the way I need you to act because you want to earn the money you're being paid."

He picked up his briefcase. "I'm heading to the office. There's a spare key and a pass card for the building on the hall table. Your name is already added to the tenant list and the doormen won't hassle you. You should introduce yourself to them, just to be sure."

"How . . . how did you do that already? It's not even eight o'clock."

"I'm on the board, and I get what I want. According to the files, you've been living here for three months. I want your resignation in my hand right after lunch, and you'll leave. I've asked for some file boxes to be delivered to my office. I don't have a lot, but you can help me pack up my personal stuff this morning. Add anything of yours to the boxes. I'll bring them here."

"I don't have much of anything at the office."

"Fine."

"Why are you packing up? You haven't been fired yet."

He flashed his smile. The one that held no warmth. The one that made the person on the receiving end acutely uncomfortable.

"I've decided to quit. It'll piss off David, and show Graham how serious I am. I'll accept your resignation, and hand them both in to David at three. It's a shame you'll be gone for the show, but I'll fill you in on all the gory details when I get home."

I gaped at him. I couldn't keep up.

"You like Italian?" His question was offhanded, as if he hadn't dropped yet another explosive bombshell.

"Um, yes."

"Great. I'll order dinner for about six, and we can spend the night talking. Tomorrow morning, you're going shopping for a suitable outfit for the barbeque, and I've made an appointment for your hair and makeup. I want you to look the part."

He turned on his heel. "See you at the office." Then he laughed, the sound making me shiver. "Sweetheart."

I sat down as the door shut, feeling dizzy.

What had I agreed to?

Ten

KATHARINE

THE MORNING WAS tense for me—even Richard felt it. He had little in the way of personal items in the office, but I helped him pack up some awards, books, and a couple shirts he kept on hand for emergencies. I shook my head as I folded one, trailing my finger over the sleeve. All his shirts were custom made, and his initials *RVR* embroidered into the cuffs; a decadent touch only he could carry off. His items only filled two file boxes. His office was as impersonal as his condo. Glancing around, I realized it didn't look any different. No one would notice, unless someone was looking.

A small piece of sculpture caught my eye and I stretched up, grabbing it off the shelf. "Did you want to take this, Richard?"

He focused his gaze on the sculpture, but before he could reply, his office door flung open and David strode in. He stopped dead, looking at us. Richard was leaning against his desk, his resignation letter in hand, me standing, holding the sculpture beside an open box. David's face was like thunder.

"What the fuck is going on here?"

Richard pushed off his desk, sauntering over to where I stood. He plucked the sculpture from my hand and smirked as he tossed it into the box and fitted the lid on top.

"I think we're done here, Katharine. Go to your desk and wait for me."

I froze in place. The sensation of his fingers drifting down my cheek startled me out of my stupor. "Sweetheart," he murmured. His voice was a low hum in my ears. "Go."

I blinked at him.

Sweetheart?

What was he doing?

He bent closer, his breath warm on my skin. "I'll be fine, go to your desk. We'll leave in a minute." His hand wrapped around my waist, pushing me forward.

Completely confounded, I did what he asked. I hadn't made it more than two feet when David started yelling. He cursed and shouted, reaching out to grab my arm.

Richard pushed him away, standing between us.

"You don't touch her, David. Do you understand me?"

"What the fuck! Are you . . . are you *fucking* her, Richard? Are you telling me you're having an affair with your assistant?"

I held my breath, unsure what would happen next.

"It's not an affair, David. We're in love."

David laughed—a dry, brittle laugh that held no humor. "In love?" he sneered. "You can't stand her. You've been trying to get rid of her for months!"

"A good cover. One you fell for—hook, line, and sinker."

David's voice dripped ice. "You just signed your death warrant with this company."

Richard smirked. "Too late." He pushed two pages of heavy company stationery in David's direction. "I quit. So does my fiancée."

David gaped. "Your fiancée? You'd throw your career away over a trashy piece of ass? A lousy, worthless fuck?"

It happened so fast, I had no time to stop it. One second David was shouting, the next, Richard was standing over his prone figure, his hand curled into a fist so tight his knuckles were white. He towered over him, chest heaving; he was the very picture of a man protecting something, or someone he loved. "You never talk about her like that, again. You never talk about her, period. We're leaving here today. I'm done with you fucking me over, dictating who I fall in love with and where. I'm done with you and Anderson Inc."

"You're going to regret this, Richard." David spat, wiping the blood off his face.

"The only thing I regret is wasting as much time as I have giving you the best fucking campaigns this company ever produced. Good luck with your success record once I'm gone."

He stepped back. "Sweetheart, get your things. We're leaving. Now."

I ran to my desk, grabbing my purse and coat. The few things I found in my desk earlier were already in Richard's boxes. I had made sure there was nothing personal on my computer and my area was tidy. I knew Richard had wiped his hard drive, chuckling as he did something, muttering, "Good luck, fuckers," then shut down the machine. I could only imagine what the IT department would discover.

He strode out of the office, ignoring David, who was screaming obscenities, threatening lawsuits and telling him he was ruined. He indicated the exit with his head, and I scurried to open the door, following him down the hall, David trailing us, still cursing and flinging insults. Other employees and executives were staring at the commotion. I kept my eyes focused on Richard's back, certain he was strutting. He held his head high, shoulders straight, not at all embarrassed by the scene he had caused.

When we reached the elevator, he pushed the button and turned to the small crowd who were watching, not knowing what was going on, but loving the drama of it all.

"It's been a pleasure, but I'm out of here. Good luck working for the bloodsucker we all know as David." The doors opened and he dropped the boxes inside, then swept his arm in a wide arc. "After you, my lady."

I stepped in, my face flushed with embarrassment. As the elevator doors began to close, he stuck his arm out, forcing them to reopen. "And by the way, so you can stop gossiping and wondering, yes, Katharine and I are together. She's the best thing this company ever did for me."

With those words, he grabbed me, dragged me to him, kissing me as the doors shut, closing off the shocked gasps.

IMMEDIATELY, RICHARD MOVED away from me. I stumbled back against the wall, breathing fast. His kiss had been hard, deliberate, with an edge of anger to it.

"Why did you do that?"

Bending down, he picked up the boxes and shrugged. "Might as well leave with a bang." He chuckled. "The way the gossip mill works in this industry, this will be everywhere by tonight." He started to laugh, his head falling back on his shoulders. "That fucker did me a huge favor and he has no idea."

The doors opened, and I followed him to his car. I waited until I sat beside him before I asked. "Favor? Did you . . . did you plan all this?"

He grinned, looking almost boyish. "No. I planned on doing it differently, but when he barged in, I went in another direction." He winked as he slid on his sunglasses. "I do that well, Katharine. The client wants it changed, you learn to think on your feet. David knew what was happening as soon as he saw the boxes. I decided a scene would be a good thing."

"Good for whom? It was embarrassing."

"It was advertising. The name of the game. In one move, not only did the entire company get to see the dissolution of my relationship with David, they also found out about us. By the time we get to Graham's place tomorrow, he will have heard about it. He'll know I punched David for talking trash about the woman I love. It's perfect. I couldn't have planned it better if I tried."

I shook my head, flabbergasted. I never would have considered what just happened as "perfect."

"Relax, Katharine." He snorted as he skillfully wove in and out of traffic. "You're done. You don't have to go back there. I'll call my lawyer and make sure we send the first volley to cut David off at the knees."

"First volley?"

"David hates negative publicity for the firm. If he thinks I'm going after him for broken promises and an unhealthy work environment, he won't try anything. It's just for insurance."

I sighed and rested my head on the cool glass.

"You have the afternoon free. Maybe you should do some shopping."

"Must I?"

"Yes. I told you—I need you to look the part. I have a personal shopper lined up. I'll call her and arrange for you to see her this afternoon. We can stick with our plans for the evening."

"Great."

He turned up the music, tapping out a rhythm on the steering wheel, ignoring my sarcasm. I hated shopping—mostly because I could never afford to buy much. Maybe not having to pay the bill, it would be fun.

I hoped so. After this morning, I needed something to distract me.

NOT LONG AFTER we arrived back at the condo, Richard signed for an envelope. He opened it and thrust a black credit card at me.

"What's this?"

"For you to shop."

I looked at the face of the card, seeing my name emblazoned in silver.

"How did . . . ? Never mind." I sighed. It was obvious, whatever Richard wanted, he got.

He sat down, reaching for the card. "Sign it and use it. I called Amanda Kelly—she's the personal shopper I told you about. She's expecting you in an hour."

"Fine."

"What's the matter?"

"Couldn't she send me a dress for tomorrow? I'm sure you've already informed her exactly what you want me to wear."

He shook his head. "This isn't solely for tomorrow, Katharine. I meant what I said. Get rid of the clothes you've been wearing. I want you in dresses, well-tailored suits, smart outfits. Decent shoes. A whole new wardrobe."

"Do I have to toss my underwear, as well?" I questioned, and even I could hear the snark.

For a minute he blinked, then started to laugh. "You do have a little backbone in there somewhere. Yes. Toss it. All new. All in keeping with the role you'll be playing."

I rolled my eyes, taking the card. "Fine. It's not as if anyone will see my undergarments, anyway."

"What is it with you?" He growled. "I've never had to beg another woman to spend my money. Usually, they can't wait to get their hands on my bank account. Why are you so fucking stubborn?"

I stood up. "Then get one of them to play your loving fiancée in this ridiculous farce." I began to walk away, stopping when his long fingers wrapped around my arm.

"Katharine."

I shook my arm free. "What?" I spat.

He held up his hands. "I don't understand the problem with outfitting you."

Wearily, I rubbed my hand over my eyes. "If tomorrow doesn't give you the result you want, you will have spent a lot of money for nothing. *All* of this *craziness* will have been for nothing."

"All of this craziness?"

I blinked away the tears I felt forming. "Pretending we're engaged. Taking me out of my home, throwing away both our jobs, subjecting yourself to having to spend time with me. Even David knew how much you disliked me, Richard. How is this possibly going to work?"

He shrugged. "If, and it's a big if, it doesn't work, you'll have a bunch of pretty new clothes to wear to your next job. Let's be honest— your hovel wasn't much of a home; we'll find you something far better. Think of it that way." He stepped forward. "And, frankly, Katharine, perhaps I judged you too quickly. I *don't* dislike you. In fact, I rather enjoy listening to you argue with me."

I didn't know what to say to his unexpected declaration.

"I think, perhaps, we need to call a truce. You're right on one thing. We need to present a united front, and we can't do that if we're on edge with each other. So I have an offer to extend."

"Okay?" I asked, almost fearful of what he was about to say.

"You go shopping, spend my money. Spend an indecent amount. Consider it a gift for all the lousy things I've done over the past year. I'll make my calls, and some arrangements I need to take care of. When you get home, we'll spend the evening talking and getting to know each other a little more. Tomorrow, we'll face the day as a couple. Okay?"

I chewed on my cheek as I studied him. "Okay."

"Good. One more thing."

"What?"

He held out his hand, a small box in his palm. "I want you to wear this."

I stared at the box, not making a move.

"It won't bite you."

"What is it?" I whispered, already knowing the answer.

"An engagement ring."

When I still didn't move, he sighed in frustration. "You had better not expect me to get down on one knee."

"No!" I gasped.

"Then take it."

My hand trembled as I reached for the box and opened it. A large solitaire in a white gold, vintage setting, shimmered under the light. It was exquisite.

I lifted my gaze to his.

"I described you to the sales woman and said I wanted something simple yet stunning. There were larger ones, but for some reason, I thought you would like this ring."

His odd, kind words touched me. "I do."

"Well, put it on. It's part of the image."

I slid it on my finger, staring at it. It was a perfect fit, but still it felt strange on my hand.

"I'll take good care of it until it's time to give it back."

He snorted. "I'm sure you'll try. Given your clumsiness, I've insured it."

I rolled my eyes, the moment of being touched passed in that second.

He looked at his watch. "Okay. The car will be outside waiting for you. Go get yourself presentable."

He turned and left the room.

I picked up my purse, the ring catching the light.

Well, it seemed I now had a fiancé.

I was engaged to a man who disliked me, but was willing to overlook it so he could get a new job and piss off his old boss.

Certainly, that was the stuff dreams were made of.

Eleven

KATHARINE

THE AFTERNOON WAS a whirlwind. Richard had indeed told Amanda precisely what he wanted, and the list was endless, it seemed. Dresses, pants, skirts, blouses, suits—a vast array of materials and colors drifted by me. There were also new bathing suits, lingerie, and nightgowns. Item after item was tried on, discussed, and either discarded or placed on the ever-growing pile of clothes to keep.

Thankfully, after watching me for a short time, the footwear she picked out was all low-heeled. Still stylish, she assured me, but I had a better chance of staying upright.

The last straw was the exercise clothing she showed me. By that point, I was beyond exasperated. I couldn't fathom a time I would need to have expensive workout clothes. He had a private gym in his apartment for God's sake. When she indicated it was on Richard's list, I threw up my hands and told her to add whatever she felt was suitable. I was done.

I walked out of the store, carrying the outfit for the next day, wearing a new pair of jeans and a silk T-shirt in a rich red color. Richard, apparently, didn't want to see me arrive back in my "old stuff."

I was silent on the car ride back, overwhelmed and tired. I carried my packages up to the condo, letting myself in with my keys. I heard music coming from down the hall. I knew Richard was busy working out, so I hung my new dress in the closet, put away the few other items I had brought back with me, then called the home to check on Penny.

Her primary nurse told me she was sleeping, but it hadn't been a good day, so I shouldn't visit. Sadness engulfed me as I sat looking out the window. I hated days like today; however, she was right. Going would only upset me further.

Instead, I went back downstairs and rummaged around in the kitchen. It was well equipped, yet held little food except for some fruit and a few condiments in the cupboards and refrigerator.

"Looking for something?"

I straightened up, startled. Richard was slouched against the doorframe, a towel draped around his broad shoulders. His skin glistened with a thin sheen of sweat, his hair damp, and he still looked perfect.

"You don't have much food."

"I have no idea how to cook. I do takeout, or my housekeeper leaves me something."

"Housekeeper?" He hadn't mentioned having a housekeeper.

He nodded, taking a drink from the bottle of water he was holding. "I need to hire one. The last one left about two weeks ago." He waved his hand. "They come and go."

I hid my amusement. That news wasn't surprising.

"I cook."

He smirked. "So you mentioned."

I ignored his sarcastic tone. "I can keep the place clean and do the shopping and cooking."

"Why?"

"Why not?"

"Why would you want to?"

"Richard," I started patiently, "I'm not working now. I have lots of time on my hands. Why would you want to hire someone else when I'm here anyway?"

His brow furrowed as he thought about it.

"It would seem natural to other people." At his confused look, I explained. "That I would look after our home. That I would look after, ah, *you*."

He scratched the back of his neck, obviously unsure. "Yeah?"

"Yes."

"Okay—for now. Use your card to pay for everything."

I nodded.

"Anything you need to keep the place clean. Buy it. If you need help, get it."

"Okay."

I felt relieved. It would feel normal to do the shopping and make dinner. Stay busy and clean the condo.

"How did your call go with the lawyer?"

"Good." He drained the bottle, tossing it in the recycle bin in the corner. "How was your shopping?"

I rolled my eyes. "Quite the list you gave her."

"I told you I wanted new everything for you."

"Well, you got it."

He stepped closer, rubbing the sleeve of my T-shirt with his long fingers. "I like this."

"Good. You bought it."

"Did you spend lots of my money?"

"Tons. Pretty sure I put you in the poor house."

To my surprise, he smiled. A real smile that lit up his eyes, making him appear boyish and younger. "Finally, you do what I tell you to do."

I snorted.

He reached past me and picked up an envelope. "Here."

Gingerly, I took the envelope; it felt hard and bulky under my fingers. "What is it?"

"The keys to your car."

"My car?" I squeaked.

"I told you I'd get you one. It's in space 709, beside my other two. Your pass is in there, as well. It gets you in and out of the garage."

"What . . .?"

"It's a Lexus. Safe. Reliable. It's red—like your shirt."

"Unnecessary."

"No. It is needed. It's all part of the image, Katharine. We're selling us as a couple—the details are important. Remember that." He shrugged. "It's got good resale value anyway, when this is done. If you don't want to keep it, you can sell it. Either way, it's yours. Part of the deal."

I shook my head. "How can you afford all this? I know you were well paid, but not *that* well paid."

His face darkened. "When my parents died, I inherited a great deal of money."

"Oh. I'm sorry, Richard. I didn't know. Did they pass recently?"

His shoulders tightened; his stance tense. "Fourteen years ago. It wasn't a great loss, so save your sympathy. It was the first time their actions benefitted me."

I wasn't sure how to respond to his statement.

"So, don't worry about the money."

He turned and walked out of the kitchen. "I'm going for a shower, then I'll order dinner. I left you a list on the table; you can look it over. We'll start talking when I come back. We need to get this all down pat."

"More image work?"

"You got it. Find a good bottle of red in the rack. I think I'm going to need it." He threw another smirk my way. "If you know a good one when you see it, that is."

On that pleasant note, he left me glaring after him.

RICHARD

WHEN I RETURNED, Katharine was perched on one of the high chairs. There was a bottle of wine opened, and she was sipping from a glass, studying the papers in front of her. I drew in a deep breath, and crossed the room. I had her list with me, so we could discuss the details. We needed to cram as much of our histories in tonight to bluff our way through tomorrow. We had to convince Graham we were the real deal. I knew it was going to be a long evening.

I was still tense from earlier—it happened every time I spoke about my parents, no matter how brief. I hated thinking about them, and my past.

Katharine's bright eyes met mine. Her hair fell over her shoulder, and I couldn't help notice how the red suited her pale complexion and deep color of her hair. Wordlessly, I poured a glass of wine and sat beside her, pushing those strange thoughts out of my head.

"Dinner will arrive soon. I ordered you some cannelloni. I hope you like it."

She nodded. "It's one of my favorites."

I held up my list with a smirk. "I know."

I took a sip of my wine, enjoying the flavor. She had picked one of my favorites.

I tapped the papers on the counter. "Shall we begin?"

HOURS LATER, I emptied the last of the wine into my glass. I was exhausted. Never one to talk about my past, or reveal too many personal details, it had been a torturous evening. Fortunately, since we had a lot of ground to cover, I didn't have to delve too deep into a lot of things. She knew I was an only child, my parents were deceased, and all the pertinent facts: where I went to school, my favorite activities, colors, foods, likes and dislikes. I was somewhat surprised to find she already knew many of those facts—she was more observant at the office than I gave her credit for being.

I learned a great deal of new information about Katharine. Whereas she was observant, to me, she had only ever been a shadow on the edge of my world. She was as reticent to discuss her past as I was, but told me enough so I could make do. She also had no siblings—her parents died when she was a teenager and she lived with her aunt who now resided in a care home. She didn't finish post-secondary school, came to work for the Anderson Inc. as a temporary job, and never left. When I questioned why, she stated, at the time she was undecided about her future and chose to work until she knew what she wanted. I let it go, even though it seemed strange. I had no idea how her mind worked.

I sat down with a sigh. Katharine tensed beside me, and I leaned my head back, regarding her with ill-concealed impatience. "I think we have the basic facts down, Katharine. I even know the name of your favorite hand cream should that come up." Her lists had been far more detailed than mine. "However, none of this is going to work if you stiffen every time I come close to you."

"I'm not used to it," she admitted. "You, ah, usually put me on edge."

"We're going to have to be close," I informed her. "Lovers are. They touch and caress. They whisper and exchange glances. There's a familiarity that comes with being intimate. I have a feeling the Gavin family is an affectionate bunch. If I can't reach for your hand without you flinching, no amount of facts will help us with Graham watching."

She fiddled with her wineglass, running her fingers over the stem repeatedly. "What are you saying?"

"I'm going to touch you, whisper things in your ear, stroke your arm, even kiss you. Call you sweetheart, other endearments. Like any other couple in love."

"I thought you said you've never been in love?"

I snickered. "I've done enough ads about it, I can fake it. Besides, I've been in lust enough, it's basically the same."

"Sex without love is just body parts and friction."

"There's nothing wrong with that kind of friction. Sex without love is the way I like it. Love does things to people. It changes them. Makes them weak. Complicates things. I have no interest in that."

"That's just sad."

"Not in my world. Now back to the task at hand. Are you prepared not to run screaming when I suddenly touch you, or kiss you? Can you handle it?" I rapped my knuckles on the lists sitting in front of us. "We need more than facts to be successful."

She lifted her chin. "Yes."

"Okay, we need to try something."

"What do you suggest?"

I stroked my chin with my finger. "Well, since fucking for fucking sake is off the table, I guess we need to figure that out. Unless you want to try?"

She rolled her eyes, but her cheeks darkened. "No. Suggest something else."

I suppressed my chuckle. She was entertaining at times. I held my hand out, palm up, in invitation. "Work with me."

Slowly, she slipped her hand into mine, and I closed my fingers around her small palm. Her skin was cool and soft, and with a grin, I squeezed her fingers before letting go. "See, I didn't burn you or anything."

Feeling restless, I stood, walking around. "We're going to have to act comfortable with each other. If I kiss your cheek or wrap my arm around your waist, you have to act as if it's normal." I tugged on my shirt hem. "You'll have to do the same. Reach for me, smile, laugh when I bend down and whisper something. Stretch up on those ridiculously short legs to kiss my cheek. Something. Do you understand?"

"Yes." Then she grinned—the most mischievous expression crossing her face.

"What?"

"If you call me sweetheart, do I get to call you something, ah, *special*, too?"

"I'm not one for nicknames. What did you have in mind?"

"Something simple."

I could live with that. "Like?"

"Dick," she stated with a straight face.

"No."

"Why not? It's a short form of your name, and it, ah, *suits you*, on so many levels."

I gave her a sharp look. I was sure she knew the nickname was attached to me in the industry and was trying to poke fun. "No. Pick something else."

"I'll have to think about it."

"You do that. Dick is off the table, though."

Her lips quirked.

I rolled my eyes. "Give it up, Katharine."

"Fine. Dick works so well, but I'll try."

I ignored her obvious humor. "No—enough." I stepped in front of her, meeting her amused gaze. "Now, shall we practice?"

"Practice?"

I picked up the remote and hit play, changing the music until a low, gentle melody hummed through the speakers. "Dance with me. Get used to how it feels to be close to me." I held out my hand, saying the one word I never used with her until the past few days. "Please."

She let me drag her to her feet and awkwardly she moved closer. With a sigh, I wound my arm around her waist, tugged her close, and breathed in the scent of her hair wafting up into the air. We began moving, and I was surprised how natural it felt. Far smaller than the women I was used to, she barely met my shoulders; her head fit under my chin. She seemed slight and fragile in my arms, yet she molded against my body well. After a few minutes, she lost the stiffness in her shoulders, letting me lead her around the room effortlessly. She was unexpectedly graceful as she moved, given how often I had watched her trip on her own feet.

A voice spoke in my head, whispering maybe what she needed all along was someone to hold her up, rather than tear her down.

That brought me up short, and I jerked back, staring down at her. She blinked up at me, filled with trepidation, and I realized she was expecting some sort of nasty remark. Instead, I cupped her cheek, and her eyes grew wider.

"What are you doing?"

"Kissing you."

"Why?"

"Practice."

Her breathy "oh," hit my mouth as my lips touched hers. They were surprisingly soft and pliant, melding to mine with ease. It wasn't an unpleasant sensation; in fact, I felt a trail of warmth run down my spine at the contact. I released her lips, only to drop my head and kiss her again, this time a fast brushing of my mouth on hers.

I stepped back, releasing my hold on her. The air around us was thick, and I smirked. "See, not so bad. It won't kill you to kiss me."

"Nor you," she retorted, a tremor in her voice.

I barked out a laugh. "I guess not. Whatever it takes to get the job done."

"Right."

I grabbed the remote, turning off the music. "Well done, Katharine. We've done enough bonding for the evening. Tomorrow is a big day, so I think we both need to get some rest."

"Okay," she whispered.

"You did a good job today. Thank you."

I turned on my heel and left her gaping after me.

Twelve

KATHARINE

I HAD TROUBLE sleeping again, so I tiptoed down the hall, pushing open Richard's door. Tonight, he was on his stomach, one arm wrapped around his pillow, the other one hanging off the edge of his massive bed. He was still snoring—his low, raspy hum I needed to hear.

I studied his face in the dim light. I traced my lips with my finger, still shocked at the fact he had kissed me, held me in his arms, and we danced. I knew it was all part of his grand scheme, but there were moments, glimpses, of a different man than I was used to seeing. The flash of a smile, a twinkle in his eye, even a kind word—they had all caught me off-guard tonight. I wished he allowed that part of himself out more, but he kept his emotions—the positive ones—locked away. I had already figured that out. I knew if I said anything, he would lock himself down even more. So, I remained silent—at least for now. I had to admit though, kissing him hadn't been bad at all. Considering the venom his mouth could produce, his lips were warm, soft, and full, and his touch gentle.

He groaned and rolled over, taking the blankets with him, his long, lean torso now exposed. I swallowed, partially in guilt for staring at him, partially in wonder. He was a beautiful man—at least on the outside. He muttered something incoherent, and I moved back, leaving the door ajar, scuttling back to my own room.

He might have been a little more pleasant at times this evening, but

I doubted he would react well to me staring at him while he slept.

Still, his quiet rumbles helped me to drift off into a peaceful slumber.

I LEFT THE condo early and went to visit Penny. She was wide-awake and in a good mood. She knew me today, tweaked my nose, and we talked and laughed until she fell asleep. I sipped my coffee while she napped, looking at some of her little pieces she'd been painting. I chose one I liked in particular of some wild flowers, and was admiring it when she stirred. She watched me, then rolled her chair over, holding out her hand for the painting.

"I like this one." I smiled. "It reminds me of when we'd go and pick flowers in the summer."

She nodded, looking distracted. "You'll have to ask my daughter if it's for sale. I'm not sure where she is."

My breath caught in my throat. She was gone again. The moments of clarity were getting further and further apart, and I knew better than to upset her.

"Perhaps I can take it and go find her."

She reached for her paintbrush, turning for her easel. "You can try. She may be at school. My Katy is a busy girl."

"Thank you for your time, Mrs. Johnson."

She gestured toward the door, dismissing me. I left the room, clutching her painting, stifling the tears. She didn't know me, yet deep in her heart, she still thought of me as her daughter. The same way I thought of her as my family.

It was a sobering reminder of why I was doing this with Richard. Pretending to be something I wasn't.

It was for her.

I wiped my eyes, and headed back to the condo.

WHEN I OPENED the door, Richard met me with a scowl on his face.

"Where were you? You have an appointment!"

I drew in a deep breath and counted to ten. "Good morning to you, too, Richard. It's only ten. My appointment is at eleven. I have plenty of time."

He ignored my greeting.

"Why didn't you answer your phone? I called. You didn't take your car, either."

"I visited Penny. The home she is in is close, so I walked."

Reaching over, he tugged on the small canvas I had clutched to my torso. "What is this?"

My grasp was ineffectual, and he held the painting in his hands, studying it.

"You aren't hanging this crap in here."

I swallowed the bitterness in my throat. "I wouldn't dream of it. I was going to put it in my room."

He pushed the small canvas back at me. "Whatever." He walked away, glancing over his shoulder. "Your clothes arrived. I put them in the closet in your room and left the bags on the bed. Burn whatever you're wearing now. I don't want to see it any longer."

Then he disappeared.

LATER THAT AFTERNOON, when I returned to the condo, I felt like a different person. I had been buffed, scrubbed, and waxed within an inch of my life. My hair had been washed with some body infusing shampoo, conditioned, cut and layered, then blown dry so it hung in long, luxurious waves down my back. Once my makeup was done, I barely recognized myself. My eyes looked huge, my mouth full and pouty, my skin like porcelain. I hurried upstairs and slipped into the new lingerie and dress Amanda and I had picked out for the afternoon; she told me it was perfect. Off-white with a flowered overlay, it was pretty and floaty, and it looked like summer. The low-heeled sandals were comfortable, and I was sure I could stay upright.

I took in a deep breath as my nerves began to tighten.

It was time to see if Richard agreed.

RICHARD

IMPATIENTLY, I DRUMMED my fingers on the counter. I heard the tapping of heels and turned my head, the glass I was about to drink from freezing part way to my mouth.

The Katharine I was used to seeing wasn't this woman. As I suspected, with the right clothes, a good haircut, and some makeup, she was quite pretty. Not like the flashy, confident women I was used to, but rather an understated beauty she carried well. Not my usual type—however, in this case, it would work.

I glanced down at her hand and frowned. "Where is your ring?"

"Oh."

She opened her small purse, took out the box, and slipped on the ring.

"You need to wear it all the time. Leave the box here."

"I took it off for a manicure. I forgot to put it back on." She smiled—a wide, almost teasing smile. "Thank you so much for reminding me, my darling."

I raised my eyebrows. *"My darling?"*

"You didn't like Dick, so I picked another endearment. You know, like *lovers*."

I crossed my arms, glaring. "I think you're laughing at me."

"I would never." She tossed her hair, the dark waves rippling down her back. "So, will I pass?"

"My money was well spent."

She picked up her purse. "You have such a way with words, Richard. So smooth and lyrical. I'm shocked women weren't lined up pretending to love you."

Her remark made me chuckle. She had a cutting sense of humor, which was something I liked.

I followed her to the door, opening it for her. She waited as I locked it, and with a smirk, I offered her my hand.

"Ready, sweetheart?"

She rolled her eyes, placing her hand in mine. "Anywhere with you, my darling."

"Let's do this."

KATHARINE ACCEPTED MY extended hand, letting me help her from my car, her eyes huge in her face as she took in the extraordinary house and grounds. Even I was impressed. Graham Gavin's estate home was lavish.

"Try to control your emotions," I murmured, tugging her close, hoping it appeared natural. She didn't fight me, leaning her body into mine as the valet drove off with my car. "You need to relax."

She looked up at me with a frown. "Maybe you're used to this sort of opulence, Richard. But I'm not." Her gaze moved around rapidly; panic beginning to show on her face. "I don't belong here," she whispered. "They're going to see right through this sham."

I bent low so I could meet her eyes. "No, they aren't," I hissed. "I'm going to stay beside you, and we're going to act as if we're in love. Everyone here will think I chose you and *us* over my career, and *you*, damn it, are going to act as though you fucking *adore* me. Got it?"

She tilted her head up, uncertainty written all over her face.

I softened my voice. "You can do this, Katharine, I know you can. We both need this to work."

She looked over my shoulder. "Graham Gavin is coming over."

"Then it's show time, sweetheart. I'm going to kiss you and you're going to act as though you like it. Pretend I just gave you a gift. In fact, I'll give you one, if you pull off this first meeting."

For a second nothing changed. Then her gaze became determined, and she beamed at me. The expression transformed her face from merely pretty to *beautiful*. The change caught me off guard, and I stared down at her, surprised at my thoughts.

"Richard!" she exclaimed. "You're too good to me!"

To say I was shocked when she reached up, threading her

fingers through my hair and yanking my mouth to hers, would be an understatement. I recovered quickly, holding her tight and kissing her far too passionately for such a public place. When I heard the clearing of a throat behind me, I smiled against her mouth and drew back. She stared up at me, then as if it was the most natural thing in the world, touched my lips.

"Passion pink isn't your color," she teased, wiping at my mouth.

I dropped another kiss on her lips. "I told you to stop wearing the stuff. I'm only going to kiss it off anyway." Keeping my arm around her, I turned to greet Graham.

"Sorry, Katharine is easily excited." I smirked. "And who am I to resist?"

He chuckled, extending his hand, introducing me to his wife, Laura. Almost as short as Katharine, her golden hair swept into an elegant bun, she was grace personified.

I, in turn, introduced Katharine as my fiancée, smiling as she blushed and greeted them both.

"You must tell me what excited you so much, Katharine." Laura smiled at her.

"Richard just told me about an unexpected gift. He's constantly surprising me. Please call me Katy. Richard insists on my full name, but I prefer Katy."

I shook my head. "It's a beautiful name for a beautiful woman."

She rolled her eyes, and Laura chuckled.

"You'll never convince him otherwise, Katy. Men are such stubborn creatures." Reaching out, she hooked arms with Katharine, tugging her away. "Come; let me introduce you to my family. Jenna is dying to meet you. Now, what is this gift he gave you?"

Following behind, I listened carefully, wondering what she would decide I had given her. Jewelry? A trip? Those were the extravagant gifts the women I dated liked to receive.

Once again, she surprised me.

"Richard made a generous donation to the 'no-kill shelter' where I volunteer. I had told him I was afraid they may close up due to lack of funds."

Laura glanced over her shoulder with a wide grin. "What a lovely gesture, Richard. Graham and I will match your donation. We both have a soft spot for animals."

Katharine gasped. "Oh, Laura, you don't have to do that!"

Laura hugged her arm. "Of course, we do. How long have you been volunteering there?"

I spoke up; thankful for the lists we'd made and the fact I had a good memory. "Three years. She's been named Volunteer of the Year twice."

"How wonderful! Graham, make sure you write out a check for Katy when you're talking to Richard later."

Those words encouraged me. If he was going to talk to me in private, I hoped it meant what I thought it did.

Graham smiled at Laura. "I will, my love."

I HAD PLANNED to stay close, but it seemed my plans were thwarted at every turn. Once introduced to Jenna, her husband Adrian, as well as their older son Adam, his wife Julia, and their two children, Katharine and I were separated. Jenna was eager to meet Katharine, her green eyes much like her father's, wide and excited. She was average height, attractive, with blonde hair and a friendly smile. Her husband resembled a linebacker, as wide as he was tall, with dark hair and eyes. Their mutual adoration was obvious—if not a little nauseating.

Jenna grabbed onto Katharine, dragging her around to meet some other women, while Graham introduced me to several key members of his staff. It was obvious Graham's intention wasn't a secret. He was letting the rest of his valued staff meet me, and I knew their opinions would matter, so I was on my best behavior, putting on the charm. For the first while, I kept glancing over to Katharine, wondering if she was saying or doing anything to jeopardize our situation, but she looked surprisingly calm, and seemed to be holding her own. Graham noticed my preoccupation and ribbed me good-naturedly.

"Relax, Richard. No one will kidnap her. I promise."

I forced a chuckle. "Of course not. She, ah, she's rather shy, that's all," I stated lamely. I couldn't tell him why I needed to stay close.

"You're protective of her."

I was? That was what he thought?

"It's been a rough few days, for both of us."

He nodded, looking serious. "I heard what happened."

Perfect.

"I couldn't let him berate her that way, or allow him to belittle our relationship. It was time to leave, regardless of how it affected my career," I stated with conviction. "I wanted our relationship—our real relationship—out in the open. I wanted the world to know we were engaged."

"You put her first."

"Always."

He clapped my shoulder. "Come meet some people, Richard."

A WHILE LATER, I walked toward the small group of people with Katharine. I had observed the Gavins and how they interacted, and I was correct in my assumption. They were a very demonstrative group. When they were close to each other, the couples were constantly touching. Both Laura and Graham were also affectionate with their children and grandchildren. I knew I needed to show the same sort of affinity with Katharine. I hoped she could respond in kind.

The women were laughing, shaking their heads. Katharine spoke up. "I know, for someone usually so health conscious, Richard is terrible. He eats far too much red meat. Every chance he gets, especially at Finlay's. The twenty-four ounce rib-eye every time." She chuckled. "I've given up trying to stop him because there's no point. At least he eats better now that I cook for him. The number of take-out menus I found in the drawer when I moved in was frightening."

Stepping up behind her, I wrapped my arm around her waist, drawing her back to my chest and dropping a quick kiss to her neck, noticing her small shiver. "What about you, Katharine?"

I glanced around at the small group of women she was talking to with a wide smile. "She worries constantly about that, yet every day, I find her eating a peanut butter and jam sandwich." I shook my head, looking back down at her. "I keep telling you, sweetheart, you need to eat more protein. You are far too tiny. I could put you in my pocket, I swear."

There was a collective sigh among the women in the group. I had obviously said something right.

"Don't hate the PB&J, my darling," Katharine insisted. "Being your assistant, I was lucky to have time to eat a sandwich."

I kissed her again. "My bad, baby. You shouldn't be so invaluable to me."

As the women around her all laughed, Jenna patted one on the shoulder with a smile.

"Look out, Amy, you've been warned. If Richard comes on board, no more lunch hours."

Amy laughed. "I'll find out all his secrets from his fiancée to keep him in line."

Ah, Amy Tanner, Brian's girlfriend, and the way things seemed to be going, my next assistant. I smiled at her—she was exactly his type: tall, pretty, and polished.

"Hello, Amy. Brian away this weekend?"

She nodded. "Another trip. He said to remind you about golf next week when he gets back."

"I'm looking forward to it."

"I hope I'm not a disappointment as an assistant after having your fiancée at your side. If, of course, you come on board."

I stiffened a little, but Katharine laughed, patting my arm. "Richard is brilliant," she enthused. "He is amazing to work with. I'm sure the two of you will get along famously."

Jenna winked at Katharine. "Spoken like a woman in love."

Katharine relaxed back into me with a small sigh. She glanced up, a gentle smile playing on her lips. Her hand traced my jaw, her voice low and husky. "Because I am."

It was an Oscar-worthy performance.

THE AFTERNOON WANED away. We ate, talked, and met many people. Often when we were with other people, I would look up to find Katharine's eyes on me. Because it amused me to watch her reaction, I would blow her a kiss or send her a wink, simply to see her cheeks flush. She did it every single time. She did the same thing when I would walk up to her, wrapping an arm around her waist, dropping a kiss to her shoulder or cheek. She played her part well, never reacting in any way except welcoming. In fact, a couple times she sought me out, leaning up on her toes to whisper in my ear. It was easy to imitate the way Adrian bent his head low to hear whatever Jenna was murmuring, with an indulgent look on his face. I had no doubt the words Jenna whispered were far more intimate than what Katharine had to tell me, but no one else knew that.

At one point, Graham drew me to the side and asked if I was available for another discussion on Monday. It was all I could do not to fist pump the air, knowing we had done it. Instead, I told him Katharine and I had an errand on Monday morning, however, I was available after lunch. I didn't want to appear too eager, but as soon as he nodded knowingly and informed me the license office was always busy on Monday so we should hold off until two o'clock to meet, I realized my mistake.

He thought we were going to apply for our marriage license. Rather than correct him, I agreed two o'clock would be a good time and shook his hand. I noticed a few other people had left, so I thanked him for his hospitality. When he reminded me of the donation, I told him we could take care of it Monday—in actuality, I didn't have a clue the name of the shelter.

Laura was talking to Katharine, when I approached. "Ready to go, sweetheart?" I asked. "I know you want to go see your aunt this afternoon, as well."

"Yes, I do." Katharine turned to our hostess. "Thank you for the lovely afternoon."

Laura beamed, and pulled her in for a hug.

"Your aunt is very lucky to have you. It was good to meet you, my dear girl. I look forward to seeing more of you. Remember what I said about your wedding!"

Katharine nodded, taking my outstretched hand. It wasn't unpleasant when Laura stretched up and pressed a kiss on my cheek. "So happy to meet you, Richard. I look forward to seeing more of you, too." She winked. "Both here and at the office."

I grinned at her. "Likewise."

"Did Graham give you a check for the five thousand?"

I blinked at her, then at Katharine.

Five thousand?

Apparently, I *had* been generous. I smirked, deciding it was well worth it.

"He's giving it to me on Monday."

"Excellent. Now you two lovebirds, enjoy the rest of your day."

I gave a low laugh, making Katharine's cheek darken and Laura's smile wider. "I plan to," I assured her with a wink as I tugged my fiancée away.

I chuckled all the way to the car.

Inside, I was celebrating. It had worked.

Thirteen

RICHARD

MONDAY MORNING, KATHARINE looked at me as if I had two heads.

"We're doing *what?*"

I sighed, folding my paper and setting it on the counter. "I didn't want to appear too eager, so I told Graham you and I had an errand to run this morning. He assumed it was to go get a marriage license, and I never corrected him."

She picked up our plates and carried them to the sink. I had to admit she was a damned good cook. I couldn't remember the last time I had eaten breakfast at home that didn't come out of a box. Yesterday she had taken her car to do "errands," and when she returned, it took two trips with me helping to bring up all the groceries she bought. I had thought she was crazy, but I was having second thoughts. Dinner last night had been some kind of delicious chicken and her scrambled eggs today were stellar. So was her coffee. I fully approved of the purchase of the new coffee maker.

She slumped against the sink, scrubbing her face. "You can let him think it, but we don't have to do it."

I shook my head. "Nope. We're doing it. I want a paper trail. We don't have to get married, just have the license."

"Richard."

I lifted the check I had written off the table. "Consider it fair trade for my donation." I arched my eyebrow at her. "My very *generous* donation."

She had the grace to look embarrassed. "I told you, I had no idea what someone in your financial bracket would consider generous. When Laura was talking about it, one of the other women was a little catty and said she wouldn't consider anything under a thousand generous." She shrugged. "Before I realized what I was saying I had blurted out you had donated five thousand. It certainly shut her up."

"I bet it did. And it's fine. Except, you owe me, so I get one real-fake marriage license."

She dumped her coffee in the sink. "Fine. I'll go get ready."

She stomped past me, and because she made me want to make her angry, I grabbed her wrist, dragging her to my lap. She gasped, pushing me away, and I laughed at her ineffectual struggle.

"Want me to come scrub your back?"

"No!"

"I'll make another donation."

She elbowed me in the ribs, making me lose my grip, and she stumbled to her feet. "Be careful, Richard, or I'll take you with me to the shelter and have you neutered!"

I burst out laughing at her indignation, letting her march away, muttering under her breath.

I had no idea why I enjoyed her outrage—but I did.

GRAHAM SHOOK MY hand, offering me a seat at his private conference table. His office, like the rest of the building, was one of understated wealth. The furniture was the best quality, the artwork tasteful and elegant. More awards and small versions of winning campaigns filled the shelves that took up an entire wall. The need to have a campaign of mine displayed there burned within me.

We waited until his assistant brought us coffee and left, shutting the door behind her. Graham smiled at me, helping himself to a cookie off the plate. "From what I hear, these are nowhere near as good as your Katy's, but help yourself."

"I've been spoiled, I'm afraid. Hers are amazing."

He chewed and swallowed, wiping his mouth. "I hope your errand was a successful one, Richard?"

I patted my pocket, trying to look smug. "The paperwork is all done. I'll have the license in three days." I snickered a little. "I only have to convince Katharine to run off to Vegas with me and make it official."

Graham frowned as he took a sip of coffee. "Forgive me for saying this, but your Katy doesn't seem the Vegas type."

I drank my coffee, stalling for time. I had no idea what "type" she was, but I couldn't tell him that. I decided to go with the shyer side of her nature.

I cleared my throat and nodded. "You're right, she isn't. Still, neither of us want a big wedding. We'll do it in private one day. Katharine is a firm believer in keeping it small—only between us."

"She has no family, except her aunt?"

"That's right."

"Laura mentioned she's in a home?"

I nodded. "She's elderly and not well. Katharine visits her a lot."

"Ah. What a shame." He looked past me to the window. "Laura and Jenna were quite taken with your girl."

I wasn't certain what to say. I didn't really want to talk about Katharine, yet it seemed I had no choice.

"That happens a lot."

He smiled wide. "I can see why. She's delightful."

"She is."

He switched gears, tapping a file folder in front of him. "I shared your idea with our team about the campaign."

"And?"

"They agreed with me. They thought it was a stroke of brilliance."

I tipped my head down, his praise making me feel good. "I'm glad."

He relaxed back in his chair, studying me. I sensed I was being judged for the final time. I met his steady gaze, waiting for him to speak.

"It's taken me many years of hard work and dedication to build this business. The work we do here means something."

I nodded silently.

"It's rare I hire outside my firm, Richard. Those who aren't family have been with me for a long time. They become *part* of my family. Here at The Gavin Group, we care about our family."

"It's a unique concept, Graham. Most employers don't treat their staff the way you do. I admit, I've never experienced it."

"I know. I have to say, I was wary when I heard your name, Richard. Your, ah, reputation precedes you."

I had the grace to look ashamed. "I can't change my past, Graham, except I can tell you, I want something different now." I hunched forward, earnest and eager. "I want to work here. I want to prove to you I belong here. Give me a chance. Let me show you what I can bring to the table."

"We work as a team here. We celebrate the victories and accept the defeats as a team."

"I know. I look forward to seeing that in action. Being *part* of something—not only being expected to bring in money and shut up."

"When did you change your mind, Richard? Was it Katy who made you want something different?"

"Yes," I answered without hesitation. "She was the catalyst. I want more now." That, at least, was the truth.

He rubbed his finger over his chin. "I think you're very talented and you could bring in a new perspective we've been missing. I still have my doubts, but Laura has been lobbying for you ever since she met you."

That surprised me. "Oh?"

"She thinks anyone as wonderful as Katy would only love someone with a huge capacity for giving. She thinks you are that person. She sees something in you."

I had no response. I wasn't sure anyone had ever "seen" something in me.

He slid the file folder toward me. "I have an offer for you, Richard. I want you to take this with you, look it over, and come see me on Friday morning."

"You don't want me to look it over now?"

"No. I want you to look it over, make sure you read *all* the stipulations, and reflect if this is what you really want. If you agree, we'll sign on Friday, and you can start the following Monday."

"I can start today."

He stroked his chin with a small laugh. "I love your enthusiasm. Except I want to be here your first few days, and I'm taking Laura away. She's been a bit blue, so I'm taking her to her favorite little resort for some R&R time. We'll return Thursday night, and I'll see you on Friday."

"I'm sorry to hear that."

"It's fine. She needs a little alone time. It's what we do for the women we love, am I correct?"

"Of course."

He swept his arm, indicating the room. "This is my business and I love it, Richard, but Laura is my life. Be sure you always know the difference. Katy will be around a long time after your career is over. Make sure you pay close attention to her needs."

Dumbfounded, all I could do was stare at him.

He stood up. "Look it over, make notes, and we'll talk Friday. Spend a couple days with your pretty girl, and then I hope we'll start on a new, exciting venture together. Deal?"

I shook his hand. "Deal."

I OPENED THE door, frowning when I heard the sound of female voices. Obviously, Katharine had someone over I didn't know. I listened carefully, and when the woman laughed, I knew.

Jenna Davis had come to visit.

Interesting.

I reached behind me, reopened the door, letting it shut with a bang.

"Katharine! Where are you, sweetheart? Come give your man a congratulatory kiss!" I shouted with a smirk.

She appeared from around the corner, looking startled. "Richard?"

I opened my arms as I went toward her. "Get over here, you."

She hurried forward and I grabbed her, swinging her around. She laughed at the unexpected move, and before she could say anything I set her on her feet, cupped her face, crashing my mouth to hers.

A strange warmth filled my chest—no doubt gratitude that she was playing along—as she tugged on the back of my neck, bringing me closer. She whimpered softly as my tongue slid in, tangling with hers, and I couldn't help the groan that escaped. Kissing her wasn't a bad perk.

The clearing of a throat behind me made me smile against her lips, and I acted startled, jerking back. "We have company?" I asked, knowing Jenna could hear everything I said.

"Yes."

"I'd say I'm sorry, but I'm not. I was too excited, sweetheart." I ran my finger down her cheek. "I couldn't wait to get home and share with you."

She stared up at me, looking every bit the loving, hopeful fiancée. "Jenna is here," she breathed out.

I turned and smiled. "Hello, Jenna."

She smirked at me. "Sorry to break up your moment. I can leave."

I wound my arm around Katharine, tucking her close. "No, it's fine. I was just . . ."

". . . excited," she finished for me. "Does that excitement have anything to do with a meeting you had with my father?"

I grinned and nodded. "I need to go over some paperwork and talk to my girl, but I think we'll be working together."

She clapped her hands and beamed at both Katharine and me. There was no other word to describe it—her face lit up like the morning sun. "I'm so pleased."

"I am, as well."

Katharine stretched up, cupping my cheek, pulling my face down toward her. "I'm proud of you," she declared, and kissed my mouth gently.

Even I bought it.

Jenna laughed. "I'm going to head out. I think you two need to be alone."

"You don't have to leave," I insisted.

"No, it's fine." She slipped on her coat. "I wanted to give Katy some decorating magazines. She had mentioned now she had time, she wanted to add a few touches to the place." She glanced around with a grimace. "Really, Richard, you should have made her do it sooner. It's so obviously a man's place."

I looked around.

It was? It looked fine to me.

"She can do whatever she wants. I keep telling her that." I hoped my reply sounded sincere.

"Excellent. Look over the magazines, Katy, and we'll go shopping." She giggled. "Maybe the other ones will inspire you, too."

Katharine's cheeks flushed, which made me curious why magazines would embarrass her.

Amid air kisses and laughter, Jenna left. Katharine and I stood, looking at each other.

"Do you want some coffee?"

"That would be great."

I followed her to the kitchen, sitting by the counter. Idly, I picked up the pile of magazines, looking at the covers. My hand froze at the bottom two. They were thick, glossy, and the words *"The Perfect Wedding"* were featured prominently on both. I glanced up at Katharine, understanding her reaction.

"Something you want to tell me?"

"She asked what our plans were. I told her we hadn't made any yet, with everything else we'd been dealing with. She thought these might help."

I took a sip from the steaming mug she handed to me with an appreciative sigh. She did make excellent coffee.

"Graham asked me about our plans, too."

"What are we going to do? They're going to keep asking. Applying for a fake wedding license was bad enough; I'm not planning a fake wedding."

I scrubbed my face with my hands. "I know. I hadn't anticipated this."

"This, meaning what?"

"I actually like Graham. I *want* to work for him. To make him proud. For some reason, it's important to me."

She studied me for a moment. "What are you saying?"

"I thought it would be easier," I acknowledged. "He'd meet you on the odd occasion, and that would be it. I hadn't anticipated you and his daughter becoming friends—or his wife adoring you." I pushed the magazines, toppling the neat pile. "I hadn't expected them to be part of my life outside the office."

"And?"

"I think this arrangement is going to have to go on a little longer than I expected. Three months isn't going to work."

She traced the edge of one of the glossy covers, her finger retracing a picture of a bookcase. "How long?"

"How would you feel about agreeing to a minimum of six months, with an option for another six?"

Her mouth fell open in shock.

"Hear me out."

She closed her mouth and nodded.

"Graham admitted he still has reservations. I read the paperwork quickly in the car. The offer is a good one, except it has a five-month trial period. I think he's going to be watching. If you leave before then, or right after, it will look suspicious."

"You think six months is the answer?"

"It might be, except I think it'll be longer. I need to know you'll stay."

She didn't say anything, and she didn't meet my eyes. I felt the stirrings of panic building in my chest. I couldn't do this without Katharine. I wanted to laugh at the irony. I had wanted to be rid of her for so long, and now I needed her more than I ever thought possible. Karma was, indeed, a bitch.

"We can rework the terms," I offered through tight lips.

She finally looked up. "Your terms are fine the way they are. I'm not asking for more money."

"You agree to stay?"

"For a year."

"Fine. I can work with that. By the end of a year, Graham will see what I bring to the table. He won't be as concerned with my private life." I drummed my fingers restlessly on the cold granite. "I do have one other thing I want to ask."

"Which is?"

"I'd like to cover all my bases. Make sure there's no room for doubt."

"I'm not following you."

I studied her for a moment, then spoke the words I never thought I'd hear myself say.

"Will you marry me, Katharine?"

Fourteen

RICHARD

SHE WAS SPEECHLESS. Her lips moved, yet no words came out. Then she did the strangest thing.

She laughed. Huge, loud peals of laughter. She clapped her hand over her mouth, but it didn't do anything to stem the flow of chortles. Tears ran down her cheeks, and still she laughed.

It was a sound I'd never heard from her, and while I had to admit, her laughter was highly infectious—I wasn't amused at why she was laughing.

I leaned back, crossing my arms. "I don't find this a laughing matter, Miss Elliott."

I thought hearing me refer to her formally would snap her out of her hysteria because that was what it had to be. The only effect it seemed to have on her, though, was she laughed harder.

I slammed my hand on the granite. "Katharine!"

She slumped against the counter, wiping her eyes. She glanced over at me, and it started all over. More gales of laughter.

I shoved off the chair and strode toward her, not certain what I would do when I got there. Shake her? Slap her? I grabbed her arms, and without another thought, crashed my mouth to hers, effectively silencing her lunacy. That strange warmth crept down my spine as I yanked her tight to my body and kissed her. I used every bit of frustration she made me feel to punish her into silence.

Except it didn't feel like punishment. It felt like pleasure.

Hot, pulsating pleasure.

With a groan, I jerked back, my chest heaving. "Are you finished?" I growled.

She gazed up at me, finally silent, then nodded.

"At the risk of starting you off again, Katharine, will you marry me?"

"No."

I shook her slightly. "You said you would if we had to."

With a sigh, she surprised me again. She cupped my cheeks, her fingers stroking my skin. "Has anyone ever told you how impetuous you are, *my darling?*"

"Spontaneity has served me well."

"I'd call it hot-headed, but you call it whatever lets you sleep at night."

"Why are you saying no?"

"Richard, think about it. Think it through. If your instinct is right, and Graham is suspicious and you marry me *right now*, it will make him more so, not less."

I stared into her blue eyes, her words sinking into my brain. I stepped back, her hands dropping from my face as I realized she was right.

"Well, *fuck.*"

"I'm right, you know I am."

I hated to admit it, but she definitely had a point.

"Yes, you are."

"I'm sorry, what did you say?" she teased.

"Don't push your luck."

She grinned, and it occurred to me, she was no longer frightened of me. I wasn't sure if it was a good thing or not.

"We are going to readdress this issue, Katharine."

She pushed off the counter, skirting around me. "Then we'll talk about it later." She lifted the magazines, tucking them under her arm. "I have some things to read. I'm going to get some ideas for my room."

She started to walk away, and I held out my hand to stop her leaving. "While you're at it, call the building super. Something is wrong with my bedroom door."

She hesitated, eyes wide. "Oh?"

I reached over for an apple from the fruit bowl, rubbing it absently on my shirt. "I never shut it tight, but it's wide open when I get up in the morning. I don't know what's wrong with it. Get it fixed."

"Oh, I, ah . . ."

I frowned. She was all red—not just her usual pink-cheeked flush either. Her chest and neck were red and the color on her face was almost purple.

"What?"

"Your door isn't broken," she burst out, speaking fast.

"How do you know?"

"Because I open it."

It was my turn to be shocked. "Why would you do that?"

"It's, ah, quiet here."

"I don't understand."

She edged closer, her fingers playing with the edge of the magazines. "I couldn't sleep the first night. Where I lived it was always noisy, from sirens, people, cars or something. In here, it was so silent that it was almost frightening. I was going past your door and I heard you—ah, you were snoring."

I narrowed my eyes. "I have a deviated septum. I don't snore—it's a wheeze."

"If I push open your door, and leave mine ajar, I can hear you, ah, *wheeze*, and I know I'm not alone. It's, well, it's comforting."

I had no idea how to respond to her bashful confession. *I was comforting?*

"Well, then, never mind."

"I won't do it again."

I waved my hand. "Whatever. I don't mind."

She turned and left, and I stared after her retreating figure. She hadn't told me not to kiss her, although she hadn't addressed the fact I had either. Instead, she confessed to being nervous and unknowingly I had helped her sleep. She also had pointed out the flaw in my idea of marrying her right away. We had each done the other a favor. We were even.

Still, later that night, after shutting off my light, I opened my door, saving her a trip. God knew how grumpy she'd be if she didn't have any sleep.

I WENT THROUGH the paperwork carefully the next day. The offer was good. The package was generous. The one thing nagging me was the five-month probationary period. Three months was the norm, and I couldn't shake the idea there was more to it in this case. I got up, pacing the floor, and ended up staring out the window at the city below me. I liked it here. I liked the fact it was a busy city, yet easy to leave behind for more open spaces. I liked being able to grab a flight with no trouble, and I liked being close to the water. Why, I had no idea, but I did.

A knock interrupted my thoughts, and I turned my head. Katharine was at the door, a cup of coffee in her hands.

"I thought you'd like this."

I accepted the mug, taking a sip. "Thank you."

"Did you go through your offer?"

I sat down, indicating she should also. "Yes."

"You don't look happy."

"No, it's fine. It's a generous base, lots of perks, and bonuses based on productivity, the usual benefits—it's all there."

"But?"

"The probation period is bothering me."

"Because it's longer than usual?"

"I think . . . I'm not sure he is convinced," I admitted. "He even said so."

She sighed. "What do you want to do?"

I gave her a pointed look. "Set a date."

"You're certain he's watching you? Do you think he would hire you if he thought you were playing a game? He doesn't seem that sort of man."

"I agree, but my gut is telling me I need—we *need*—to move forward." I inhaled deeply. "Name your terms, Katharine. My future is entirely in your hands right now."

She studied me for a moment. I waited to see what she would say. What huge dollar amount and demands she would lay on the table. I could afford it, but I was still curious.

She retraced a design on the top of my desk, not saying a word. Finally, I couldn't take it anymore. "Just tell me."

"If I agree to marry you," she began, "you want at least a year?"

"Yes. Maybe eighteen months." When her eyes widened, I hastened to add. "Two years, tops."

"*Two years*," she mouthed silently.

"It may not take that long. I'm just throwing it out there."

"With a minimum of one year?"

"Yes."

She tossed her hair, a stubborn look crossing her face. "There are things I want."

I rolled my eyes. "I'm not surprised. You have me right where you want me, Katharine. You know you hold the upper hand right now. Lay it on the table."

"I want to make a few changes here."

"Changes?"

"To the living area, my room. Add some color, some softness. Make it homier."

I nodded in agreement. "Fine. Do whatever you want to the place— no fucking pink. I hate pink. What else?"

"A table in the empty space in the kitchen would be nice."

"Buy one."

"Can I buy a waffle iron? I always wanted a waffle iron."

I blinked. She wanted a fucking waffle iron? *That* was what she wanted?

"Never mind all the little shit. What do you *really* want to agree to this? A bonus? A house for after we split?"

She frowned. "I told you I wasn't looking for more money. Your, ah, terms, are fine."

"You want something. You're nervous and fidgety. Just say it."

"I want the same thing I wanted before. No cheating."

I huffed out a large puff of air. I knew what she wanted—my celibacy.

Resting my chin on my fingers, I studied her. She was a contradiction. Every woman I knew would have hit me up for a large sum of money. A house. Jewelry. Easy things for me to give. She wanted something of no monetary value, but a huge sacrifice on my part. I wondered how she felt about me turning the tables.

"I would ask the same of you."

She raised her chin. "That isn't an issue."

"You won't miss not having sex for two years?"

Color saturated her cheeks; however, she didn't look away. "You can't miss what you've never had, Richard."

Shock rendered me speechless. I hadn't expected her frank confession.

"Ah," was all I managed to croak out.

"Can you handle that?" she demanded, an edge to her voice. "I can't abide cheating."

I stood, then sat down on the edge of my desk in front of her. "Are you sure you wouldn't like a nice house instead? Maybe a generous lump payment big enough you never have to worry about working for an ass like me again?"

"No."

I sighed. "Is there nothing else I can give you as an alternative?"

"No."

I gave in. I really had no choice. "On two conditions."

"What?"

"You marry me this weekend after I sign with Graham. I'll tell him we were so caught up in celebrating, we got married. He'll buy that."

"And the second?"

I smirked at her. "We'll be married, Katharine. Legal. I want to know if you'd be willing to discuss, ah, expanding our boundaries at some point further into our relationship."

Her eyes grew large. "You said you didn't want to sleep with me."

"Two years is a long time for a man like me."

"You have hands."

I burst out laughing at her candid remark. "Something for which I'm already grateful. I'm not saying it's a given. I *am* asking if it could be discussed"—I winked at her—"should the need arise."

"You don't find me attractive. You don't even like me! Why would you want to sleep with me?"

"I already told you I think I may have misjudged you. I do like you. You make me laugh. As for the attractive part, again, I was wrong. You're quite pretty when you're not dressed in rags and sporting an old woman hairstyle."

She rolled her eyes. "Thanks. Keep up with the sweet words; I may not be able to control myself around you."

I grinned. "It wouldn't be all that awful, you know. I'm a good-looking man, I know my way around the bedroom, and I can make sure you enjoy yourself."

"Wow. Hard to believe I'm the only one you ever convinced to marry you. You make it sound *so* great, *so* romantic."

I chuckled. I did like the way she argued with me at times. "Do you agree to my terms?"

She pursed her lips. "If you agree to mine."

"Then, Miss Elliott, I guess we're getting married on Saturday."

"Saturday?"

"We'll have the license tomorrow; I'll sign on Friday—the timing is perfect. We'll go to city hall, say the words, snap a couple pictures, and the deed is done."

"My dream wedding," she murmured sarcastically.

I shrugged. "Wear a nice dress. I bought you lots of them."

"Well, then, with an offer like that, how can I refuse?"

I held out my hand. "A pleasure doing business with you."

Tentatively, she grasped my outstretched palm. She gasped when I yanked her close, wrapping my arm around her, pressing my lips to her ear. "I guarantee your pleasure, Katharine. Remember that."

Releasing her, I sat back down at my desk, laughing as she stormed out.

At least the next two years wouldn't be completely dull.

Given what she had shared . . . they could prove to be interesting.

Fifteen

RICHARD

I T WAS A night to celebrate. I had done it. I was a certified employee of The Gavin Group. I met with Graham, signed the offer, and much to his delight, I told him I wanted to stay and get started right away. My office was set up, I officially met my assistant, Amy, and Graham had already placed some folders on my desk. I dove into them with vigor, making preliminary notes, jotting down ideas and thoughts as they came to me.

When he told me there was a small gathering after the office closed, I had texted Katharine to inform her I wouldn't be home, so I was surprised when I saw her walk in carrying, of all things, a tray of cookies. Looking over at the lavish buffet spread out, I wanted to roll my eyes. She brought homemade cookies to an event like this? And why was she here? I hadn't asked her to come.

The answer became obvious rather quick. Jenna clapped her hands and hurried over to Katharine.

"You came! And you brought the cookies as I asked! You're the best!" Jenna then proceeded to hug her, making a huge fuss over the fact my fiancée was present.

Schooling my features, I crossed the room, ever aware their eyes were on me. I wound my arm around Katharine's waist, drawing her close. I nuzzled her hair as I murmured to her.

"You never told me, sweetheart. If I'd known you were coming, I would have been downstairs waiting for you." I tightened my arm. "You never even answered my text."

She looked at me, and I could see the apprehension in her eyes. "Jenna insisted I surprise you."

"I was afraid if you knew she was bringing your favorite cookies, you'd kidnap her *and* them," Jenna teased.

I smirked at her impish tone. "I'd share the cookies before I shared her."

Jenna giggled, and I knew I'd said the right thing. She grabbed Katharine's arm. "Break it up, you two. Mom wants to see Katy again, and I want to pick her brain about your wedding plans." She dragged her off. I made a big show of pouting, then went and got another scotch. I did take a couple cookies, though.

That was how the evening unfolded. It felt as though I wasn't even there. I drifted from group to group, chatted with Graham, Adrian, and Adam, all of whom teased me about trying to talk about work, insisting this was a social occasion. Graham grinned as he clapped me on the shoulder and told me he was thrilled I was so anxious, but Monday would be soon enough. I listened to their plans for the weekend, the way they talked about their wives, and their lives, wondering how anyone could be so attached to another person. It seemed to be the same for every one of them. They all watched their respective spouses with adoration-filled gazes. It made me a little nauseous, but I followed their example, watching Katharine as she walked around the room, talking to people, usually with Jenna or Laura by her side. She seemed to be the star of the show. Everyone wanted to talk to my fiancée. Her cookies were a huge hit, disappearing long before any of the other desserts.

When had she become more important than I was? She was the sidekick. I was the star. I was always the one who commanded the room. How had it changed? I frowned as I thought about it. It had been the same last week. When she was beside me, people spoke to me, engaged me in conversation. When we were separated, they were polite, but distant—there was no small talk or personal observations. Instead, it revolved around business. It was what I knew best. Katharine brought a warmth and ease to the interactions. Somehow, she made me more likable; her softness was doing exactly what I wanted it to do.

It was what I needed, yet somehow, it still angered me. It made me feel as if I needed *her*.

I didn't need anyone.

Graham chuckled. "Okay, Richard, quit glowering at the accounting department. They're only being friendly to your lovely Katy. No need to be shooting daggers in their direction."

I dropped my gaze. I wasn't shooting daggers at *them*. I found myself irritated by Katharine, even though she was doing what I asked. Yet, it also drew the attention away from me, and my ego didn't like it.

I forced a chuckle. "She draws them like a moth to a flame."

"She's delightful. You're a lucky man, and we've kept you apart long enough. Go get your fiancée and have something to eat."

With a smile I hoped was real, I made my way toward Katharine. She saw me coming, and to her credit, she looked happy to see me. When I held out my hand, she took it and let me tuck her close. I'd had enough to drink; I lowered my mouth to hers, nuzzling her lips, and murmuring against them. "Sweetheart, you've been too far away for too long."

She giggled a little, cupping my face easily. It was obvious, she'd had a few glasses of wine herself, and she felt loose and relaxed in my arms. "I was wondering when you'd make your way over."

"Don't worry, my lovely, I was watching you." I buried my face into her neck. I had to admit, she always smelled enticing. It was light and feminine, not overpowering.

And it was true—for some reason, even when I didn't want it to happen, my gaze drifted to where she was in the room.

Jenna laughed. "The two of you can't keep your hands off each other."

I lifted my head. "Can you blame me? I had to hide it so long. It feels good to be able to show my affection."

Her face creased into a frown. "That must have been difficult."

Nodding, I pulled Katharine tighter. "You have no idea."

"Well, I hate to do this to you, but there are other people who want to meet your lady."

I couldn't resist. "They don't want to meet me?"

Jenna shook her head. "They know who you are, Richard. And you're welcome to come along, but Katharine is the star tonight."

She tugged on Katharine's hand, and dutifully, but silently, I followed. My mood had gone from irritated to downright pissed off. Jenna had summed it up perfectly.

I signaled for another scotch, ignoring Katharine's warning look. If she were to be the star, then I'd be at her side.

The adoring fiancé—who couldn't keep his hands to himself.

She'd hate it.

"RICHARD!" KATHARINE WARNED, moving my hands from her ass again. "People are looking!"

I grinned against the soft skin of her neck. She really did smell good. "Let them look."

She turned, glaring at me. She leaned up on her toes, and I bent my head down to hear what she had to say. To anyone looking at us we were trading secrets, lovers whispering sweet words to each other. The truth was far different.

"You aren't paying me enough to let you grope me in public all night," she hissed into my ear.

I smirked as I yanked her tighter to my side, my arm like a piece of iron around her waist. "I pay you to act like a loving fiancée—so play your part. If I want to grope you, I will."

"You already got the job. Why are you trying so hard?"

I forced her closer. "I want to keep it—act as if you can't wait to get me home and fuck my brains out, and we can leave soon."

Her head fell back, her eyes startled. Up close, I was amazed to see the rim of gold around her irises, small flecks of sunshine in the blue sea. Her hair was loose again tonight, and I buried my hand in the thick tresses. "You have great hair," I murmured.

"Wh–what?"

I dropped my face lower. I could sense the stares all around us. "I'm going to kiss you now."

I didn't give her a chance to speak. I crashed my mouth to hers, holding her head tight in my hand, kissing her hard. Because I was angry and she was the cause, I deepened the kiss, slipping my tongue inside and stroking hers.

What I didn't expect, was the burst of intense heat that flared between us—or how her hands slipped up my arms and around my neck, holding me just as tight. Nothing prepared me for the flash of desire, or the desperate wish that we were alone, not surrounded by a group of people watching me kiss my fiancée. Hastily, I drew back, my gaze finding Adrian's and Jenna's amused expressions. I shrugged, kissed the end of Katharine's nose, and stepped back, releasing her from my iron grip. She stumbled and gasped a little, and my arm shot out, holding her upright. I steadied her, looking down with what I hoped was a concerned expression.

"Sweetheart?"

She glanced up, her mouth pink and moist from my tongue, cheeks infused with color and her eyes dazed. At my amused face, she shook off my hold, smoothing back her hair.

"I think we need to go home."

I winked at her. "I've been waiting for you to say that."

She glared, and I wanted to laugh. Whether she knew it or not, she had just made certain everyone thought the same thing.

My plan had worked.

"Oh, no, you aren't leaving for another hour." Jenna shook her head. "It's not even nine. Mom and I still haven't finished talking to Katy about the wedding. She won't commit to anything! I swear she's hiding something!"

"Fine," I acquiesced. "You have an hour, then she's mine. All mine. Understood?"

She muttered something about selfish, impatient bastards, and dragged Katharine off. I watched them go, feeling a little off-kilter myself.

Adrian caught my eye and winked. I returned his with one of my own and went back to the bar.

Scotch was the answer.

I COULDN'T DRIVE. I was smart enough to know that. Katharine had taken a cab, so Graham insisted on sending us home in his car, and I didn't argue. I wasn't drunk, but I was well on my way.

I'd had far too much scotch. It helped soothe the burn I felt every time I heard Katharine laugh. Saw her smile. Watched as she made—yet another—instant friend.

I didn't understand why I cared, or why it bothered me. She was charming people. If they liked her, they would give me a chance because no one would believe someone that good and kind could be in love with the bastard my reputation upheld.

Except it did.

All the way home in the car, she was quiet, yet watchful. She made sure I got out of the car without trouble, and wrapped her arm around my waist. When we got inside, she helped me off with my jacket, looking concerned.

"You barely touched anything at the party, Richard. Let me make you a bite to eat."

"No, I'm fine. I ate a couple of your cookies."

"That's not a meal—or even a snack. I'll make you a sandwich and some coffee. You'll feel better."

I waved my hand. "Stop acting as though you care how I feel, or what I need." I walked over to the bar and grabbed the scotch. "I said I'm fine. I'll have another drink."

"That's not a good idea."

"Why?"

"Because you've had enough. You need to eat something." She took the bottle from my hand and started to walk toward the kitchen.

Without thinking, I grabbed her arm, spinning her around. "You don't make decisions for me. If I want to drink, I'll drink."

She gasped and released the bottle I was reaching for, shaking her head. "Why are you drinking this much, Richard? You should be pleased! You fooled the Gavins, you got the job, and you screwed over

David! Why are you acting like someone pissed on your cornflakes?"

It exploded. Everything I'd been feeling all evening. The annoyance at how easily they accepted her into their *family*. The frustration that I was the one on the outside. The strange way I reacted when she was close—as if I almost liked it.

I shouldn't like it. I didn't like it. I didn't like her.

"Tell me, Katharine, what do you get out of this? Do you have some twisted sense of martyrdom?"

She stared at me, her eyes wide, the blue orbs glistening in the dim light.

"Do you have some sick sense of thinking you're better than me? You put up with my shit for a year, and without barely blinking, you agreed to this masquerade." I stepped closer, my rage boiling to the surface. "You think your sacrifice is going to make me a better man or some sort of shit?" I spat. "You think I'm somehow going to magically fall in love with you and life will be a bed of *fucking* roses?" I grabbed her arm, shaking her with more force than I knew I should. "Is that what you think?"

Her head shook furiously.

"Then, why did you agree? Why are you doing this for me?"

She remained silent, her teeth chewing away at her cheek so hard I thought she'd draw blood. With a curse, I pushed her away. "Get out of my goddamn sight."

I blindly grabbed the bottle of scotch, pouring a generous shot into my glass. I threw back the liquor, the burn of it warming my throat and chest. I refilled it and stepped toward the window, gazing out into the dark of Victoria, the lights of the city shining bright in the inky blackness.

Behind me, Katharine hadn't moved. I was about to tell her to leave again, when she spoke.

"Penny Johnson isn't my real aunt. I simply call her that so I don't have to explain our relationship all the time. When I was twelve, my parents were killed in a car crash. I had no other family, so I ended up in the foster system."

That news surprised me, although I remained quiet. I knew her parents had died, but she had never mentioned foster care.

"Twelve-year-old girls aren't exactly on the most desired list to be adopted or even fostered, and I went through a few places. The last one wasn't, ah, very nice."

Something in her voice made me turn around. She was standing where I left her, her head down, hair covering her face so I couldn't see anything.

"I ran away. I was on the streets for a while and one day I met Penny Johnson. She was an older woman, very kind, and she took me home, cleaned me up, and for some reason, decided I was going to stay with her. She petitioned the province to become my foster parent. She was everything to me—mother, father, friend, teacher. She didn't have much, but what she had, we made the best of it. I got a paper route, we'd collect bottles and cans—things to help make money stretch a little more. She had a way of making every job we did like a game, so it didn't seem as hard. She loved to paint and we'd spend hours in the little room she had set up—she'd paint and I'd read. It was a peaceful life, and for the first time since my parents died, I felt safe—and loved."

Her fingers ran over the back of the sofa in front of her. Up and down in a restless motion, finally stilling. "I even got to go to university. I had almost perfect grades in high school, and I got a scholarship."

"You never finished." I remembered that fact from her pages of notes.

Her voice was quiet and sad when she spoke. "Penny became ill. I lived with her while I went to school and she began acting odd. She was diagnosed with Alzheimer's. Then she fell and broke her hip, and went downhill quickly. She needed constant care. The home where she was placed was awful—she was neglected and unhappy. I fought to have her moved and the next place was just as bad."

"None of this explains anything."

She looked up, her eyes narrowing at me. "Stop being so impatient, Richard. I *am* trying to explain it to you."

I held up my hands. "Sorry, just want to make sure there was a point here."

"The point is, I realized she needed more care. A decent place. I knew I had to leave school, get a job, and provide that for her. A friend of mine told me about a temporary position with Anderson as a PA—the money was good, and if I was careful and found another job right away, I could move Penny into a nicer place. So, I took the job, and it became permanent. One day, Mr. Anderson called me in and offered me the job as your PA—with a pay increase, since you were notoriously hard to work for—being 'The Dick' and all."

"Money talks."

She shook her head. "Not usually for me. Except the pay increase meant I could move Penny into a private room. The money meant when I went to see her, she was surrounded by her canvases and pictures that were somehow still familiar to her. She was well cared-for and safe. I gave her the same gift she gave to me all those years ago. It didn't matter how shit my day was—often because of you—since at the end, I got to see the woman who took such good care of me, get the same in return."

I blinked at her, stunned.

"I didn't spend money on clothes or fancy shoes because I didn't have it. As good as it was, all my salary went to pay for Penny's room. I lived in a tiny, awful place because it's what I could afford. I shopped at discount stores and second-hand places because that was what I had to do. I made sure I was neat and presentable every day for you. I took all the horrid things you said and did, and ignored them, so I could keep my job, because by doing so, I made sure Penny was safe.

"I agreed to be your fiancée because the money you're paying me *guarantees,* until she dies, she will *never* be afraid or cold or not properly cared-for. I don't care what you say or do, because your opinion means *nothing.* This is simply a job to me. As much as I hate it, I have to let you be the ass you are, because sadly, I need you as much as you need me right now."

She turned to leave but stopped. "Do I hope I can make you a better man and somehow fantasize you'll fall in love with me? Not once has the thought even crossed my mind, Richard. You need a soul to love—and even an 'emaciated scarecrow' such as myself can see you don't have one." She drew in a deep breath. "And when this farce is over,

I'll walk away and start again somewhere else. When I no longer have to be subjected to your cruel jibes and uncaring ways, my life will be a much better place."

With that, she hurried up the stairs, and I was left at a loss for words.

Sixteen

RICHARD

I WOKE UP, confused. After a moment, I realized I was on the sofa. I sat up, grimacing, holding my aching head. I deserved it, but it still sucked. Cautiously, I raised my eyes, surprised to see a bottle of water and Tylenol on the table in front of me. Reaching for it, I swallowed two pills and drained the bottle. As I stood up, the blanket draped across my torso fell to the floor. I bent to pick it up, when realization dawned in my sluggish brain.

After Katharine had stormed away, I had tossed back more scotch, her words on a constant loop in my head. At some point, I must have passed out, and she had obviously come and covered me up, leaving the drugs and water, knowing I'd be suffering when I awoke.

Despite being even a bigger prick to her than usual, she still looked after me. My legs were shaking as I sat down, recalling the words she had flung at me last night—why she had agreed to help me. Why she scrimped and saved—to look after a woman who took her in and gave her a safe place and a home. I had looked down my nose and belittled her for it, never bothering to ask her for the details. Never really seeing her for the good person she was inside.

A wave of nausea hit me, and I tore upstairs, emptying my stomach of the copious amounts of scotch still lingering. After, I had a shower, and more Tylenol. I kept hearing her words, and the pain behind them. My behavior of the past year played on repeat in my head. My cruel jibes, my harsh words, and my ignorant manner. Despite how I treated her, she had put the needs of someone else first and kept her head up. She did her job, and I had to admit she did it well, with pride, and zero positive input from me.

I studied my face in the mirror, my hand too shaky to lift a razor to the scruff on my chin. For the first time in my life, I felt the heat of shame burn through me, and I dropped my gaze.

I had two choices.

Ignore what happened last night and hope Katharine would continue with our arrangement. I knew if I didn't bring it up, she wouldn't either. She would assume I didn't remember what had occurred.

Or, act like a mature adult and find her, apologize, and try to move forward. In order to do that, I needed to make a concerted effort, and at the very least, understand her. I had no doubt, the wedding was now off the table, but we could still continue as an engaged couple.

I pushed off the counter, ignoring the thumping of my head.

It was time to find out more about my fiancée.

"RICHARD, I DIDN'T expect to see you today. Or at least not this early."

I looked up from my computer screen. "Oh, Graham." I tugged on my cowlick and ran my hand over my neck nervously. "I had a few things I wanted to get, and, ah, pick up my car."

He came into my office, sitting down in front of my desk. I folded my hands on the dark wood, trying to stop my fingers from twitching.

"I need to apologize for last night. I drank too much. Trust me, that wasn't normal behavior for me."

He laughed, waving his hand. "We've all been there, Richard. After everything you've gone through and starting with us, then of course, your big day today, I think you deserved to cut loose."

"I hope I didn't do anything inappropriate."

He shook his head. "No, you were fine. I think you drove poor Katy around the bend a little. It was amusing to watch."

I thought of my conversation with her and grimaced. "She wasn't happy with me." Then I frowned as his words sank in. "I'm sorry, Graham, what did you mean by 'my big day' when you said that?"

He smirked. "You rather let it out of the bag you were getting married this afternoon, Richard."

"I–I said that?"

"You did. Katy kept trying to shush you, but you seemed determined to let out the secret."

"No wonder she was ready to kill me. I don't even remember."

"I think she'll forgive you." He winked. "I'm not certain my wife and Jenna will, however. They wanted to help Katy with the wedding."

"I'm sorry?" I offered.

"It's fine. They're happy with the dinner you agreed to afterward."

I swallowed. *Holy shit.* How could I remember the entire conversation with Katharine and not recall a single word of this verbal diarrhea I had with the Gavins? *What the hell else had I said?*

"Dinner?"

"Katy explained how private you both wanted your actual ceremony. You were so eloquent when you added your thoughts on why you wanted it to be the two of you, it made Laura tear up."

I blinked at him. *I did that?*

"After they agreed not to crash your day, you agreed to allow us to host a dinner for you tonight." He ran his hands over his thighs. "Are you sure you don't want to take the next week off for a honeymoon?"

"Ah, no. We have other plans. Katharine wants to get to work on making my place, ah, our place, a little homier. I'll take her away once we're more settled."

He nodded, stood, and held out his hand. "Congratulations, Richard. I hope today is everything you want it to be."

I took his hand, shaking it firmly. "Thank you."

"I think today is the start of a new, great life for you." He flashed me a smile. "I'm thrilled to be a part of the new direction."

He walked out, leaving me staring after him.

After last night, I wasn't sure Katharine would even speak to me today, never mind marry me. She was out when I left, and she hadn't answered her phone when I tried to call earlier.

I turned back to my computer. I had narrowed down my search, and I was sure I had found the home where Penny Johnson now resided. It was close to my place, private, and from the information I found on the website, expensive. I picked up the phone and dialed the number.

"Golden Oaks."

"Good morning," I replied. "I want to bring my fiancée's aunt some flowers when I visit this morning, and I want to make sure she isn't allergic to anything. I forgot to check with Katharine before she left."

"The resident's name?"

"Penny Johnson."

"I'm sorry—did you say your fiancée, Katy?"

"Yes."

"I wasn't aware Katy was engaged."

I cleared my throat. "It's a fairly recent development."

"Well, I'll have to congratulate her. Penny isn't allergic to any flowers, but if you really want to get in her good graces, be sure to bring Joey a treat."

"Joey?"

"Her parrot."

"Oh, and what does one bring a parrot, if I may ask?"

"Joey's favorite treat is a mango, but he loves any fresh fruit, or popcorn."

I felt as though I was in *The Twilight Zone*. Never in my wildest dreams would I have expected to wake up on a Saturday morning with plans to get married to Miss Elliott, after stopping to buy fruit and popcorn for a bird who belonged to a woman I had never met.

"Mangoes and popcorn. Got it."

"The caregivers like chocolate, Mr., ah . . . ?"

"VanRyan. Richard VanRyan. Has Katharine been in today?"

"Not yet. She'll be along soon, I imagine."

"Okay. Thank you, ah, Miss . . . ?"

"Tami. My name is Tami. Penny is one of my favorite residents."

"Good to know. See you soon."

I hung up. I had some shopping to do.

Along with lots of groveling.

I STOPPED IN the doorway of Penny Johnson's room, taking in her appearance. She was a small woman, plump, with pure white hair and raisins set into her chubby cheeks for eyes. Those eyes lifted at my knock, regarding me with suspicion.

"Can I help you?"

I stepped in, holding out a large bouquet. "Hello, Penny. I'm Richard VanRyan, a friend of Katharine's."

"Are you now?" She reached for the flowers. From the corner, a colorful parrot flapped his wings, squawking loudly. "My name is Penelope. I haven't given you permission to use Penny yet."

"My apologies, Penelope."

I winced a little at the noise from the bird, and held out my other purchase. "I brought Joey a treat."

"What did you bring?"

I dug into the shopping bag. "I brought him a mango. Should I put it in his cage?"

She pursed her lips, looking up at me. "Not the brightest button in the box, are you?"

"Pardon?"

"He can't eat a whole mango, young man. It needs to be cut."

I looked at the mango, then at the bird. "Oh." From the bag, I lifted out a package of microwave popcorn I had grabbed from the cupboard. Katharine ate a lot of popcorn. "I suppose I should have cooked this, too."

She began to laugh. Loud peals of amusement echoed off the walls. "Katy must like you for your looks because it can't be for your brains."

I couldn't help but grin at her sharp tongue. She reminded me of someone—the woman I once called Nana. In the brief time I had known Nana, she was the one person who cared about me. She was blunt, direct, and had no problem expressing her opinion.

Reaching to her left, she pressed a button on the wall to bring a caregiver to her room. "Tami will put these in water, and cut the mango for poor Joey. If I ask her nicely, she'll bring us some coffee."

I fumbled in the bag, and held out some chocolates. At least I got that part right. "Maybe these would help."

She arched an eyebrow at me. "There may be hope for you yet. Now, sit down, and tell me how you know my Katy—and why you call her Katharine." She smiled when I produced a second box of chocolates. "If those are for me, then you have my permission to call me Penny."

PENNY JOHNSON WAS bright, smart, and as I learned, filled with stories of Katharine as a teenager. However, I discovered, her short-term memories were shaky at best.

More than once, I saw a veil come over her eyes, and she would stumble over her words if I asked something about the present. I would steer her back to a more cohesive time by questioning her about meeting Katharine. She beamed and gave me a longer version of the story than I had heard last night. She described the thin, scared girl she had found rooting in a dumpster for food. She talked about the pain and need she saw in Katharine's blue eyes, and how she knew she was meant to find her that fateful day. I could feel the love she had for the younger Katharine, and I found I liked hearing about her life.

Penny wavered in her thoughts after that, asking for something to drink. By the time I found Tami, she showed me the kitchen area, and I went back to the room, Penny was dozing in her chair. Her bird was still in the corner, flapping around, and the music she had playing when I arrived was a gentle noise in the room.

Looking around, it was easy to understand why Katharine wanted her here and why she worked so hard to achieve that long-term. Penny's room was light and airy, with large windows, and filled with easels, boxes of charcoals, pencils, and watercolors. There were books and photographs on the shelves, and many pieces of her work hanging on the walls.

An unaccustomed wave of guilt drifted through me as I remembered the small canvas Katharine had been carrying that first Saturday. I had been my usual caustic self, telling her she couldn't hang it up in the condo. The wave of guilt and shame became a tsunami, engulfing my brain, its prickly tentacles piercing at my skin. I shifted in my chair, unused to the strange emotions.

"Richard?" Katharine's shocked voice startled me. "What are you doing here?"

I stood up, more guilt flooding my head. She looked exhausted, and I knew it was because of me. "I came to meet Penny."

"Why?"

"I felt it was important."

"I'm surprised to see you up and about."

I cleared my throat, feeling more uncomfortable. "About that—"

She held up her hand. "Not here."

I approached her in slow steps. "Will you give me the chance to talk to you? I owe you an apology." I sighed. "Many, I think."

"I'm not looking for your pity."

"And you're not getting it. All I'm asking is the chance for a civilized conversation."

"*Can* you be civilized?"

"I want to try. Please, Katharine."

She pursed her lips. "Does this have anything to do with what is supposed to happen this afternoon?"

"I don't expect you to still marry me today."

"You don't?"

"After my behavior last night, absolutely not." I sucked in a deep breath, rubbing the back of my neck. "I would appreciate it if you would, but I don't expect it."

"You sort of announced it last night. I tried to stop you." She waved her hand. "You seemed determined."

"I know. I drank far too much, and my mouth seemed to have a mind of its own. I'll deal with it." I ran a hand over my aching temple. "At this point, I'm lucky you're speaking with me."

She worried the inside of her cheek, the way she always did when she was nervous. Before she could speak again, Penny stirred and looked up.

"Hello, my Katy."

Katharine moved past me, dropping a kiss on Penny's cheek. "How are you today?"

Penny reached up and tweaked her nose. "I'm fine." She jerked her chin in my direction. "Why haven't I heard about this one until today?"

Katharine smiled and shook her head. "I think I did say something."

"Not overly smart, but he's easy on the eyes—and he has good taste in chocolates and flowers."

I chuckled at the shocked look on Katharine's face. I was grateful Penny was still with us and lucid. Tami told me she drifted in and out, often confused and lost when she woke up from a nap. I didn't want to think I had been the one to see her lucid today and rob Katharine of her chance. I wasn't sure I could take any more guilt.

I picked up my coat. "I'll leave you ladies to it."

I bent down, lifting Penny's hand and kissing the back of it, her veins like blue spider webs blooming under the thin, powdery skin. "Penny, it was an honor."

"If you bring more chocolates, you can come back."

"I'll be sure to do that." I rested her hand back onto her lap. "Katharine, may I speak to you for a moment?"

We stepped into the hall.

"Did you drive?" I asked, thinking I would wait for her if she had walked.

"Yes."

I glanced down at her hand. "Where is your ring?"

"I don't wear it when I come here. It would confuse Penny. It's safe in my purse."

That made sense. I was relieved she didn't tell me it was because the entire deal was off.

"Okay. Good. I'll see you later at the condo?"

She hesitated, remaining silent.

"What?"

"If I . . . if I agreed to marry you today, would you give me something? Think of it as a wedding gift."

"What do you want?"

"I want to know your story. Your childhood."

"I don't talk about my past." The conviction in my voice said it wasn't up for discussion.

She drew herself to her full height, holding her shoulders rigid. "Then go marry yourself, VanRyan. I'll see you at the condo later."

I caught her arm before she could leave. "Katharine," I began wearily.

Our eyes met. I saw her determination.

"All right. Marry me today, and I'll tell you."

"You promise me?"

"Yes."

"I want you to wear a ring."

"Fine," I huffed. "Nothing fancy."

"You can go pick it out yourself."

"Anything else you want as a gift?" My voice laced with snark.

"No, your story and a ring."

"I'll go get one now."

"Then I'll marry you today."

I was momentarily stunned. I had expected screaming, accusations, and arguments. Maybe even tears and her telling me to go fuck myself, for real this time. Her agreement surprised me.

"Thank you. Three o'clock?"

"I'll meet you at home." She turned and went back into Penny's room, leaving me staring after her, dumbfounded.

When had Miss Elliott become such a force to be reckoned with?

I had no idea, but for the first time, I felt grateful she was on my side.

Seventeen

RICHARD

I WAITED IN the kitchen, pacing and fidgeting with my tie. Damn thing wouldn't lay flat no matter what I did, as if I had forgotten how to tie a proper Windsor knot. It wasn't as though I was nervous. I had nothing to be nervous about—Katharine and I were simply going to say a few words, sign a piece of paper, and be done with the formality of marriage. It was another layer in my plans. Simple. It meant nothing.

I yanked at the silk again. Why wouldn't this fucking tie lay flat?

"Keep pulling it like that and there won't be any material left, Richard. What did that tie ever do to you?"

I glanced up, startled. Katharine stood in the doorway, looking equally as nervous, however, much prettier. "Whoa!"

She was wearing a simple off-white dress that hugged her narrow waist and exploded in a froth of material at her knees. The top was lacy and showed off her slender neck and arms. Her hair was pinned back, hanging to one side in a cascade of curls. The champagne hue of her dress accented her coloring. I looked down, grinning at her shoes—small with a tiny heel, they were perfect. I had gotten used to the way she fit under my arm, and now, I didn't want her any taller.

I approached her, lifting her hand, kissing it. "You look lovely."

She lowered her eyes, then straightened her shoulders. "Thank you."

"No. Thank you."

"For?"

"Where would you like me to start? For agreeing to this arrangement in the first place. For sticking to your word, even though you had every right to tell me to go to hell." Reaching over, I twisted a long curl around my finger, rubbing the soft strands of her hair, releasing it, letting it curl back into place. "For being a better person than I am," I added with complete honesty.

Her eyes were bright. "That's the nicest thing you have ever said to me."

"I know. I haven't tried very hard not to be such an asshole, have I?" I met her gaze, refusing to look away. "I'll try harder."

She worked away at the inside of her cheek furiously.

"Hey. Enough." I chuckled, drawing my finger down her cheek. "No blood on our wedding day."

The corners of her lips curled into a smile. I bent over and picked up the small gift I had gotten for her, holding out the bouquet of flowers.

"For you."

"Richard!"

"I thought you would like them," I said, feeling self-conscious.

She buried her nose in the small bouquet. "I love them." She frowned. "What about you?"

"I'm not carrying a bouquet." I smirked, wanting to lighten the serious tone we had taken.

She shook her head with a grin, and went over to the drawer, rummaging around. She picked through her bouquet and snipped one of the roses, then carefully pinned it to my lapel. Her small fingers twisted, and smoothed my tie into place. She patted the material, looking pleased. "There. Now you're ready."

"Are *you* ready?" I asked, almost fearful of her answer.

"Yes."

I crooked my arm. "Let's get married."

IT WAS A simple ceremony. Solely the two of us, with witnesses neither of us knew. Words were spoken, short vows exchanged, and we were pronounced husband and wife. I slipped a slim band on with her diamond, and as she requested, I allowed her to put an unassuming platinum band onto my finger. I stared down at my hand, flexing my fingers, and tightening my fist, the cold metal touch alien on my skin. Katharine watched me, and I grinned at her. "Marked as taken now, so I guess it's official."

The Justice of the Peace chuckled. "It is once you kiss your bride."

I lowered my head, our gazes locking. I brushed my mouth over hers, wrapping my hand around her neck, drawing her tight to me and kissing her deeply. It was my right, after all—she was my wife. When I drew back, she opened her eyes, and I was startled at the honest gentleness of her gaze. Her smile was a genuine one and I returned it fully, dropping another swift kiss on her full lips.

"We're married, Richard."

I wasn't sure why those words pleased me, yet they did.

"We are. Now, we have to go have dinner with the Gavin family. What are the chances they're keeping it low-key?"

"Slim to none—but you were the one who agreed to it."

"I know. Don't remind me. Let's sign the papers and go face the music."

"Okay."

WE PULLED UP in front of the house. I shifted into park and glanced around with a sigh of relief. "No extra cars."

"Thank goodness."

I looked over at Miss Elliott.

Katharine.

Mrs. VanRyan.

My wife.

Holy shit. I was married.

"Richard? What is it? You've gone pale."

I shook my head. "Thank you. I mean it, Katharine. I really do."

"I know."

"I don't suppose I could—"

"No."

"You don't know what I was going to say."

"You were trying to get me to forget about hearing the story of your childhood."

"It's the usual parental BS, Katharine. Why dredge it up?"

"I feel it's important."

I dropped my head in my hands with a groan at the way she used my own words back at me.

"Please, Richard."

"Fine." I huffed. "Later."

"I'll wait."

"All right. Let's get this shit over with."

She rolled her eyes with a huff of impatience. "Well, that effort lasted all of three minutes."

I gripped the back of my neck. "This is not an easy subject for me."

"I'm gathering that, but we're not talking about it at the moment. Right now, your new boss and his family are having a celebration dinner for us. Get your head out of your ass, smile, and act like you fucking adore me," she insisted, once again throwing back my words at me.

With those words, she got out of the car and bent down.

"Are you coming?"

Stunned, I could only nod.

IT WAS PROBABLY as toned-down as the Gavins could handle. The back deck was set up with an extravagant table, with tulle and small lights wrapped around the area, flowers and candles flickering in the light breeze. In the corner, there was another small table with a wedding cake. Katharine's eyes were huge when she looked at me. "How did they do this in a day?"

"The benefit of money and connections," I muttered. I had to admit, I was impressed.

Our hosts beamed at us when we arrived, Laura wrapping Katharine up in a tight hug. Graham clapped me on the shoulder, congratulating me, and I suffered through the hugs and handshakes from the rest of the family. They were certainly a touchy bunch. I stepped back, grabbing Katharine's hand like a talisman. Maybe if I touched her, they'd all stop hugging me.

Dinner was extravagant, the champagne was plentiful, but this time, I kept my head. I only sipped at the wine, and consumed water most of the evening. There might not have been any pictures at the ceremony, but Jenna and Laura made up for it with their phones, constantly snapping pictures and calling out for kisses. Luckily, Katharine had drunk enough this time, she didn't seem to mind. In fact, she tilted up her face eagerly, smiling and accepting my caresses. Copying the other couples at the table, I kept my arm around her most of the time, running my fingers over her exposed skin. On occasion, I would turn and drop a kiss to the softness of her shoulder or neck and whisper some inane comment into her ear, making her smile or laugh. We were the picture of a happy couple in love.

Jenna turned to her at one point. "Oh, Katy! I almost forgot. I teach yoga classes and a new one starts next week! Please come! You'll love it."

Julia nodded. "Adam looks after the kids. I go to all the classes—even the beginners—I love it so much. Jenna is an amazing teacher."

Katharine's eyes flared with interest. "Oh, I'd like that! I've always wanted to try it. When?"

"Tuesday nights—it's an eight week course for beginners. There's a break, then we move onto the next level."

The light in her eyes dimmed. "I can't—Tuesday is music night at the home. Local groups come in and entertain the residents. I take Penny to all of them; she loves going. I would hate not to be with her; she might not go without me."

I had noticed the list on Penny's bulletin board while I was there. This week was jazz night. I loved jazz music. The fact going to yoga was something Katharine wanted, made me want to give it to her, so I spoke up. "I'll go with her."

"What?"

"You go to the class. You've been saying you wanted to try yoga. I'll go have dinner with Penny and take her to the lounge." I nudged her carefully. "You know I love jazz music." I winked, teasing her. "Maybe it will help you with your balance."

"It's great for that!" Jenna enthused.

"It's *every* Tuesday," Katharine pointed out.

"That's fine." I liked all types of music, except heavy metal, and I doubted that genre would be included in the lineups. "I guess Penny and I have a date every Tuesday for a while."

She leaned closer, and whispered, "Are you sure?"

"Yes," I murmured back. "I'd like to spend some more time with Penny." I met her eyes. "Honestly."

She kissed my cheek. "Thank you," she breathed in my ear.

Turning, I caught her mouth. "You're welcome."

I sat back with a sigh. I was pleased I could do something for her. I saw Graham looking at me, nodding his approval. I looked down, almost flustered over his silent support.

What an odd, emotional day.

After dinner, Laura had us move the table off to one side, freeing up the space, insisting we needed to dance. Grateful we had practiced, I held out my hand, grinning at Katharine.

"Ready to dance with your husband?"

Her smile was shy, but real, as she slipped her hand into mine. "I am, my darling. Just don't use all your energy on the dance floor."

I winked. "Don't worry about that, sweetheart."

I twirled her onto the dance floor amid the laughter. She nestled into me as we moved to the music. Once again, it struck me how well she fit to me—the way her head was the perfect height to tuck under my chin. I could smell her soft scent, and enjoyed the silk of her hair on my skin. I beamed as we spun around, our steps in sync.

I had chosen the perfect fake wife.

THERE WERE MORE hugs, well wishes, and catcalls when we left. We were both quiet in the car. I kept glancing over at Katharine.

"Are you all right?"

"Hmmm."

"Is your head okay?"

Leaning against the headrest, she nodded. "I'm fine. It was a nice day."

"Okay for a shotgun wedding to an asshole?"

"Ranks right up in my top ten."

I chuckled. Her humorous side came out more every day. I liked it.

"How much older is Adam than Jenna?"

"Ten years, I think. She told me she was a bit of a surprise."

"The baby of the family."

"The spitfire, I think. Adam is far more sedate."

"Like Graham," she mused. "I like them all. They're a wonderful group."

"They like you."

"I'm trying not to feel guilty," she admitted. "They are being so kind."

"No one is going to get hurt here, Katharine. I'm going to do my best for Graham. He'll get someone as committed as any of his family is to making sure his company thrives."

"Still, after . . ."

"Let's worry about that later. It's months away—longer. Don't dwell on it."

She was quiet for a moment.

"Thank you for offering to spend time with Penny."

I shrugged. I was grateful she had let it go. "As I said, I liked her. I need to know her more. As your husband, I should. It would only be natural."

She hummed in agreement. "I think you convinced them. Even Graham," she added. "He was watching us, and I think he liked what he saw."

"I agree. Thank you. Another excellent job, Miss Elliott."

"That's Mrs. VanRyan, thank you."

An odd ripple went through my chest at her words.

"I stand corrected. Mrs. VanRyan."

She turned her face, looking out the window.

"And it wasn't only a job," she whispered so low, I almost missed it.

I had no reply to her statement. For some reason, though, I found her hand in the darkness and squeezed it.

It stayed clasped with hers all the way home.

SHE FELL ASLEEP before we arrived at our building. I knew she was exhausted after last night, and the events of the day, so I decided to let her sleep. I eased open the door, lifting her out and carrying her up to the condo. She was small in my arms, with her head resting on my shoulder. I found myself unable to look away from her as the elevator whisked us upward. Once in her room, I laid her on the bed, unsure what to do about her dress. She roused a little, and with my encouragement, we managed to get the dress over her head, then she fell back, already asleep.

I crouched beside the bed, taking in her sleeping form. Lace that matched her dress, covered her breasts, a triangle of the same silk hid her untouched sex from my eyes. Although I had always thought she wasn't my type, to my surprise, I found the delicate curves and dips of her body sexy. Carefully, I traced a finger over her collarbone, down her chest, across her stomach. Her skin was like satin under my touch. She shivered in her sleep, curling up on her side, mumbling something incoherent. She bent and curled her toes, resuming her sleep.

I pushed back the dark curls of her hair, and studied her face. The face I had called plain. It was anything but plain. Her cheekbones were too prominent and she was still too thin, yet I knew now she was in a safe place, able to eat properly, and have fewer worries, all of her would fill out more. The weariness would be erased from under her eyes and the quiet, honest beauty others saw, and I had finally discovered, would shine through.

I shook my head at the weird thoughts I was having regarding

Katharine. Today had been filled with emotions I rarely, if ever, felt. I knew, without a doubt, it was because of the woman in front of me. Still, I didn't understand *why*.

My body stirred at the sight of her, and a fresh wave of shame hit me. I shouldn't be ogling her while she slept, no matter how appealing she looked in her half-naked state. Hastily, I dragged up her duvet to her chin and switched off the light. I left her door open and retired to my own room, getting ready for the night of restless sleep. Her giving into the exhaustion she felt in the car was only a brief reprieve. I knew in the morning she would ask for her story. I also knew I would give it to her, because the bottom line was, I owed her.

After I showered, I looked in the mirror at my reflection. The outside shell envied by many. The one that covered up the empty, lost person inside. I had ignored and buried him for many years, and now Katharine was going to bring him to the surface.

I shuddered, dropping my towel on the floor. I dreaded the conversation.

Crossing the room, I opened my door wide, even though I knew there would be no comforting wheezes for her tonight.

I slid into bed, a strange yearning drifting through my head.

Wishing she were lying there, waiting for me.

Eighteen

RICHARD

I WAS SITTING at the counter, nursing my third cup of coffee when she came downstairs Sunday morning. She fixed herself a mug—I still hadn't attempted to use the coffee maker that had appeared one day last week, so she had to make do. I could sense her stolen glances as she waited for the Keurig to perform its magic.

"What?" I sighed.

"I fell asleep."

"You were exhausted."

"I woke up in my bed. With my dress off."

I arched my eyebrow at her. "It is customary for a husband to carry his wife over the threshold and remove her wedding dress the night they are married, I believe."

Deep crimson flashed across the top of her cheeks, highlighting the delicate bones.

I grinned and shook my head. "You helped me, Katharine. You fell back asleep; I covered you up and left the room. I thought you might be uncomfortable otherwise."

"Oh."

She sat beside me, and sipped her coffee before noticing the wrapped package on the counter. "What is that?"

I pushed the box toward her.

"A present."

"For me?"

"Yes."

I discovered she was a ripper—no gentle peeling back of tape and carefully removing the paper. She grabbed at the corner and tore it off with the glee of a child on Christmas morning. It brought a small smile to my face. She stared down at the box.

"What?" I smirked at her confusion.

"It's a waffle iron."

"You said you wanted one so I got it for you. Like a wedding gift." I chuckled. "I couldn't fit a table into a gift bag. I guess you'll have to pick one out yourself."

She lifted her gaze to mine. "The gift I wanted costs no more than a small piece of your time."

She was wrong on that. I knew what she wanted, what I had promised in order to get her to marry me.

"You won't let this go, will you?"

"No. You know my story. I want to know yours." She lifted her stubborn chin, the cleft standing out. "You promised."

My coffee mug hit the granite with a little too much force. "Fine."

I slid off the stool, tense and agitated. I stomped over to the window, looking at the city, the figures small and distant—much the way I wanted these memories to be.

Yet, Katharine wanted them brought into the open.

"My father was a playboy. Rich, spoiled, and a real bastard." I barked out a laugh, turning to look at her with an intense glare. "Like father, like son."

Katharine moved to the sofa, sat down, remaining silent. I turned back to the window, not wanting to make much eye contact.

"He played hard, traveled a lot, basically did what he wanted, until my grandfather called him on it. He told him to grow up and threatened to cut him off financially."

"Oh dear," she murmured.

"He and my mother married a short time later."

"Well, your grandfather must have been pleased."

"Not pleased enough. Not much else changed. Now they partied together, still traveling, spending lots of money." I moved and sat across from her on the ottoman. "He was furious, and gave them an ultimatum: unless he had a grandchild to bounce on his knee within a year, he was pulling the plug on both of them. He also threatened to change his will, cutting out my father completely."

"Your grandfather sounds a little bossy."

"I come by it honestly."

She rolled her eyes, and indicated I should continue.

"So, I was born."

"Obviously."

I met her gaze. "I wasn't born out of love, Katharine. I was born out of greed. I wasn't wanted. I was *never* wanted."

"Your parents didn't love you?"

"No."

"Richard—"

I held up my hand. "My entire childhood, my entire *life*, I heard about what an inconvenience I was—to both of them. How they had me to make sure the money kept coming. I was raised by nannies, tutors, and as soon as I was old enough, shipped off to boarding school."

She began to worry the inside of her cheek, not saying a word.

"All my life I was taught the one person you could rely on was yourself. Even when I went home during school breaks, I wasn't welcome."

Bending forward, I gripped my knees. "I tried. I tried so hard to get them to love me. I was obedient. I excelled at school. I did everything I could do to make them notice me. I got nothing. The gifts I made at school for Mother's and Father's Day were discarded. My drawings were trashed. I can't remember goodnight hugs or kisses, or having a parent read me a bedtime story. There was no sympathy for scraped knees or bad days. My birthday was marked with an envelope of cash. Christmas was much the same."

A tear slipped down her cheek, the sight of it startling me.

"I learned very early in life, love was an emotion that didn't interest me. It made me weak. So I stopped trying."

"There was no one?" she whispered.

"Only one. A caregiver when I was about six. Her name was Nancy, but I called her Nana. She was older, kind, and she was different with me. She would read to me, talk, play, listen to my childish nattering. She told me she loved me. She stood up to my parents, and tried to get them to pay more attention to me. She lasted longer than some, which is why my memory of her is sharper than others. She left, though; they all did." I exhaled hard. "I think my parents thought she was spoiling me, so they dismissed her. I heard her arguing with my mother about how isolated they kept me and I deserved more. I woke up a couple days later to a new nanny."

"Is she the one Penny reminds you of?"

"Yes."

"And since then?"

"No one."

"You weren't close to your grandfather, either? He was the one who seemed to want you the most."

I shook my head. "He wanted me to continue the VanRyan line. I rarely saw him."

Her brow furrowed, but she remained silent.

I stood, pacing around the room, my stomach in knots as I allowed myself to remember. "Eventually, my parents could barely tolerate each other, let alone me. My grandfather died, and they separated. I was sent back and forth between them for years." I gripped the back of my neck as the pain in my chest threatened to overwhelm me. "Neither of them wanted me. I went from place to place, only to be ignored. My mother flitted around, traveling and socializing. There were many times I would wake up to a stranger there to babysit, while she went on her merry way. My father went from woman to woman; I never knew who I'd run into in the hall or the kitchen." I grimaced. "I was actually grateful when they sent me away to school. At least there I could forget."

"Could you?"

I nodded. "I learned early in life to compartmentalize. I meant nothing to them. They told me often enough, showed it in their neglect." I huffed out a huge gust of air. "I had no feelings for them, either. They were the people who paid for things I needed. Our contact was almost always limited to a discussion of money."

"That's terrible."

"It's the way it was, all my life."

"Neither of them remarried?" she asked after a few beats of silence.

I laughed; the sound was bitter and harsh. "My grandfather had put a stipulation in his will: if they divorced, my father was locked into an allowance. My mother couldn't touch the money, so they stayed legally married. My father didn't care; he had plenty of resources. He fucked around when they were married, and he continued when they separated. They settled on a monthly figure, and she lived life the way she wanted and he did, too. A win-win situation."

"And you were lost in the shuffle."

"Katharine, I was *never* in the shuffle. I was the discarded Joker in the deck. However, in the end, it didn't matter."

"Why?"

"When I was almost eighteen, my parents were at a function together. I forget what it was—some society thing. They were big on those. For some reason, they left together, I suppose he was taking her home, and a drunk driver hit them head-on. Both of them were killed instantly."

"Were you sad?"

"No."

"You must have felt something?"

"The one thing I felt was relief. I didn't have to go places I wasn't wanted, but sent to for appearance sake. More importantly, though, I didn't have to pretend to care about two people who never gave a shit about me."

She made a strange noise low in her throat, bowing her head for a moment. Her reaction struck me as odd. She seemed so upset.

"Since they were still legally married, and their wills had never changed, I inherited it all," I continued. "Every last dime, which is rather ironic, considering the only time they did anything good for me was by dying."

"Is that how you afford your lifestyle?"

"Not really. I rarely dip into my holdings. I used it for important things, like to buy this place and to pay for my education. I never wanted the life my parents had—frivolous and wasteful. I enjoy working and knowing I can survive on my own. I am beholden to no one."

"Is that what you're using to pay me?"

I rubbed the back of my neck, feeling the slight dampness of stress lingering. "I consider you important, yes."

Again, she bowed her head, her hair falling forward and covering her face. I sat down beside her, and faced her straight on.

"Hey. Look at me."

She lifted her face. Her cheeks were wet with tears, her eyes wide, and her hands clutched the cushions of the sofa so hard her knuckles were white.

"Why are you this upset?"

"You expect me to remain calm after hearing how neglected you were your entire life?"

I shrugged. "It's the past, Katharine. I told you it wasn't pretty. Still, it doesn't concern the here and now."

"I disagree. I think it does, Richard."

I shook my head. "Nothing will change because I told you my story."

"Perhaps not for you."

"I don't understand."

"No, I'm not surprised."

"What the hell does that mean?"

"It explains a lot to me. Why you are the way you are when you interact with people. Why you don't get close to anyone in your life. And why you don't let people in."

I glared. "Don't start to analyze me."

"I'm not. I'm stating what I think, that's all."

"I don't want your tears, or your sympathy."

"That's too bad, Richard—because you have them both. Your parents were horrible people, and you—no child—deserves to be mistreated or ignored." She smiled sadly. "But you choose the way to live your life now. You think you've let go of the past, but you haven't. The way you see the world, the way you treat people is colored by how *you* were treated." She stood, brushing her cheeks. "If you let yourself try, I think you'd discover people aren't always as horrid as you think we are. Some of us are actually worthy."

Her words stopped me cold. "I don't think you're horrid, Katharine—quite the opposite, in fact. I'm the despicable person."

"No, Richard. You aren't despicable. I think you're lost. You haven't let yourself feel. Once you do, once you allow yourself to connect to someone, I think you'll find this world is a much better place. Love doesn't make you weak. Real, honest love—it makes you strong."

With those words, she bent down and brushed a kiss on my cheek. I felt the evidence of her sadness on my skin, the wetness of her tears lingering.

"Thank you for telling me. And, for the record, I don't think you're anything like your father. You only think so because you don't know any other way. I think, if you try, you could be a great man."

She turned and left the room, leaving me with much to think about.

Nineteen

RICHARD

I WAS UNSURE what to do with myself after the conversation with Katharine. Her words kept echoing in my head, making me question the truths I held onto for all these years. I felt drained, and I needed to stop the barrage of thoughts, so I changed, hitting my gym. I pushed myself hard, showered, then headed straight to my den. I expected Katharine to approach me wanting to continue the conversation, which I hoped to avoid, but she was busy in the kitchen, not bothering to look my way as I went past.

Waiting on my desk was a plate of sandwiches and a thermos of coffee. I stared at the offering for a moment, then with a shrug, dug in as I lost myself in the files I had brought home. It wasn't until early evening I saw her again.

"Dinner is ready, if you're hungry."

I looked up, squinting.

"Richard, you need some light." She crossed over, snapping on my desk lamp. She shook her head. "And maybe a pair of reading glasses. I've been noticing how close you hold things to your face to read."

I looked down, realizing she was right.

"I'll make an appointment for you," she offered, a grin tugging on her lips. "I doubt that falls under your assistant's job listing, either."

I had to chuckle, even as I rolled my eyes. When I met with Amy on Friday, listing out my expectations, she had surprised me with her own list. PAs at The Gavin Group were a vastly different species than at Anderson Inc. She was there to provide back up, keep me organized, and even, *on occasion*, fetch me lunch, but she was not there to make me coffee, toast a bagel, or pick up my dry cleaning. To say I was put in my place would be an understatement. She was kind enough to show me the large employee lounge, how to use the coffee machine, and where I could find the bagels and other assorted foods Graham kept on hand for his staff.

Katharine had to leave the room to hide her laughter when I told her the story.

"It's not funny!" I yelled after her.

"Oh, but it is." Her dry reply drifted down the hall.

I had to admit, she was right. In retrospect, it didn't kill me to get up and grab a coffee. It was a good way to stretch my legs. I had a sense Amy would be skimpy with the cream cheese on my bagel, anyway. Katharine always piled it on the way I liked it.

"Christ, I'm getting old," I grumbled. "Reading glasses."

She laughed. "Yes, thirty-two is ancient. You'll be fine. I'm sure you'll make them look good."

I quirked my eyebrow at her. "Oh yeah? Are you saying I'll look even sexier wearing glasses?"

"I'm saying nothing. Your ego is big enough. Dinner is in the kitchen if you want it."

With a snicker, I switched off the light, following her to the kitchen, still wary. Some of my clearest memories of my childhood were of my parents' constant disagreements. My mother was like a dog with a bone, refusing to give an inch. She would harp away at my father who would eventually explode. I was worried Katharine would attempt to pick up the threads of our earlier conversation, but she said nothing. Instead, as we were eating she slid a paint chip my way.

"What do you think?"

I studied the greenish color. "A bit feminine for my taste."

"It's for my room."

"If you like it, then go for it."

She slid another one to me, and I picked it up. The deep claret hue was strong and vibrant. I liked it. "For?"

"I thought the wall around the fireplace. To anchor the room."

Anchor the room? What the hell did that mean?

"Just the one wall?"

"I thought I'd paint the others a deep cream."

I could live with that. "Fine."

A swatch of material appeared next. It was tweed with the same claret color woven in it and the deep brown of the sofas. "What is this for?"

"A couple chairs for the room."

"I like my furniture."

"I do, too. It's quite comfortable. I thought I would add to it; change it up a little. They would look nice by the fireplace."

"What else?"

"A few pillows, some other touches. Nothing major."

"No frills or girly shit out here. Do what you want in your room."

She grinned. "No girly shit. I promise."

"Who is doing the painting?"

"What?"

"Who did you hire?"

"I'm doing it."

"No."

"Why?"

I turned in my chair, indicating the vast space. "These walls are twelve feet tall, Katharine. I don't want you on a ladder."

"My room has regular height ceilings. I like to paint. Penny and I did it together, and I'm pretty good at it."

I tapped the top of the counter with one of the paint chips. How could I make her understand she didn't have to do these things anymore? I kept my voice patient as I tried again. "You don't have to paint it. I'll pay to have it done."

"But I like doing it. I'll be careful."

"I'll make you a deal. Paint your room, and we'll discuss this one when it's time."

"Okay."

Another swatch of material caught my eye. Leaning over, I picked it up, fingering the thickness of the weave. Bold navy and brilliant green plaid woven on a rich background. I held it up, studying it. It didn't look like something for either room.

"Do you like that?"

"I do. It's striking. What's it for?"

She looked down at the table, color bleeding and gathering under her skin.

"What?"

"I thought maybe you might want your room done when I finished the others. I saw it and it reminded me of you."

"I look like plaid?"

"No," she answered with a small laugh. "The colors, they're like your eyes. The green and the blue mixing together—such an amazing combination."

I had no response, but for some reason, I felt as if I was the one blushing now. I pushed the swatch her way and stood. "We'll see how the rest comes out. Anything else?"

"I, ah, I need to move my clothes in the closet. I don't want paint getting on them."

"My closet is massive. I don't even use half of it. Hang your stuff in there. There are some really high rods—your dresses can go there."

"You wouldn't mind?"

"It's fine."

"Thank you."

I inclined my head and went back to the den. I mulled over the conversation in my head, chuckling when I realized how domestic the whole thing seemed. Discussing paint chips and material over dinner with my wife. I should have hated it.

Yet, somehow, I didn't.

THUNDER ROLLED, AND the clouds hung low and heavy overhead. I turned my chair, gazing outside into the darkened skies of the late afternoon. Grimacing, I rubbed the back of my neck, recognizing the telltale signs of a headache. They were rare, but I knew the beginnings of them well—the unexpected storm the determining factor.

The office was calm that afternoon, the usual hum of activity absent. Adrian had left on a last-minute business trip, Adam was with clients, and Jenna was out of the office. Graham had whisked Laura away for a surprise weekend, and the rest of the staff was busy within their own spaces.

In the time I had been at The Gavin Group, I discovered a completely new atmosphere in the business world. The energy was still high, the place buzzed with voices, meetings, and strategies, but it was a different sort of energy than had been at Anderson Inc. It was positive, almost nurturing. As Graham told me, they worked together as a team: administrators, PAs, designers—everyone was involved and treated equally. Amy was as important of an asset as I was. It took some getting used to, but I was beginning to acclimate myself.

With a sigh, I realized I was acclimatizing myself in other ways. Before Katharine, I worked late nights, attended many business dinners, and dated a lot of women. When I was at the condo, I used the gym, watched the occasional TV program, and entered the kitchen only to grab a coffee or a plate for the evening's takeout dinner. Otherwise, I spent the time in the den working or reading. Seldom did I have company; and it was rare I brought a woman home. My condo was my private space. If needed, either we went to her place, or I rented a hotel room. The rare time my relationships lasted longer than a few dates, I invited them over for dinner, but they went home at the end of the evening, and they never made it up the staircase.

Now, business dinners I attended, Katharine was on my arm, and the table filled with my colleagues, their spouses, and of course, the Gavin family.

One such dinner, I'd looked up, meeting the frosty glare of David across the room.

I knew David had heard of my marriage, and my name was not to be spoken in the hallowed halls of Anderson Inc. I found his anger entertaining. I tightened my hand on Katharine's shoulder, causing her to look up at me.

"What?" she whispered.

"David," I muttered.

She stole a glance his way, turning toward me. "I think I need a kiss now."

"You read my mind."

With a wicked smile, I lowered my head. Her fingers threaded into the back of my hair as she tugged me close, pressing her mouth to mine. It was hard, deep, and far too short; enough to anger David even further, but not embarrass Graham. When we broke apart, Jenna was giggling, and David was headed for the exit. I dropped another kiss on Katharine's lips.

"Well done."

Most evenings, I ate dinner with Katharine and found myself talking about my day, sharing my projects with her, wanting to hear her thoughts. She knew me better than anyone at the office, and often she came up with a word or a concept I hadn't considered. Instead of sitting in the den, I often brought my laptop into the living room, working while she watched TV or read. I found I liked her quiet company.

Twice, we had Adrian and Jenna over for dinner, using the new table that now resided in the once empty space. Katharine assured me it was what a normal couple did—they socialized with other couples. I discovered a very competitive side to her when Jenna announced she'd brought some board games over for after dinner. I'd rolled my eyes at the thought of game night yet found myself enjoying the camaraderie of it. Adrian and I beat them at *Trivial Pursuit*, but they wiped the table with us on *Pictionary* and *Scrabble*. After a couple glasses of wine, Katharine became lippy and liked to trash talk, which I found quite amusing. It reminded me of Penny.

I'd now had four "dates" with Penny while Katharine went to yoga. She was surprised to see me show up the first Tuesday, but once I flashed the rich chocolate-covered cherries Katharine told me she loved, I was welcome. The jazz trio was surprisingly good, and we both enjoyed the music before going back to her room for tea and a chat. I liked listening to her talk and hearing the memories she liked to share with me. She would drop tidbits about herself and Katharine, I could store away for future reference. On the following Thursday, I stole back to see her at lunch, sneaking her in a cheeseburger she'd confessed to craving.

Our next two dates were local choirs, and we cut out early for tea, more stories of Katharine, and whatever goodie I had picked up for her that day.

The past Tuesday had been a classical group, but she was fitful and anxious, and far more forgetful. Partway through, I took her back to her room, hoping the familiar surroundings would comfort her. She calmed some, but still seemed upset. When I hunted down Tami, she told me that had been happening a great deal more often and usually Katharine could soothe her best. I called her, and she came to the home, leaving her yoga class right away. When she arrived, Penny was asleep in her chair, waking up when she heard Katharine's voice.

"Oh, my Katy! I was looking for you!"

"I'm right here, Penny. Richard called me."

"Who?"

"Richard."

I peered around Katharine. "Hello."

She frowned. "Do I know you?"

I felt a small fissure in my heart open, but I held out my hand. "I'm a friend of Katharine's."

"Oh. It's nice to meet you. I want some time with my daughter if you'd excuse us."

I stood up. "Of course."

Katharine smiled sadly. "I'll see you soon."

Even though I knew it was part of the disease, it bothered me to the point I went to see Penny the next day. I picked up a bunch of her favorite flowers—daisies—and presented them to her with a bow. Her dark eyes twinkled in her chubby cheeks and she let me kiss the downy skin.

"I see why my Katy is so taken with you, Richard."

"Is she now? Well, I am a charmer." I smirked down at her, relieved.

She pursed her lips. "I think there is more there than that."

Ignoring her words, I stayed until she fell asleep. I left somewhat calmer. I could imagine if it upset me when she didn't know my face, how much it must affect Katharine.

It struck me odd I should be worried about that. Nevertheless, I was. I decided I needed to start tagging along for more visits with

Katharine, as well as going to some on my own.

I turned back to the file in front of me. The Kenner Footwear campaign I had pitched to Graham had been met with huge enthusiasm by the client, and I was still working up all the different concepts. I rubbed my temple, wishing I could concentrate more. When I spoke with him on the phone earlier, Graham had told me to cut out early, and I closed the file, shutting down my laptop. Maybe I would take him up on his offer. I could go home and see what changes had occurred today—see what my wife was up to.

My wife.

Katharine.

Somehow, since we had exchanged vows, we had come to an unspoken truce. The things I always found annoying, no longer bothered me. Maybe it was because I understood where they came from. Maybe I was more patient because she understood *me*.

Between our talks, Penny, yoga, paint chips, dinners and games, we had become . . . allies. Maybe even friends. We had a common goal, and instead of fighting and pulling, we had almost settled into a life, together. I knew my tongue wasn't as sharp. What before was nasty, now became teasing. I liked hearing her laugh. I looked forward to sharing my day with her. When she felt sad about a bad day with Penny, I wanted to cheer her up. I had taken her out to dinner a few times, simply to have her dress up and enjoy herself.

I found myself wanting to be affectionate with her. It felt natural to hold her hand, drop a kiss to her brow, or brush a caress over her lips— and not always when we were in public. She often pressed a kiss to my head when heading upstairs, and there were times I slipped my arms around her for a hug or dragged my lips over her soft cheek in thanks for dinner or to say goodnight. They were actions without thought—all simply a part of being with her now.

Maybe tonight, I'd surprise her. Offer to take her out if she wanted. We could drop by, visit Penny, and take her some decadent treat she loved—or we could order in. Afterward, I could relax, she could watch one of the shows she liked, or we could watch a movie. Maybe a quiet night would help ease my head.

I'd ask her what *she* wanted.

I still liked seeing the surprise and confusion cross her face when I offered *her* the choice.

I OPENED THE door, hearing voices. I recognized them both, and smirked. Jenna was over—again.

"Katharine, sweetheart!"

Hurried footsteps headed my way and she came around the corner. She looked unusually frazzled. I was used to seeing her calm and was surprised when she wrapped her arms around my neck, pulling me close.

"Are you okay?" I murmured into her ear.

"Jenna is frightened of storms—Adrian is away. She asked if she could stay here until the storms break."

The warning behind her words hit me.

"Your room?" I asked, worried.

"Yes."

I drew back. "Is it . . . ?"

"All ready, yes."

"Okay."

"I–I didn't—" she floundered.

"It's fine."

I walked ahead of her, pulling her behind me. "Hey, Jenna."

The woman I was used to seeing flitting around, enthusiastic and vibrant, was curled into the corner of my sofa, looking anything but vibrant. She was pale and looked scared to death.

"I'm sorry, Richard. Storms terrify me. With both my parents and Adrian away, I didn't know what else to do. The house is so big when he's gone."

I sat beside her and patted her leg awkwardly. "It's fine. I'm glad you came."

"Katy said you had no plans I'm interrupting?"

"No. In fact, I have a headache. I was looking forward to a peaceful night at home. We'll sit it out together, okay?"

She clasped my hand with her shaky one. "Thank you."

I stood up. "No problem. I'm going to change and grab a shower."

"I'll bring you some Tylenol," Katharine offered. "You're rather pale, Richard. Are you sure you're okay?"

"It'll pass. I may grab a nap."

"I'll bring a cold compress, too."

I went past her, stopping to drop a grateful kiss to her head. "Thank you—that will help."

Upstairs, I peeked in her room, not having looked while she was redoing it. There had been some delays with the furniture she ordered, so the room took longer than she had planned, only being finished this week. There was a bag on the floor I assumed was Jenna's. The room was complete, looking like what Jenna would think was a guest room. Empty. None of Katharine's personal possessions were scattered around. She had added a bookshelf and unpacked her few boxes, the knickknacks and books filled the shelves. A new chaise lounge sat in the corner, a small table, and lamp beside it. Some of Penny's watercolors adorned the walls. I pulled open the dresser drawers and closet, seeing they were empty, aside from a couple of boxes stored in the closet. The bed was made up with the new linens she had bought. It was staged well.

I went to my room and had to pause for a moment. Katharine was everywhere. Her robe was draped across the end of the bed, the deep red silk shimmering in the light. A few pictures of Penny and us were sprinkled around. The once empty night table had books and a half-full glass on it. The top of the dresser had her favorite perfume, jars, and bottles strewn around. Without even looking, I knew the bottom drawers of the dresser now held her clothes, and the closet still housed the contents of hers she had planned on moving back this week. In the bathroom, her toothbrush was beside mine; her daily skin care items were on the counter. She must have moved like a tornado, to make sure it looked like this was her room, too.

She was waiting when I got out of the shower, holding the cold compress and pills. She had shut the door, giving us some privacy.

"How much time did you have?" I asked, keeping my voice low.

"About fifty minutes. A bunch of items are in the boxes I had unpacked. I switched things around as fast as I could when she called, crying, asking if she could come. She called the cell phone—I told her I was out and would be home in an hour. I didn't know how to say no."

"You couldn't," I acknowledged.

"Are you okay with this?"

I sighed and held out my hand for the pills. "It's fine. Thank God, it's a king-sized bed. You stick to your half, I'll stick to mine." I smirked. "You can have a close encounter of the wheezing."

Her eyes grew round, making me snicker. She'd been so anxious to set the scene, she hadn't thought about what happened later. Swallowing the pills, I reached for the bottle of water she was holding.

"Unless, of course, you'd like to revisit the whole 'fucking, no fucking' topic. You've already resisted me for a month."

She glowered, and I couldn't resist bending down and brushing her mouth. "Think about it, sweetheart," I murmured against her softness.

I *was* getting weary of my hand.

She slammed her hands on her hips. "I doubt you're up to your usual *stellar* performance at this moment. Especially being so out of practice—and having a *headache*."

I smirked as I collapsed onto the mattress, groaning with relief when she laid the compress on my head.

"I'd be willing to put forth my best effort."

I was shocked to feel her mouth on mine again.

"Go fuck yourself, VanRyan."

Her words had no venom, and my offer was bullshit. We both knew it, and we both laughed, the sound of our joint amusement low in the room.

"Rest, I'll come get you for dinner."

I caught her hand and kissed it.

"You're going soft," she chided, running her hand over my aching head.

I shut my eyes and surrendered to her gentle touch.

"All your fault," I mumbled.

"I know," she replied as the door closed.

Twenty

RICHARD

SPENDING AN EVENING with two nervous, tense females proved to be interesting.

Jenna was unnaturally still, which was disconcerting itself, but Katharine was the bigger surprise. I had gotten used to her quiet nature, but tonight, she rambled.

Incessantly.

Between showing Jenna her plans for the living area, "our room," asking endless questions about the history of yoga, the general inquiries about every member of the Gavin family and office, as well as any other subject that seemed to filter through her brain, she talked non-stop. Also, she never sat down. She flitted around the room, using her hands to demonstrate her ideas. She picked, moved, tidied, and straightened every object in the room at least twice. She kept patting Jenna's shoulder, making sure she was okay, and the cold compress she kept on my neck was switched out every twenty minutes. I didn't think it ever reached room temperature. I had to admit, when she stood behind me, chatting, I didn't mind the way her fingers felt as she massaged my neck, or the way she tilted my head back to the softness of her stomach and ran her fingers through my hair repeatedly. The soothing action felt good, and my headache began to dissipate, despite the constant chatter.

Still, her behavior was perplexing. Even Jenna quirked her eyebrow at me more than once. I shrugged one shoulder, offering the only thing I felt made sense when Katharine was out of earshot.

"She doesn't like storms, either."

My explanation seemed to satisfy her curiosity.

Around ten, the storm lessened, the thunder tapering to a low occasional growl, although the rain continued to beat on the glass around us.

Jenna stood. "I'm going to go stick in my ear buds, turn up the music, and put on a night mask. Maybe I can fall asleep before the next wave hits."

Katharine stood, as well. "Are you sure you'll be okay? I can sleep on the chaise and be close."

Jenna shook her head and kissed her on the cheek. "I'll be okay. Knowing you're across the hall will help. I just can't be alone. Usually Mom and Dad are around if Adrian is away. Adam and Julia are so busy with the kids, I hate bothering them. You guys were a lifesaver tonight." She bent down and kissed my cheek. "Thanks, Richard. I know you see enough of me in the office. I really appreciate it."

"Not a problem."

"If you need me, come and get me," Katharine offered.

"I'll try not to."

She walked up the steps, leaving Katharine and me. I studied her body language. Tense was an understatement. If she held herself any tighter, she'd be the one with the headache soon.

"Hey."

She startled and looked at me, her eyes wide.

"What's wrong?"

"Nothing. Why would you ask?"

I snickered. "You've been like a cat on a hot tin roof all night."

She bustled around, tidying up her already neat files, straightening the newspaper I'd been trying to read, and picking up the glasses to take to the kitchen.

"I don't know what you're talking about. Are you hungry?"

"No."

"I can make you a sandwich."

"No."

"Do you want coffee? I bought some decaf. Or, maybe some toast or something? You didn't eat much dinner."

"Katharine," I warned, my voice becoming impatient.

She set down the glasses she was holding. "I'm going to bed."

She bolted up the stairs, leaving me more confused than ever.

I FOLLOWED NOT long after, leaving a couple lights on in case Jenna needed to prowl around the condo. The last thing I needed was to have to call Adrian and tell him his wife fell down the stairs in the night, and I had to take her to the hospital. Graham and Laura wouldn't be overly impressed, either.

The rain was picking up again, the storm gathering strength outside. I wondered if any of us would get much sleep on this strange night.

Upstairs, I shut my door behind me, the sight of the small lump in my bed reminding me I wouldn't be alone tonight. Katharine was huddled under the duvet as close to the edge of her side of the bed as she could get without falling off. Suddenly, her strange behavior made sense. We were sharing a bed tonight, and she was nervous. An odd feeling—one of tenderness—swept through me.

It struck me as I watched her tonight what a gentle soul she must have. She lost her parents, survived what I knew must have been a rough time after they passed, although she hadn't given me a great deal of information. She never discussed her time living on the street, which must have been horrific. She put up with me, cared for Penny, and thought nothing of helping a friend, even if she had to shift her entire life to do so—and she did it all with one of her warm smiles. She was amazing.

I found a pair of sleep pants and a T-shirt. I preferred sleeping only in boxers, but I didn't want Katharine any more uncomfortable than she clearly was already. After getting ready, I slipped in beside her, waiting for her to say something. There was only silence.

Rising up on my elbow, I peeked over her shoulder, drawing the heavy veil of hair away from her face. She didn't speak or move, staying still, and her eyes remained firmly shut. Her chest moved far too rapidly for her to be asleep, though. I bent low over her, close to her ear.

"Faker," I whispered.

She shivered, burrowing her face farther into the pillow. I dropped a kiss on her bare shoulder, and pulled up the duvet. "Relax, Katharine. I'll be a perfect gentleman."

I shifted over, shut off the light and lay there, listening to her short, nervous breaths. It should have felt strange having her in my bed, and yet, it wasn't unpleasant. I could feel her warmth, and smell her light perfume.

The bed felt wrong, though, somehow. It took me a few moments to realize why. There was a constant vibration—just enough to make the mattress quiver. I looked over at her, studying her small huddled mass. She was shaking.

Was she *that* afraid of me?

I rolled to my side, reaching out and wrapping my arm around her, drawing her back to my body. She let out a shocked squeak, her body rigid. Tremors ran through her constantly, and her hands clutching my arm were like ice.

"Katharine, stop this," I murmured. "I'm not going to do anything."

"It's not that. Well, not just that."

"Is it the storm?"

"It's . . . it's the wind," she confessed. "I hate the howling sound of it."

I tucked her closer, and another shiver raced through her whole body. "Why?"

"The night my parents died, there was a storm. It was like this one. Loud. The wind pushed the car around as if it was a feather. My dad lost control and the car flipped."

My heart began to beat faster. "You were with your parents that night?"

"I was in the back seat. When it happened, the windows exploded and the wind was so loud, and I was scared. I kept losing consciousness, but I was so cold, and I could hear the wind howling . . . it never stopped." Her voice dropped. "I knew they were dead, and I was alone and trapped."

My throat felt tight at the pain in her voice. She had never told me any of that until now.

"Were you hurt?"

Silently, she took my hand and pressed it to the top of her leg. Under the thin material of her nightgown, I could feel a long, twisted scar running down the outside of her thigh. "I had a concussion and my leg was crushed when the car flipped. It took two operations, but I survived." She cleared her throat. "That's why I sometimes trip or lose my balance. It buckles."

All the times I mocked her, rolled my eyes, and watched her struggle to her feet, filled my mind. Shame, hot and blistering, made me tighten my arms, and I dropped my face into her neck. "I'm sorry, sweetheart."

"It's not your fault."

"No. I am sorry for what you went through, but that's not what I'm talking about."

"Oh," she breathed, knowing the reason for my apology. "Well, you didn't know."

"I never bothered to ask, though, did I?"

"I guess not."

The next words out of my mouth shocked me. "Forgive me for that."

"I did."

I rolled her onto her back, hovering over her, staring down into her face in the darkness. The lightning flashes lit up her pale face, and the tears stood out in her eyes. "Forgive me for all of it, Katharine."

"I have."

"How?" I whispered. "How can you be this forgiving? How can you even stand to be around me?"

"Because you're trying."

"It's that easy for you? A little effort on my part and you forgive?"

"I had to forgive you to do this with you."

"In order to make sure Penny was looked after."

Hesitantly, she lifted her hand, cupping my cheek, her fingers stroking my skin. "That was one reason."

"What was the other?"

"I saw something—the day you told me about meeting with Graham. I saw a different side of you. I thought . . ."

"Thought what?" I asked when her voice trailed off.

"I thought if I could help you get away from the poisonous atmosphere of Anderson, maybe you could find the real Richard."

"The real Richard?"

"I think . . . I think you're more than you let people see. More than you let yourself see. I see more and more of the real you coming out."

I leaned into her touch, letting her words soak in. Idly, I twisted a lock of her hair in my fingers, brushing the silkiness of it between my fingers.

"What is the real me like?" I asked, my voice low, almost pleading. I wanted to know her feelings—what she thought of me.

"Strong, caring. Capable. Talented." She paused and sighed. "Kind."

"You see things that aren't there."

"No, they are. You aren't ready to see them yet. You will," she assured me.

I stared at her in wonder. Gentle didn't describe her soul. Not even close. I wasn't sure I knew a word that did. Angelic, maybe? Whatever it was, whatever *she* was, I didn't deserve her forgiveness, the high opinion she had of me—and I certainly didn't deserve her.

A huge gust of wind shook the glass in the long windows, the rain furious in its rage as it beat against the panes. Katharine tensed up, her gaze flying toward the sound.

I bent low and kissed her. It was tender, nothing but a brush of our lips; hers trembling and soft pressed to my humble, unworthy mouth. I kissed her with the gentleness I should have always used when speaking to her.

I moved, tucking her back to my chest.

"Sleep, sweetheart. You're safe. Nothing will hurt you, I promise."

"I've never slept with someone like this, Richard."

I dropped another kiss to her neck, wanting her to understand, to know something about me that made me worthy of her faith. "Neither have I, Katharine. You are the first woman I've ever had in this bed."

"Oh, ah . . ."

I smiled into her skin. "I've never let anyone stay here. This is my safe place. Only mine." I tightened my embrace. "Now, let it be yours. Sleep. I've got you."

Closing my eyes, I relaxed into her warmth. Our bodies melded from chest to hips, our flesh seeking and finding something from the other.

Comfort.

WHISPERS. I COULD hear whispers as I woke, drowsy and warm—almost too warm. I was surrounded by heat and something that smelled enticingly good. My pillow tickled my face and I twitched my nose, trying to ease the itch, burrowing deeper into the welcome softness. My pillow giggled a little, and the whispers started again. I forced open my eyes. The light was dull, the skies still heavy and rain-soaked outside. I lifted my head and met the amused gaze of Jenna, who was sitting on the floor beside the bed, coffee cup in hand.

"Morning," she said with a smirk.

"Is the storm that bad you had to hide in here?"

"I came to get Katharine, but she couldn't escape your clutches, so we were having coffee right here," she teased.

I looked down, realizing she was right. I was wrapped around Katharine as tight as possible. Every inch of me touched her body. I had one hand fisted in her hair, and the other held her to me like an iron bar. My legs intertwined with hers and my cock—my fully erect, desperate-for-release cock—was pressed into her ass. Her firm, accommodating ass, which felt like heaven nestled into my aching erection. I buried my face back into Katharine's neck, marveling at how natural it felt to wake with her this way.

"Go away, Jenna," I mumbled.

Katharine pushed against my arm. "Let me go."

I kissed her neck, liking the shiver that happened this morning.

Unlike the fearful tremors last night, this was one of pleasure. It rippled down her spine, her torso flexing, her ass snuggling tighter to my cock.

"Five minutes, Jenna. Give me five minutes," I added in a throaty voice.

It was only going to take two.

She stood up, laughing. "Men," she snorted. "I'll meet you downstairs."

As soon as the door shut, I flipped Katharine, crashing my mouth to hers. I kissed her hard, needing to feel her lips beneath mine. I stroked her tongue, tracing the contours of her mouth, teasing, yet desperate. I pulled back, gasping.

"You are killing me."

"I was sleeping," she protested. "*Sleeping.*"

"You feel too good." I thrust against her hip. "*Jesus*, Katharine."

Her eyes widened; the glimmer of fear piercing the lust in which I was drowning.

What the hell was I doing?

I flung myself off her, my chest heaving. I threw my arm over my face.

"Go downstairs. I need a shower. A long, cold one."

"I'm sorry."

"It's fine," I groaned, grabbing her arm. "Wait. Don't go yet. Just . . . just stay there for a moment or two. I don't want Jenna to think I am, ah, lacking stamina."

Her mouth opened, but no sound came out.

Lifting my arm, I flexed my fingers as I glared at her. "I swear I'm getting carpal tunnel syndrome. I'm going to need surgery."

Katharine began to chuckle. Her shoulders vibrated as she buried her face in the pillow, her chuckles turning into full out peals of laughter. The bed shook with the force of her amusement.

The corners of my mouth twitched. "It's not a laughing matter."

She didn't stop, and I started laughing with her. Purposely, I hauled myself over the top of her, letting my heavy, hard cock drag across her body. I lifted her face from the pillow; her cheeks flushed and pink, her eyes bright with fun. I kissed her again.

"We need to talk about expanding our boundaries. Before I explode."

I left her lying there, speechless.

But, she was still smiling.

And, she didn't say no.

Twenty-One

RICHARD

J ENNA RECEIVED A call from Adrian while we were having
breakfast, telling her he wouldn't be home until Sunday. With the
storm still all around us, we assured her she was welcome to stay
until he came to pick her up the next day. There was no other option.
Besides, she made Katharine laugh, and I liked hearing the sound. I
wanted to make it happen more often.

The three of us went to see Penny while the storm simmered,
low and tame. I insisted on cheeseburgers, letting it slip how often I
snuck them in for her. Katharine was shocked to realize the number
of times I'd been to the home without saying a word. Her eyes shone
with appreciation when she stretched up and kissed me, catching me
off guard. I yanked her close and took full advantage of the fact we had
a captive audience with Jenna, kissing her until she was pink-cheeked
and embarrassed. Jenna caught my eye with a wink as I accepted the
heavy bag of burgers with a wide grin.

Penny was quiet but lucid when we arrived. She laughed at my
offering of grapes for Joey. He liked to pick at them, and I didn't have
to cut up anything or bribe Tami to do it for me. The chocolate shop
I frequented certainly had a boom in sales the past few weeks, and the
staff looked forward to what I brought each visit. I never disappointed
them.

Jenna was more like her usual self, bubbly and chatty, entertaining
Penny with stories of her family. It gave me the chance to sit back

and watch Katharine with Penny. She sat next to her, holding her hand. She would cup her cheek, run her hand over Penny's forehead, smoothing away the flyaway hairs as she talked or laughed. She teased and encouraged Penny to eat, tucking a napkin under her chin as she scolded her for being messy. Penny tweaked her nose back. "You stop being so bossy, my Katy."

"She is bossy," I muttered. "She tells me what to do all the time."

"Payback," Katharine mused.

"That's what wives are for!" Jenna laughed.

Both Katharine and I froze. We had never mentioned being married to Penny. Our gazes met over her head, unsure what to do next.

Penny sat up, her lunch forgotten. She looked between us. "You're married?" She turned to Katharine. "You got married, and you didn't tell me? Katy, are you pregnant?"

Katharine shook her head. "No, Penny. I'm not pregnant."

"But you're married."

"Yes."

Penny looked at me, pushing away her lunch tray. "I'd like to speak to my daughter in private."

I PACED THE hall, my eyes on the closed door. With a groan, I slumped against the wall, letting my head fall back on the hard surface.

"Richard, I'm sorry," Jenna pleaded. "I had no idea she didn't know. It never occurred to me she wouldn't have been told."

"Of course it wouldn't."

"She didn't know? She hadn't simply forgotten?"

I wanted to lie and tell her we had told Penny. That the disease was at fault, not us. Except, I was getting tired of the lies. I pushed away from the wall, rubbing the back of my neck.

"Katharine had a rough time in her teens. There is more to her story than you know, but it's her story to tell. Penny is the world to her, and she was trying to protect her wellbeing."

She nodded, waiting for me to continue.

"I was the instigator, Jenna. I pursued *her*. I was way ahead of her this whole relationship. She didn't want me to meet Penny at first, until she was sure." I tugged on my cowlick roughly. "I forced the issue and came to see Penny without her knowing. I wanted to know more about the woman who helped Katharine. I pushed everything forward. I married her quickly—before she could change her mind. Katharine was worried Penny would think it was too fast, so we decided to stay quiet for a while and let Penny get used to me."

"And I blew it."

I shrugged. "We should have bitten the bullet and told her ourselves. This is on us."

The door opened, and Katharine stepped out. "Richard, can you come in?"

"Shit," I cursed under my breath. "If I don't make it out in one piece, look after Katharine for me."

Jenna gave me a sympathetic smile and patted my shoulder.

At the door, Katharine laid her hand on my arm. "I'm sorry."

I squeezed her fingers. "It's fine."

I stepped in, Katharine close behind me.

I had faced angry clients in boardrooms. Stood in front of conference rooms filled with unfriendly faces waiting for me to fail in my presentation. I had done it all without breaking a sweat. Yet, standing in front of the stern-looking old woman, I was sweating, and gripping my wife's hand like a talisman.

Penny fixed me a look. "You married my Katy."

"Yes."

"Without my permission."

"Yes."

"Why?"

"I've never done this before. I didn't know I had to ask—"

She waved her hand. "Oh, you really aren't that swift at times, are you, young man?"

I swallowed. "Sorry?"

"Why did you marry her?"

"I couldn't be without her."

"And you didn't say anything because?"

I had no idea what Katharine had said, but I sensed I needed to stick close to the truth.

I crouched down, meeting Penny's eyes. "I married her fast because I didn't want to lose her. I need her in my life. We were worried you wouldn't approve, but I hoped once you got to know me, you might be okay with the thought of her marrying me."

"She's too good for you."

I laughed because it was the truth. "I'm well aware of that."

"You should have asked me first."

"You're right, I should have. I apologize."

"She says she's happy."

"I am, too." I glanced over at Katharine, surprised at the fact it was the truth. "She constantly amazes me."

Penny sniffed. "Just wait. You haven't seen anything yet."

"I can only imagine."

She pursed her lips. "I'm watching you."

"Duly noted."

"Fine. Now you owe me cake."

"Cake?"

Katharine stepped forward, laying a hand on my shoulder. I noticed her rings were now in place, the sight of them making me smile for some reason. I hadn't taken mine off, and Penny had never questioned it. Without thinking, I pressed a kiss to her hand, the action making Penny beam.

"We always celebrated good things with cake."

"So, it's a good thing? I'm a good thing?"

Penny patted my cheek. "I'm depending on you to take care of her for me."

"I will."

"Now, that cake?"

There was a bakery down the street.

"I'm on it."

"Chocolate," Penny insisted.

I brushed her downy cheek. "As if there was any other kind."

KATHARINE CAME IN, carrying a cup of coffee that I gratefully accepted. I indicated she should sit down.

"Where's Jenna?"

"Having a nap. I think she's taking advantage of the lull in the storm. I don't think she slept well last night."

"I slept like a baby."

She rolled her eyes. "A clingy baby."

I grinned. "Not my fault you're so perfect to snuggle up to. You smell good."

"Your, ah, *wheezing*, is much louder up close."

I narrowed my eyes. "Cute."

She smirked. "Sorry." Her expression turned serious. "I *am* sorry about this morning."

I scratched the back of my neck. "I guess it was bound to happen."

"There's a good chance she'll forget. We may have the conversation again."

"At least we can say we did tell her, and maybe she won't be so upset."

"I suppose."

I took a sip of coffee. "What did she say to you?"

"She was worried I was pregnant."

"That's not an issue. Never will be." I couldn't resist teasing her on the subject. "Even if we expand our boundaries."

"Are you not able to father children?"

"I have no idea. I've never attempted to procreate, and I never plan to. I am always protected, and I make sure my partners are, too."

She tilted her head, confused. "You don't want children?"

"Katharine, I don't have the capacity to actually be in a real relationship. I have no interest in being a father and bringing another emotionally stunted person into this world. I would never be able to connect with a child, which is why I have no desire for children. Ever."

"I think you're wrong."

"Wrong?"

"I think you have the capacity. I think you could connect—love—a child. If you loved their mother."

I barked a laugh. "Since that's never going to happen, I stick to my original statement."

"Why are you so certain you can't fall in love?"

I was getting impatient. "I told you. Love makes you weak. It makes you need people. Depend on them. I won't allow that to happen."

"Sometimes things happen that are beyond our control."

I waved my hand. "Not in this case. There is no love or children in my future."

"That sounds lonely."

"I have my work, and it fulfills me. It's sufficient."

She studied me, a frown on her face. "Is it?"

"Stop trying to analyze me, Katharine."

"I'm not. I'm trying to understand you."

"Don't."

"Why?"

I leaned forward, my hands fisted on the desk. "I don't pay you to understand me. I'm paying you to act out a role."

"One that gets more complex every day."

"What are you talking about?"

"Don't you get tired of it, Richard? The lies? We seem to add more all the time. It's like a snowball that grows as it rolls down a snowy hill." She sighed. "It was supposed to be a simple thing—me pretending to be your fiancée. Now it has grown and escalated to the point I don't even recognize myself! I hate lying to people—and I'm lying to everyone! Penny, the Gavin family, people at the care home . . . It's one huge mountain of lies!"

"It's a means to an end. No one is getting hurt."

"Really? I think you're wrong."

"How do you figure that?" I waved my hand around the room. "Graham isn't suffering, Penny is being looked after, you're living in a better place, and you don't have to work. Who is getting hurt?"

Her voice dropped to a whisper. "I feel guilty—more so every day."

"Why?"

"I like these people. I really like Jenna; we've become friends. Knowing I'm lying to her bothers me. Graham and Laura have been nothing but kind. It's as if I'm betraying them with this farce. The people at the home think we're married."

"We are," I insisted. "It's not a farce. Our marriage is legal."

"They think it's *real*. They think we're in love. And Penny . . . I never wanted Penny to know. I didn't want to have to lie to her of all people. I hate lying to her the most."

"You know she'll probably forget."

Katharine rolled her eyes. "It's still a lie. Tami and others will keep reminding her, so she may not forget. And there's Adrian, Adam, Julia . . ." She huffed in exasperation. "The list grows."

Drumming my fingers on the desk, I shrugged. "It's bigger than I expected, I'll give you that much. Even Brian thinks I had a change of heart. When we played golf the other day, he congratulated me on finally finding my 'human side.'"

"It doesn't bother you? How many people this lie touches? How many people it will affect when it's done?"

"Katharine, stop being overdramatic. Marriages break up all the time. The world will go on. We'll figure out the hows and whys when we decide the time is right."

"And, in the meantime, we keep lying."

I was done with this inane conversation. I rubbed my head and scowled. "Yes. We keep lying. I'm still paying you, and it's still a job. Until further notice, you are my wife. Keep acting the part. Pretend you like me. Dig deep, and imagine you love me. Do whatever you need to do to keep up the 'farce,' as you call it."

She rose to her feet, shaking her head. "That's the rub here, Richard. I don't always have to pretend to like you. When you stop acting like such an asshole, you're a decent man. You respond to people. You're kind and generous to Penny. For some reason, you forget to be that asshole you show the rest of the world when you're around her. Sometimes, you forget even when you're around me." Her expression was sad and her voice dejected. "Sometimes, I forget you dislike me and

I think we're actually friends."

She strode to the door, paused, and looked back. "I like those times. They make the rest of the days easier to take."

Then she walked out, leaving me stunned.

Twenty-Two

RICHARD

KATHARINE WAS QUIET the rest of the evening. The rain came and went, eventually easing off around midnight. Jenna sensed the turmoil in the air and tried to be discreet. At one point, she asked me if Katharine was all right.

"We, ah, had a disagreement," I admitted. Couples argued; my response—it seemed probable.

"Because of what happened earlier?"

"Yes." I didn't tell her to which earlier occurrence it pertained. I let her think it was what happened with Penny.

"Do you want me to leave?"

"No, it's fine."

"Don't go to bed angry. Talk it out," she encouraged. "I'll head up soon and give you some privacy."

Unsure how else to respond, I nodded. I had no idea what to say to Katharine, but as soon as Jenna went upstairs, she followed. I waited a while, shut off the TV, and joined her in my bedroom. She was already in bed, curled up and close to the edge. I got ready and slipped in behind her small, warm body. I hesitated, then reached over, tugging her back to my torso.

"Don't be angry with me."

"I'm not, just sad." She sighed.

"I can't change who I am."

She rolled in the dark to face me. "I think in some ways you *have* changed."

"Maybe," I admitted. "Still, it doesn't change how I feel about certain things—children and love are two of them."

"Everything is black and white with you."

"It has to be. It's how I deal with life."

"You miss so much."

I trailed my finger down her cheek, touching the softness of her skin in the dark. A trace of dampness lingered, and I knew she'd been crying. It bothered me, thinking of her lying there, upset.

"Katharine," I began.

"What?" she whispered.

"I know this got bigger and more complex. I know you're a better person than I am, and it bothers you. I didn't expect the Gavins to be part of our life outside the office. I hadn't planned on meeting Penny and being fond of her. There isn't anything we can do about that now except go with the flow. I can't change my outlook because it's what I believe. There is something you're wrong about, however."

"What is that?"

I cupped her cheek, bringing her face close to mine. "I don't dislike you. Far from it. I regret every nasty word, every lousy fucking errand I sent you on, and every dirty job I got you to do. I think you're incredibly brave to have agreed to do this with me, and the reasons you did it are astonishing to me. You are selfless and kind, and the fact you've become so *important* to me is a testament to how special you are."

Hot tears ran down her face. I groaned, unable to handle more emotion today. "Jeez, woman." I growled playfully. "I try to be nice and you cry. I give up. I'll go back to being a jerk."

She patted my hand. "No, it's fine. I'll stop." She sniffed. "That was unexpected. That's all."

"I'm trying to apologize."

She lifted her face, brushing her mouth to mine. "Accepted."

I buried my hands in her hair, holding her close. I pressed my mouth to hers, wanting to taste her once more. She responded with a low sigh, her breath drifting over my face. Long moments passed as our lips moved together, tongues touched and teased. Desire built, slow and heavy, and my body hummed with need. With a moan, I drew back, staring down at her. Her lips were swollen, her breathing fast. I traced her bottom lip with my finger.

"Katharine," I murmured in a husky voice as I ran my hand up her bare leg.

She lifted her head, and just as her mouth met mine, we heard it. A crack of unexpected thunder followed by a crash in the guest room and a loud yell.

I groaned, dropping my head to her shoulder. "Fucking Jenna, *again.*"

She huffed out a huge exhale of air. "Well, hell. I think she broke my damn lamp. I *liked* that lamp."

I began to laugh at her rare colorful statement. I rolled off her, throwing an arm over my face. "Go see what your *friend* has done now."

She slid out of bed, hesitating. The dim moonlight behind her highlighted her silhouette through her wispy nightgown. She had filled out a little, her body softening with curves. With her hair tumbled over her shoulders, her eyes wide with desire, she looked sexy. Sexy as hell, in fact.

"Go." I growled. "If you don't, I won't be responsible for what happens next."

Pivoting, she hurried to the door.

"Katharine," I called.

She turned, her hand resting on the doorknob.

I gentled my voice. "If the lamp is broken, I'll buy you a new one."

Her smile was brilliant. "Okay."

I flopped back on the bed.

What the hell was I doing? That was twice today I had wanted to fuck her thoroughly—the woman I once wanted out of my life. Now, she was all around me. In every aspect of my life. In my bed.

The strangest part? I didn't mind any of it.

"KATHARINE, SYRUP IS a condiment. Not a food group."

She looked up from her plate, already shaking her head. "Each hole needs to be filled with syrup, Richard. It's a rule."

I snorted as I lifted my mug to my mouth. "You're drowning the waffle. There's more syrup than food on your plate."

"It's better like this."

I groaned. "And you add bacon?"

She hummed around her mouthful. "Perfect."

Jenna chuckled as she cut into her breakfast. "Not a syrup fan, Richard?"

"I added a reasonable amount. I want to taste the waffle, too."

Katharine held out a forkful in my direction. "Try it."

"No."

"Please?"

I speared a piece of my far dryer waffle. "Then you try mine."

We fed each other pieces of breakfast. Hers was dripping in syrup and butter, way sweeter than I was used to. I grimaced. "That is god-awful."

She grinned. "Better than yours." Looking down, she cursed. "Darn it, I got syrup on my shirt. Excuse me."

She hurried out of the kitchen. I waited until she had disappeared and grabbed the bottle of syrup, adding more to my waffle.

Jenna giggled. "The two of you are so sweet. Have you never eaten waffles together?"

I had to think fast. "No, Katharine always made pancakes. I bought her the waffle iron for a wedding gift."

Jenna gaped at me "You gave her a waffle iron for a *wedding gift*?"

"She wanted one!"

"Good Lord, Richard, you have a lot to learn about romance."

"She got me."

Jenna picked up her coffee mug. "Hmmph. Maybe the waffle iron was the better gift."

I glared. "When are you going home?"

She smirked. "Adrian will be here soon."

"Good."

She pushed on my arm with a playful wink. "I interrupted your make-up session last night. Sorry. The thunder caught me off guard."

"I have no idea what you're talking about."

"Of course not. Katharine is always that, ah, disheveled."

I smirked. She had looked rather rumpled when she left the bedroom last night.

I winked at Jenna. "We have the rest of the day to make out. I mean up. Or both."

She rolled her eyes, muttering about men and one-track minds.

I kept eating my now syrup-laden waffle.

I CAME OUT of the den, looking for Katharine. Jenna had left mid-afternoon, and I had gotten busy with some work, then had a call from Graham. I heard noises down the hall and went to investigate. The door to the smallest bedroom was open. I used the room for storage now. At one time, it held a bed, and I used it for my female guests and the after dinner activities, since I didn't ever take them upstairs. I had gotten rid of the bed when Katharine moved in—all that remained were boxes and files.

I leaned on the doorframe, watching her for a few moments, an indulgent smile tugging on my lips. "What are you doing?"

She indicated a few framed pictures. "You have some nice prints in here."

"I wasn't sure where to put those."

"They'd look great in the front room." She lifted some photographs from the box she'd been sorting. "These are lovely shots—shame to see them packed away."

I held out my hand, and she placed the stack of photos in it.

I shuffled through the pictures, feeling somewhat embarrassed. "I took these."

"You did?"

"Yeah. I went through a phase where I tried my hand at photography. It didn't last long." I handed them back to her. "I wasn't any good."

"I think they're great."

"Help yourself."

"Do you have the negatives?"

I shook my head. "All digital. One of those boxes has my camera and all the SD cards inside."

"Okay."

"Listen, Graham called. He wants me to go with him out of town to see a client. I think he's feeling guilty Adrian went the last two times."

"When are you going?"

"Tomorrow."

"How long?"

"That's the thing. I'll be gone until Thursday, which means I'll miss Tuesday with Penny."

She grinned impishly. "Not a problem—I can miss yoga. I'm not that good at it."

"Tell her I'll come see her Friday for lunch. I'll bring her favorite cheeseburgers."

"She'll love that."

"What will you do while I'm gone?"

"Work on the living room."

"You have painters coming right? No ladders?" She did an amazing job in her room, but the living room was too big a job for her alone. The thought of Katharine on such a tall ladder made me nervous—especially if I was going to be out of town.

"I have professionals coming in, Richard. It'll be finished in two days. You'll miss all the fun."

"What a shame."

She stood up, brushing off her pants. "I'll help you pack. I need to change the bedding and move my things back."

The word was out before I could stop it. "Don't."

"What?"

"Sleep in my room while I'm gone. Don't worry about the laundry. You have enough to do."

She chewed the inside of her cheek. "And tonight?"

"We share again."

"I . . ."

I took her hand. "It makes sense. Saves you some work."

A mischievous grin curled her lips. "You're a snuggler. You like to snuggle with me!"

I scoffed. "I'm simply being practical."

"Admit it, and I'll sleep with you."

I arched my eyebrow. "You want to rephrase that?"

"Oh, I—"

There it was—the flush that amused me. It bloomed on her chest and stained her cheeks. She pushed at my arm, teasing. "Admit it, and I'll sleep in your bed while you're gone."

"*And* tonight?"

The flush deepened.

"Yes."

I bent down, brushing my mouth across her cheek over to her ear. "I like snuggling with you. You're all warm and you smell good."

It was the truth. I had woken up again this morning with my body wrapped around hers. I was rested and relaxed; even if I had to deal with the after effects of her soft figure pressed to mine.

She brushed past me. "Fine. If that's what you want."

I grinned. It was, in fact, exactly what I wanted.

"WHAT ARE YOU smiling about?" Graham asked. The trip was going well, and the client had been enthusiastic today. I had spent the afternoon adding to my outlines and ideas in preparation for another meeting in the morning. Graham insisted we go to dinner to celebrate.

I looked up from my phone and handed it to him. "Oh, I sent a massive chocolate caramel cheesecake to Penny to make up for not being there tonight. Katharine sent a picture of them enjoying it."

He chuckled, and passed it back. "You're very fond of Penny."

"She reminds me of someone from my childhood."

"A relative?"

I shifted in my chair. "No."

He regarded me shrewdly over the rim of his glass. "You don't like to talk about yourself. Specifically your past."

"No, I don't."

"Do you talk to anyone about it?"

"Katharine."

"Your catalyst. The woman who changed your life—who changed you."

I tilted my head in acknowledgment, hoping he would take the hint and drop the subject. He was silent for a moment, then reached in and took an envelope from his pocket, sliding it across the table.

"What is this?"

He tapped the heavy cream-colored stationery. "You've been outstanding since you came on board, Richard. You've surpassed my expectations. All of our expectations. Your work on the Kenner Footwear campaign, the way you've pitched in and been a key part of the team. Coming on this trip last minute. All of it."

I shrugged in unusual modesty at his praise; his words warmed me. I wondered if that was how it felt to a boy basking in the glow of his father's pride—something I had never experienced. Graham was quick to compliment, and rarely criticized—his remarks more often teaching, as opposed to condemning. I had been amazed how fast I had slipped into my role at The Gavin Group. I enjoyed the positive energy and the entire "working with and not against" attitude they shared. His words, however, meant a great deal. My throat felt tight, and I took a sip of water to clear the thickness before speaking. "Thank you. It's been remarkable for me, as well."

He pushed the envelope closer. "For you."

Inside was a sizable check—my eyes widened at the generous amount—along with the copy of my contract. What really got my attention, though, was that clause six was crossed out and initialed. I lifted my eyes to his with a questioning look. "I don't understand."

He grinned. "The check is your bonus for an exceptional job. Kenner signed a multiple year deal with us all because of your idea. They want you on every campaign."

I held up the contract. "You crossed off my trial period."

"I did. I had only put it in place to be sure I was right in my gut instinct you would fit in with us. You have more than proven yourself to be what you stated you were: a changed man. Your Katy has indeed brought forth the real Richard." He held out his hand. "You have a place with my company for as long as you want it, Richard. I hope we have many years ahead of us."

Reeling, I shook his hand. I had pulled it off. I had done it.

I should have been gloating, euphoric. All my plans, all the arrangements had led to this moment. I had secured my position with The Gavin Group and screwed over David.

Mission accomplished.

Yet, while I was thrilled, it wasn't for the reasons I had thought. I found I didn't care one way or another about David or how he felt. He could walk in, offer me a partnership and more money than I ever dreamed of, and I wouldn't be tempted to leave. Instead, I only wanted to bask in the approval from Graham. I wanted to make him proud. I wanted to keep working for him and to hear his kind, praise-filled words. Along with those thoughts came an emotion I wasn't used to having: guilt. Guilt for how this started and why I was sitting here now. Guilt for the deception I had used to get to this moment.

As I stared at the papers, I wondered how much the fact Jenna had stayed with us had to do with his decision. She had certainly seen enough of us acting like a normal married couple to convince anyone we were real. She thought I couldn't keep my hands off Katharine, we had a great sex life, we argued and made up—everything other couples shared. Maybe the storm had not only brought Katharine and I closer, but also eliminated any doubts that still lingered in Graham's mind.

Internally, I shook my head. It didn't matter. What mattered was I would keep working hard and proving myself to Graham and his company. No matter how it began, I would earn it—and keep it.

"Thank you."

He clapped my shoulder. "I am sure Katy will be happy."

Another odd emotion bubbled in my chest—the anticipation of telling her, sharing this victory with her. I grinned, knowing how positively she would react. "I'd love to tell her, but I think I'll wait until

I get home." I looked down at my bonus. "I think I need to buy her something to celebrate. I thought that last week she needed a present. This is the perfect excuse."

He nodded. "That's a great idea. I know a wonderful jewelry store down the street."

My eyebrows shot up. Jewelry. I hadn't thought of that, but it was . . .

"Perfect."

Twenty-Three

RICHARD

I SLID MY key in the lock, entering the condo quietly. I was shocked to realize how much I had missed being home. How much I had missed Katharine.

I found myself texting her, checking she was okay, that Penny was well, or she remembered to lock the condo door. Her return texts made me smile, always a little cheeky and sweet. She had adored the cheesecake, telling me how the staff all dove in and helped her and Penny eat it. She found it amusing I had also sent a fruit arrangement for Joey's snack. When she mentioned Penny seemed more tired than usual, I had phoned the home to check up on her twice, making Tami chuckle at my worry.

I had to laugh at myself. It seemed, even without trying, Katharine's presence in my life brought forth more emotion all the time.

I should hate it, yet somehow, I didn't.

I was anxious to get home, see her, visit Penny, and get back to the office. When the client had agreed sooner than expected to our pitch, we had both agreed to head home early and caught the last flight out. The cab dropped me off, Graham laughing at my exuberance as I grabbed my case.

"*I don't expect to see you in the office first thing, Richard. Enjoy the morning with Katy. I'll see you in the afternoon.*"

I nodded. "Thank you."

I put down my case, flicked on the light, and froze.

I wasn't in the same room I left days earlier. The bold claret color Katharine had picked out now graced the massive wall around the fireplace and highlighted the wood mantle. The cream of the other walls was rich and attractive. She had added some cushions, the two chairs she had shown me, and the result of the transformation made it warm and inviting. Homey.

The biggest surprise was the artwork she had hung. She had used some of the prints she found, but on the red wall, she had some of my photographs, printed, double-matted, and framed. I was stunned by how great they looked and amazed she had chosen my favorite ones to use. The entire room looked spectacular.

I ran my hand over the curve of the chairs she'd added. They were strong pieces. The effect was still masculine, yet softened by what she had created. On the mantle was a picture of us, taken by Jenna on our wedding day. I picked it up, studying the candid photograph. Katharine was smiling into the lens, her face almost glowing. My forehead rested on hers, and I was smiling. We both looked happy. Like a couple in love. I ran my finger over her image, unsure of the odd sensation in my chest.

Placing it back on the mantle, I picked up my bag and climbed the stairs. In my doorway, I stopped, surprised to see Katharine asleep in my bed. I was sure she would have moved back into her own room by now. She hugged my pillow, her hands fisted in the material as she slumbered, her dark hair a wave of chocolate behind her on the crisp, white sheets. I studied her as she slept. She looked young and vulnerable. I remembered thinking she was weak. She was anything but. Knowing her now the way I did, I knew she had a core of steel—without it, she'd have folded up long ago—yet she hadn't.

She survived losing her parents, living on the streets, the pain of watching Penny become ill, and me—in all my selfish, shortsighted, egotistical glory.

She shifted, the covers dragging back with her movement. I grinned when I saw she was wearing the T-shirt I'd had on the day before I left.

My wife was in my bed, wearing my clothes.

I found I was more than okay with both facts.

With a muffled sigh, I put down my bag, grabbed some sleep pants, and got ready for bed, making sure to stay silent. Carefully, I slipped in behind her and tugged her back to my chest. She startled awake, stiffening in my embrace.

"Relax, sweetheart. It's me."

"Why are you home?"

"Business went well. Very well. We wrapped up early."

She struggled to get up. "I'll go to my room."

I pulled her back down. "Stay. You're fine." With a grin, I dropped a kiss to her neck. "I'm a snuggler, remember?"

She burrowed down with a contented little sound. "Your bed is comfy."

I couldn't help teasing her. "And my T-shirt?" I asked, fingering the worn cotton. "Is it comfy, too?"

She brushed my hand away. "I've been busy. I hadn't got around to doing the laundry. It was lying there, so I used it."

"I saw how busy you've been."

"Do you like it?" Her voice was shy and hesitant.

I dropped a kiss on her forehead. "Good job, Mrs. VanRyan."

She giggled into her pillow. "I'm glad you're pleased, Mr. VanRyan."

I tucked her closer. "I am. Go to sleep. I'll tell you everything in the morning about the trip."

"Okay." She hummed sleepily. "Night."

"Night."

KATHARINE STARED AT me over her coffee and picked up the contract again. "Just like that? He canceled your trial period?"

I nodded, my mouth full of scrambled eggs. Chewing, I swallowed and grinned. "I have an idea Jenna's little visit may have had something to do with it."

She chewed on the end of her nail, and I reached over, smacking her hand. "Stop that."

"Why do you think Jenna being here had anything to do with it?"

"Think about it, Katharine. Think of what she saw. Us in the same bed, me all over you. We got along well. She even knew we had a fight and made up. I'm pretty sure she told Graham he was wrong to have any doubts."

"Makes sense, I suppose."

"Plus, he said I'd done a great job—I surpassed expectations. It was his way of rewarding me." I took a sip of coffee. "Well, the end of my probation, and a generous bonus."

Her smile was warm. "I knew you'd blow them away with your work. It doesn't surprise me. You've always been brilliant with your ideas."

Her praise did strange things to me. I rubbed my chest, as if I could move around the warmth radiated by her words, and I smiled at her, my voice sincere. "You've always been supportive. Thank you."

The smile she returned was wide and open. I looked down at my plate, as the normalcy of our situation registered. Was this what marriage was like? A real marriage? Small moments of sharing that made you feel whole—connected.

I dug in my pocket, and slid the small box her way. "For you," I said gruffly, picking up my mug.

She made no move to touch it. I had never met a woman like Katharine. My wealth had always been a magnet for the women I dated. They would be all over me for gifts—wanting them, dropping hints, showing me items on the internet. Practically ripping any offering from my hand if I decided to purchase something. Not Katharine, though.

"*Your* bonus," I insisted and nudged the box closer. "Open it. It won't bite."

Her hand shook as she reached for the box. She hesitated once it was in her palm, as if anticipating the moment of opening the lid. Appreciating the mystery. I liked watching her expressions as they flitted across her face.

Her eyes grew round as she looked at the ring inside. As soon as I saw it, I knew she would love it. Small and delicate, the diamonds were set into different shaped frames. Tiny squares, ovals, circles, and rectangles made up a ring as unique and different as her. It wasn't the most expensive ring the store had, and certainly not the biggest, but it suited Katharine. Even Graham had nodded his approval the second my finger tapped on the glass case.

"That one, please. I would like to see that one."

Katharine looked up at me. "I don't understand."

"It's a gift, Katharine."

"Why?"

I shrugged. "Because you deserve it." I touched the contract envelope. "None of this would have happened without you. I wanted to say thank you." I added, completely sincere. It was important she believed me—that she knew I was aware of how much she had done for me.

"It's beautiful."

"Put it on."

She slid the ring on her right hand and twisted her wrist in the way women did when admiring a ring on their finger. "It fits!"

Reaching over, I took her hand and studied it. It fit well and it suited her perfectly. I set down her hand on the counter, patting it awkwardly.

"Do you like it?"

"It's . . ." Her voice was thick. "It's gorgeous."

"I was thinking of earrings, but I noticed Jenna and Laura have rings on their right hands, so I thought you'd like one, too. We could get earrings, if you prefer."

She shook her head. "No. It's perfect."

The air around us swirled with emotion. She kept looking at her hand and blinking fast. Oh God—was she going to cry? Over a present? I wasn't sure I would be able to handle it if she started crying. Emotion like that made me extremely edgy.

I clapped my hands. "Good choice, then. I'll save the earrings for another time. Maybe a six-month anniversary or something. I'm sure the Gavins celebrate milestones like those. I'll have to keep up."

She cleared her throat and slid off her stool. "I guess so."

I was shocked when she stopped by my chair after dumping her coffee in the sink. She cupped my cheek and pressed her lips to it, lightly.

"Thank you, Richard," she murmured, then kept walking.

I turned in my chair to watch her climb the steps. It was only when I shifted back that I realized my hand covered my face where her lips had touched, as if I was holding her kiss to my skin.

How odd.

Twenty-Four

RICHARD

I GLANCED OVER at Penny with a frown. I had been excited the same jazz trio we'd seen before was doing an encore performance this evening, but she'd been off the entire night. More than once, she had lifted her hand, wiping away a tear as it rolled down her cheek. When I asked, concerned, if she was all right, she waved me away with an impatient hand.

"I'm fine."

Yet, she seemed to be anything except fine.

I wheeled her back to her room, hoping the treat I had waiting would pick up her spirits.

Katharine mentioned Penny wasn't eating well the past couple days and seemed tired. Tonight, her caregiver told me she picked at her dinner and had only eaten lunch because Katharine fed it to her.

I knew Katharine was worried. She had considered canceling her yoga class, but I encouraged her to go. I reminded her only two classes remained, then she could join us every Tuesday. I would miss my time with Penny, but the classes started again a month later, so it would be back to us at that point. My favorite part of the night was listening to Penny tell stories of Katharine. There were so many—some Katharine herself had undoubtedly forgotten. They often contained humorous, embarrassing moments that made me chuckle.

I sat beside Penny, sliding the pizza box open with a smile. "Voila!"

When I discovered, next to cheeseburgers, pizza was her favorite food, I started bringing it to her regularly. It was fine with the home, and I made sure I had plenty for the staff on occasion. One day I brought enough pizza so any resident who wanted some could enjoy it. I was a hero that day.

Today, however, it was only for Penny.

She took a slice yet made no move to eat it. With a sigh, I took her slice back and returned it to the box. I wrapped my hand around her fragile wrist, rubbing the delicate skin of her palm.

"Penny, what is it? What's wrong?"

She heaved a deep exhale of air, the sound drained and resigned. "I'm tired."

"You want me to get Connie? She can get you ready for bed." Tami was off tonight, but she liked Connie.

"No. I don't want to go to bed."

"I don't understand."

Withdrawing her hand, she rubbed it over her face in a weary manner. "I'm tired of all this."

"Your room?" If she wanted a different one, I'd get it for her.

"Of being here. In this . . . *life,* if you can call it that."

I had never heard her talk this way. "*Penny—*"

She reached out and wrapped her hand around mine.

"I forget things, Richard. Time goes on and I don't know if it's the same day that it was only a moment ago. Katy comes to visit and I can't remember if she was here hours ago, days ago, or if she just left the room for a minute. Some days, I don't recognize anything, and I'm scared. I know there are days I don't know *her.*" Her voice shook, eyes glimmering with tears. "I don't know myself most days."

"She's here. Every day, she comes to see you, and even if you forget *her,* she knows *you.* She stays and sits with you."

"I'm a burden to her."

"No," I insisted. "You aren't a burden to her. She loves you."

"You must resent me."

"*What?* No. Not at all. I love spending time with you. You're part of my family now, Penny. You became that when I married Katharine." As the words left my mouth, I realized I was telling her the truth.

"She should be doing other things, traveling, having babies, making friends, not babysitting an old woman."

"Why are you talking like this? You know Katharine would do anything for you. So would I." I lifted her hand up and pressed a kiss to the thin skin. "Please, Penny, if she heard you . . ."

"I miss Burt."

"I know," I soothed. "You were married a long time. Of course, you miss him."

"Forty years. We weren't rich, but we had love." She smiled softly. "I loved watching him cook. He was a chef—did you know that?"

"Yes, you told me."

"I was a teacher. We had a good life. When he died, I didn't know how I was going to carry on. But then, I found Katy. She became my reason."

"She needed you."

"She doesn't need me anymore."

"You're wrong. She does."

"Will you look after her?"

"Don't. Don't give in yet, Penny. Katharine—she'd be devastated."

She shut her eyes as her shoulders sagged. "I'm just so tired."

I panicked when I realized she wasn't referring to wanting to go to bed. She was tired of life and being trapped in a body that no longer worked, with a mind that left her confused and forgetful.

I bent close, lowering my voice. "I'll look after her. I promise. She won't want for anything." I could promise her that. I would make sure Katharine was all right. "Don't give up. She *does* need you."

Her eyes opened, her gaze drifting past me. "Can you give me that picture?"

I turned and handed her the picture to which she pointed. After coming clean about being married, Katharine brought her a picture of us on our wedding day, and one Tami had snapped when we were visiting. Katharine was holding her hand, Penny was tweaking her nose and laughing, and I sat beside them, smiling. We looked like a family.

She traced our faces. "She's been my life since I lost Burt."

"I know."

"She is everything I knew she would be—smart, loving, strong."

"I agree. Beautiful, too. Tough as nails. You had a lot to do with that, Penny."

That made her smile. The first real one I'd seen tonight.

She stretched up and patted my cheek. "You're a good boy."

Those words made me chuckle. No one had *ever* said them to me.

"When you get older, Richard, you realize life is made up of moments. All sorts of them. Sad ones, good ones, and great ones. They make up the tapestry that is your life. Hold on to all of them—especially the great ones. They make the others easy to take."

I covered her hand with mine. "Stay," I urged. "For her. Give her more great moments, Penny."

With a sigh, she nodded. "I want to go to bed now."

Turning my face, I kissed her palm. "I'll get Connie."

She met my eyes, a fierce gaze that trapped and held mine. "Love, Richard. Make sure you surround her with love."

I could only nod.

She tweaked my nose. That was what she did to Katharine—her way of saying, "I love you."

My eyes stung all the way to the desk to get Connie.

MY PHONE VIBRATED on the wooden table and I picked it up, stifling a grin at the number. Golden Oaks. I wondered what Penny was asking Tami for now. Since our unsettling evening last week, she had wanted something daily, and I made sure she got it. I never told Katharine about our conversation. She was already plenty worried. Penny was obviously slowing down, and her mind giving out more often. She had been more like herself last night, but had fallen asleep as soon as I got her back to her room. I left her in her caregiver's capable hands with a kiss on her downy cheek.

I declined the call, planning to return it when the meeting was over. I focused my attention back to Graham, who was pointing out a client's desires for their next campaign, when my phone went off again.

Glancing over, I saw it was Golden Oaks. A small pit of worry began in my stomach. Tami knew I would call her back. Why was she being so insistent?

I glanced up at Graham, who had paused his speaking.

"Do you need to take that, Richard?"

"I think it may be important."

He nodded. "Five minute break, everyone."

I accepted the call. "Tami?"

"Mr. VanRyan, I'm sorry to interrupt." Her voice sent ripples of anxiety down my back. "I have some terrible news."

I had no recollection of standing, but suddenly I was on my feet. "What happened?"

"Penny Johnson passed away about an hour ago."

I shut my eyes against the sudden burn. I gripped my phone tighter, my voice thick. "Has my wife been told?"

"Yes. She was here this morning, and had only left a short time before I went in to check on Penny. I called her back."

"Is she there now?"

"Yes. I tried to ask her about arrangements, but I can't get her to talk. I wasn't sure what to do, so I called you."

"No, you did the right thing. I'm on my way. Don't let her leave, Tami. I'll handle all the arrangements."

I hung up, dropping my phone, the sound of it hitting the table, a dull thud breaking the roar in my head. I felt a hand on my shoulder and looked up into Graham's concerned face.

"Richard, I'm sorry."

"I have to . . ." My voice trailed off.

"Let me drive you."

I felt odd. Off balance. My mind was chaotic, my stomach in knots, and my eyes burned. One thought clarified, her name burning in my brain. "Katharine."

"She needs you. I'll take you to her."

I nodded. "Yes."

AT THE HOME, I didn't hesitate, rushing through the hallways. I saw Tami outside Penny's room, the door closed.

"Is she in there?"

"Yes."

"What do you need?"

"I need to know if there was anything arranged, pre-planning, what her wishes were for when she passed?"

"I know she wanted to be cremated. I don't think Katharine had made any pre-arrangements." I ran my hand over the back of my neck. "I have no experience with this, Tami."

Graham's voice came from behind me. "Let me help, Richard."

I turned in surprise. I thought he had dropped me off and left.

He extended his hand to Tami, introducing himself. She smiled in acknowledgement. He turned back to me.

"Go to your wife. I have a good friend who has a string of funeral homes. I'll contact him and start things for you—Tami can advise me."

She nodded. "Of course." She laid her hand on my arm. "When you're ready, I'll get Joey and take him to the lounge. He is staying here with us."

"All right."

"I'll help Mr. Gavin as best I can."

"I'd appreciate it—so will Katy."

Graham smiled. "So rarely you call her that. Go—she needs you."

I slipped into the room, quietly pushing the door shut. The room seemed so wrong. There was no music, no Penny sitting at one of her canvasses, humming away. Even Joey was silent, huddled on his perch, his head buried in his wing. The curtains were drawn, the room dimmed in sadness.

Katharine was a huddled figure sitting beside Penny's bed, holding her hand. I moved beside her, allowing myself a moment to gaze down at the woman who had changed my life. Penny looked as if she was asleep, her face peaceful. She would no longer be confused or agitated, no longer searching for something she couldn't remember.

No longer able to tell me stories of the woman who was now grieving for her.

I lowered myself beside my wife, covering the hand clutching Penny's with mine. "Katharine," I murmured.

She didn't move. She remained frozen, her face blank, not speaking.

I slid my arm around her stiff shoulders, bringing her close. "I'm sorry, sweetheart. I know how much you loved her."

"I just left," she whispered. "I was halfway home, and they called. I shouldn't have left."

"You didn't know."

"She said she was tired and wanted to rest. She didn't want to paint. She asked me to turn off the music. I should have known something was wrong," she insisted.

"Don't do this to yourself."

"I should have been with her when she—"

"You *were* with her. You know how she felt about this, sweetheart. She said it all the time—when she was ready, she was going. You were here, the person she loved the most—the person she would want to be the last one she saw, and she was ready." I ran my hand over her hair. "She's been ready for a while, baby. I think she was waiting to make sure you were going to be okay."

"I didn't say goodbye."

I tugged her head to my shoulder. "Did you kiss her?"

"Yes."

"Did she tweak your nose?"

"Yes."

"Then you said goodbye. That's how you two did it. You didn't need words, any more than you had to tell her you loved her. She knew, sweetheart. She always knew."

"I don't . . . I don't know what to do now."

Her entire body shuddered, and unable to take her intensifying pain, I stood, lifted her, sitting back down before she could protest. She still clutched Penny's hand, and I could feel her trembling.

"Let me help, sweetheart. Graham is here, too. We'll figure out what we need to do."

Her head fell to my chest, and I felt the wet of her tears. I pressed a kiss to her head, holding her until I felt her body relax and she released

Penny's hand, gently letting it rest on the quilt. We sat in silence as I stroked my hand up and down her back.

There was a knock at the door, and I called out for them to enter. Graham came in, crouching beside us.

"Katy, dear girl, I am so sorry."

Her voice was a mere whisper. "Thank you."

"Laura is here. We would like to help you and Richard with the arrangements, if you are willing."

She nodded, another shiver running down her spine.

"I think I need to take her home."

Graham stood up. "Of course."

I bent my head lower. "Are you ready, sweetheart? Or do you want to stay longer?"

She looked up at Graham, her lips quivering. "What is going to happen?"

"My friend, Conrad, will come pick her up. According to Richard, she wanted to be cremated?"

"Yes."

"He will arrange everything, and we can discuss what sort of service you would like."

"I want to celebrate her life."

"We can do that."

"What about"—she swallowed—"her things?"

"I'll arrange to have everything packed up and brought to the condo, sweetheart," I assured her. "Tami said Joey was staying here?"

"The other residents like him—they'll look after him. I'd like to donate some of her things to the residents who don't have as much as she did—her clothes and wheelchair, things like that."

"Okay, I'll make the arrangements. When you're ready you can go through everything, and I'll make sure it happens."

She was silent, looking at Penny. She nodded. "Okay."

I stood up, taking her with me. I didn't like the trembling in her body or the shakiness in her voice. I felt better holding her, and she didn't protest.

I looked down at Penny, saying my own silent thank you and

goodbye. Feeling the burn of emotion in my eyes, I blinked it away. I had to stay strong for Katharine.

"I'll get the car," Graham offered, and left the room.

I met Katharine's gaze, her eyes wide with pain and sadness. A rush of overwhelming tenderness ran through me, and the need to ease her hurt filled my entire being.

I pressed my lips to her forehead, murmuring against her skin. "I've got you. We'll get through this together. I promise."

She leaned in to my caress, her quiet need touching.

"Are you ready?"

Nodding, she buried her head into my chest, tightening her grip on my jacket.

I strode from the room, knowing both our lives were about to change.

Once again, I had no idea how to cope with it.

Twenty-Five

RICHARD

THE CONDO WAS quiet. Katharine, after another night of silence, had gone to bed. She hadn't eaten much dinner, barely sipped her wine, and answered my questions with small hums or shakes of her head. I heard her moving around upstairs, the sound of drawers opening and closing, and I knew she was probably rearranging and organizing. She did that when she was upset.

Worry ate away at my nerves; it was something I'd never experienced. I wasn't used to caring about anyone. I wondered how to help her to feel better, how to help her talk. She needed to talk.

The memorial had been small but special. Since Laura and Graham handled most of the arrangements, it wasn't surprising. Laura sat with Katharine and helped her pick out some photos, which they placed around the room. Her favorite one of Penny they positioned by the urn that was decorated with wildflowers. There were flowers sent by different people, the largest arrangement came from Katharine and myself. All of Penny's favorites filled the vase beside her picture; the majority of the flowers were daisies.

Most of the staff from The Gavin Group came to pay their respects. I stood by Katharine, my arm wrapped around her waist, holding her rigid body close to mine, in silent support. I shook hands, accepting the murmured words of condolences; aware of the way her figure shook at times. Some care workers and staff from Golden Oaks attended, and Katharine accepted their hugs and whispered words of shared grief, then always stepped back beside me, as if seeking the shelter of my embrace. There were few of Penny's friends left to attend—those who did, Katharine gave preferential treatment. She crouched low to speak in hushed tones to those in wheelchairs, made sure the ones with walkers were escorted to a seat quickly, and after the brief ceremony, spent time with them all.

I kept my eye on her and stayed close, worried over the lack of tears and the constant shake of her hands. I had never experienced grief until that day. When my parents died, I had felt nothing except relief after all they put me through. I had been sad when Nana left the house, but it was the sadness of a child. The pain I felt for Penny was a scorching ache in my chest. It welled and spilled over in the strangest of ways. Unshed tears burned in my eyes when I least expected them. When the boxes containing her possessions arrived, I had to stay in the storage room, overcome with an emotion I couldn't explain. I found myself thinking of our talks, the way her eyes would light up when I mentioned Katharine's name. Her sweet, funny stories of their life together. My calendar still showed all my Tuesday evenings blocked out with the name Penny across them. Somehow, I couldn't bring myself to erase them yet. On top of the already strange emotions I felt was the concern for my wife.

I thought she was handling everything. I knew she was grieving the loss of the woman she loved like a mother, yet she had been calm. Steady. She had cried once, but I hadn't seen her weep since the day Penny passed. Since the memorial earlier today, she had shut down. She had gone out for a walk, silently shaking her head at my offer to accompany her. When she returned, she went straight to her room until I went to get her to eat dinner.

Now, with my limited knowledge of helping other people, I was at a loss. It wasn't as if I could call Jenna or Graham and ask them what I should do for my own wife. They thought we were close and would assume I would know exactly what to do. Today, when we left the funeral home, Jenna had hugged me and whispered, "Take care of her." I wanted to, but I didn't know how. I had no experience with such intense emotions.

I paced the living room and kitchen, restlessly prowling the floor, sipping my wine. I knew I could go and work out to relieve some of my tension, except I wasn't in the mood. Somehow, the gym seemed too far away from Katharine, and in case she needed me, I wanted to be close.

I sat down on the sofa, and the plump cushion beside me made me smile. Another one of Katharine's touches. Silky blankets, downy pillows, warm colors on the walls and the artwork she had added, made the condo feel like home. I paused as I lifted my glass. Had I ever told her I liked what she did?

With a groan, I drained my wine, setting down the glass on the table. Bending forward, I clutched my hair, tugging on it until it was painful. I had improved over the past weeks, of that I was certain, but had I changed enough? I knew my tongue wasn't as sharp. I knew I'd been a better person. Even so, I wasn't sure if it was sufficient. If she was struggling, did she trust me enough to turn to me?

I was shocked to realize how much I wanted that. I wanted to be her rock. To be the person she could depend on. I knew I had come to rely on her—for many things in my life.

Giving up, I snapped off the lights and went to my room. I changed into my sleep pants and walked over to the bed, hesitating, then left my room. I went to her door, not surprised to see it partially open. How my "night noises," as she politely called them, brought her comfort, I didn't understand, but ever since the day she admitted needing them, I never shut it at night.

For a moment, I felt odd standing outside her door, unsure why I was there. Until I heard it. The sound of muffled weeping. Without another thought, I slipped in her room. Her blind was open, the moonlight spilling in her window. She was curled in a ball, crying. Her body shook so hard with the force of her sobs, I could see the bed moving. Lifting the blanket, I slipped my arms around her, holding her close and carrying her to my room. Cradling her, I lowered us to the bed, tucking the covers around us. She stiffened, but I held her tight.

"Let it out, Katharine. You'll feel better, sweetheart."

She melted into me, her body molded to mine. Her hands clutched at my bare shoulders, her tears hot on my skin as she wept uncontrollably. I stroked my hand over her back, my fingers through her hair, and made, what I hoped were, comforting noises. Despite the reason, I liked having her close. I missed her softness melded to my hardness. She fit to me so well.

Eventually, her sobs began to taper, the terrible shudders easing from her frame. I leaned over, grabbing some tissues and pressing a bunch into her hand.

"I–I'm s–sorry," she stuttered in a whisper.

"You have nothing to be sorry for, sweetheart."

"I disturbed you."

"No, you didn't. I want to help you. I keep telling you—anything you need, all you have to do is ask." I hesitated. "I'm your husband. It's my job to help you."

"You've been so nice. Kind, even."

I winced a little at the shock in her voice. I knew I deserved it, but I still didn't like it.

"I'm trying to be better."

She shifted a little, tilting up her head to study me. "Why?"

"You deserve it, and you just lost someone you love. You're grieving. I want to help you. I don't know how, though. I'm new to all of this, Katy." Using my thumb, I gently wiped away the fresh tears leaking from the corner of her eyes.

"You called me Katy."

"I guess it rubbed off. Penny called you that all the time. So does everyone else."

"She liked you."

My throat felt strangely thick as I studied her face in the pale light from the window. "I liked her," I stated, quiet but honest. "She was a wonderful woman."

"I know."

"I know you'll miss her, sweetheart, but . . ." I didn't want to say the same platitudes I'd heard uttered to her over the past few days. "She would have hated being a burden to you."

"She wasn't!"

"She would have argued with you. You worked hard to make her feel safe. You sacrificed so much."

"She did the same for me. She always put me first." She shuddered. "I–I don't know where I'd be today if it hadn't been for her finding me and taking me in."

I didn't want to think about that either. Penny's actions had affected both our lives—for the better.

"She did it because she loved you."

"I loved her."

"I know." I cupped her face, staring into her pain-filled eyes. "You loved her so much you married a total asshole who treated you like shit so you could make sure she was looked after properly."

"You stopped being a total asshole a few weeks ago."

I shook my head. "I should never have been an asshole to you at all." To my shock, I felt tears gather in my eyes. "I'm sorry, sweetheart."

"You miss her, too."

Unable to speak, I nodded.

She pulled me down, my head resting in the crook of her neck. I couldn't remember the last time I cried—most likely when I was a child—but I cried now. I cried for the loss of a woman I only knew for a brief time, yet came to mean so much to me. Who, with her stories and fractured memories, brought to life the woman I was married to—her words showed me Katy's goodness and light.

She and Katy showed me it was okay to feel, to trust . . . and to love.

Because, in that one moment, I knew I was in love with my wife.

I yanked Katy to me, holding her tight. When my tears dried, I lifted my head, meeting her gentle gaze. The air between us changed from one of comfort and care to something charged and alive.

The lust and longing I had denied myself ignited. My body burned for the woman I was holding, and Katy's eyes widened, the same desire flaring in their vivid blue color.

Giving her the chance to say no, I lowered my head, pausing over her quivering lips.

"Please?" I whispered, not certain what I was asking.

Her feather-soft whimper was all I needed, and my mouth met hers with a hunger I had never experienced.

It wasn't only lust and desire. It was need and longing. It was redemption and forgiveness. All of it wrapped up in one tiny woman.

It was like being reborn in a fiery burst of flames that licked and snapped at my spine. Every single nerve hummed in my body. I could feel every inch of her pressed to me; every curve fit to me as if she were made for me and me alone. Her tongue was like velvet against mine, her breath like gusts of pure life filling my lungs. I couldn't get close enough. I couldn't kiss her deep enough. Her ridiculous nightshirt vanished under my fists, the material ripping easily. I had to touch her skin. I needed to feel all of her. Using her feet, she pushed down my pants; my erection released, trapped between us. We both groaned as our skin met. Soft, smooth skin, rubbed my rougher, harder body.

She was like cream—fluid and sweet, wrapping around me. Using my hands and tongue, I discovered her everywhere. The dips and hollows hidden from the world were now mine to explore. I feasted on her taste, each discovery new and exotic. Her breasts were full and lush in my hands, her nipples pert and sensitive. She moaned as I tongued them to stiff peaks, tugging on them gently with my teeth. She squirmed and whimpered as I drifted lower, swirling my tongue on her stomach, down to her tiny belly button, and beyond, until I found her, wet and ready for me.

"Richard," she gasped. The word was static and frantic as I closed my mouth around her and tasted her sweetness. Her body bowed, arching and stretching as I explored, using my tongue to delve and tease. She buried her hand in my hair, pushing me closer and tugging me back as I built a rhythm. Her moans and whimpers were like music to my ears. I slid a finger, then two, inside, stroking her deeply.

"God, sweetheart, you're so tight," I moaned into her heat.

"I've . . . I've never been with a man."

I stilled, lifted my head, her words sinking in. She was a virgin. I needed to remember that, to be gentle with her and treat her with respect. That she would bestow that gift to me, of all people, made me ache with emotions I couldn't identify. I shouldn't be surprised, yet, as always, she continued to confound me.

"Don't stop," she pleaded.

"Katy—"

"I want this, Richard, with you. I want you."

I crawled up her body, cradling her head; kissing her mouth with a reverence I had never felt or shown another person. "Are you sure?"

She drew me back to her mouth. "Yes."

I moved over her carefully; I wanted to make her first time memorable. To show her with my body what I was experiencing with my soul.

To make her mine in every sense of the word.

I worshipped her with my touch, keeping it light and gentle, her skin like silk under my hands. Loving her with my mouth, I learned every part of her in the most intimate ways, memorizing her taste and the feel of her. I stroked her passion with my own until she was pleading for me.

I groaned and hissed as she became bolder, touching and discovering me with her teasing lips and tender hands. Her name fell like a prayer from my mouth as her fingers stroked my shoulders, down my spine, then encased my cock. Finally, I hovered over her, covering her with my body, sinking deep into her tight warmth, holding her until she begged me to move, and then, and only then, did I let my passion fly. I thrust powerfully, driving into her over and again. I kissed her hard as I took her, needing her taste in my mouth as much as I needed her body wrapped around me. Katy held me tight, groaning my name, her fingers digging into my back as she grasped me hard.

"Oh, God, Richard, *please*. Oh, I need . . ."

"Tell me," I urged. "Tell me what you need."

"You . . . *more* . . . please!"

"I've got you, baby." I moaned, pushing her leg higher and sinking deeper. "Only me. You're only ever going to have me."

She cried out, her head flung back, body tensing. She was beautiful in her release, her neck stretched taut, a slight sheen of sweat on her skin. My own orgasm flickered, and I buried my face in Katy's neck as the force of my pleasure rocked my world. I turned my head, grabbed her chin, bringing her mouth to mine, kissing her as the shockwaves rippled then calmed in my body. I rolled, tugging her to my chest, nuzzling her hair. She sighed, burrowing close.

"Thank you," she breathed out.

"Trust me, sweetheart. The pleasure was all mine."

"Well, not *all* yours."

I chuckled against her head, pressing a kiss to her warm skin.

"Sleep, Katy."

"I should go—"

I tightened my arms, not wanting her to leave. "No. Stay here with me."

She sighed, her body giving a long, slow shudder.

"Front or back?" I murmured. She liked to sleep with her back pressed to my chest. I liked waking up with my face buried in her warm neck and her body connected to mine.

"Back."

"Okay." I loosened my arms so she could roll over. Bringing her back to me, I kissed her gently. "Go to sleep. We have a lot to talk about tomorrow."

"I—"

"Tomorrow. We'll figure out the next step tomorrow."

"Okay."

I shut my eyes, breathing her in. Tomorrow I would tell her everything. Ask her to tell me what she was thinking. I wanted to tell her what I was feeling—that I was in love with her. Clear the air for both of us. Then help her move her things into my room, making it *our* room.

I didn't want to be without her beside me again.

With a sigh of contentment I didn't think I'd ever experience, I fell asleep.

I WOKE UP alone, my hand on cold, empty sheets. I wasn't surprised— Katy had been more restless than usual the past few nights, and even more so last night. More than once I had pulled her back to me, feeling the sobs she was trying to hide. I had held her, letting her emotions drain from her body.

I ran a hand over my face and sat up. I would have a shower, then find her in the kitchen. I had to talk to her. There was so much to clear up—a great many things I needed to apologize for, so we could move forward—together.

I swung my legs off the bed, grabbed my robe, and stood up. I began walking to the bathroom and stopped. My bedroom door was shut tight. Why was it closed? Was Katy worried about disturbing me? I shook my head. She was one of the quietest people I knew, especially in the morning.

I crossed the room and opened the door. Silence greeted me. No music or any sounds from the kitchen met my ears. I glanced over toward Katy's room. Her door was standing ajar, but there were no sounds from her room, either. Something in my stomach tightened, and I couldn't shake it off. Crossing the hall, I looked inside. The bed was made, the room tidy and spotless. It felt empty.

I headed to the stairs, taking them two at a time, making a beeline for the kitchen, calling for Katy. She didn't respond, and the room was deserted.

I stood, panicked. She must have gone out—maybe to the store. There were several reasons for her to have left the condo. I hurried to the entryway. Her car keys were on the hook.

She must have gone for a walk, I told myself.

I headed back to the kitchen toward the coffee maker. She had shown me how to use it, so at least I could make a pot of coffee. It was misty out, the clouds low and dark. She'd need the heat of a hot drink when she returned.

Except, when I reached for the pot, I saw her phone sitting on the counter. Beside it, her condo keys. My hand shook as I picked them up. Why would she leave her keys? How would she get into the condo?

I looked back to the counter. It was all there. The bankcards and the checkbook I'd given her. The copy of her contract. She had left it all because she had left me.

A glint of light caught my eye, and I leaned forward to pick up her rings.

My memory flashed with images of Katy. Handing her the box and telling her I wasn't going down on one knee. The look on her face when I slid the band on her finger the day I married her for circumstance and not love. She had looked beautiful, but I never told her. There were many things I never told her.

So many things I would never have the chance to tell her—because she was gone.

Twenty-Six

RICHARD

I KNEW SHE wasn't there, yet I still checked every inch of the condo. When I looked in her dresser and closet, most of the new clothes I purchased for her remained, but some were missing. Her two still-to-be-unpacked boxes were in her closet, some of her toiletries were in the bathroom, but the one suitcase she had was missing. I remembered hearing drawers opening and shutting last night. What I thought was her organizing and moving things, was in fact, her preparing to leave me.

I sat down on the edge of her bed with my head in my hands.

Why? Why would she sleep with me when she knew she was going to leave? Why did she leave?

I cursed under my breath—the answer to that was obvious. Penny was dead. She no longer had to provide for her, which meant she no longer had to keep up the pretense of being in love with me.

We had, I thought, been getting along well. I was sure she was feeling something. Why hadn't she talked to me?

I barked out a laugh in the empty room. Of course, she wouldn't come and talk to me. When had I ever let her know she could? We had become friendly enemies, united in our common goal. Now that goal had changed for her. I might have planned to talk to her, but she had no idea of how I felt. I still couldn't wrap my head around it; how much my emotions had changed.

The question I kept shouting in my head, the one that didn't make sense was: *Why did she sleep with me?*

The air in my lungs turned to ice as memories of last night played in my head. She had been a virgin—and I hadn't worn protection. I'd been so caught up in the moment—in Katy—I hadn't thought about it until this instant. I had taken her with no condom. I always wore a condom—there was never any discussion with my partners.

What were the chances of her being on birth control? I gripped the back of my neck in panic. What were the chances of her getting pregnant?

She was gone. I had no idea where she was, no idea if she was pregnant. Nor did I have any idea how I would react if she *were* expecting my baby.

Would she even think about that probability?

I hurried to the den, my anxiety now higher than ever, switching on the laptop. I did a quick history check, wondering if she had used it to book a flight or a train ticket, but I found nothing. I did a check of our bank accounts, sitting back in amazement when I saw she had withdrawn twenty thousand dollars yesterday. I remembered the walk she took in the afternoon, and how she insisted on going alone. She had gone to the bank and withdrawn or transferred the money. Two months' "salary" was all she took. As I scrolled through her account, I noticed that, other than expenses for Penny, she had never touched a cent of the money. She had spent nothing on herself. She hadn't taken anything for her future.

I was more confused than ever. She didn't want my money. She didn't want me. What did she want?

I drummed my fingers restlessly on the desk. She had left her keys and pass, which meant she couldn't get in the building or condo. I knew she would eventually be in contact with me to ask for the boxes she left behind, and I would insist on seeing her first. My gaze strayed to the shelf in the den, and I realized Penny's ashes were gone. Wherever she went, she'd taken them—but I knew her well enough to know she would want her pictures and the contents of those boxes upstairs; they contained sentimental items—things she deemed important.

My mind started spinning, working the way it always did when I had a problem. I began to compartmentalize and figure out solutions. I could tell the Gavins she had gone away for a few weeks. That the shock of Penny's death was too much and she needed a break. I could say I sent her to a warm place to relax and recover. It would buy me some time. When she got in touch, I could convince her to come back and we could figure something out. We could stay married. I'd get her a place close by, and the only time she'd have to see me was when the occasion called for it. I could convince her to do that. I stood up, staring out the window into the dull light. The overcast day was the perfect foil for my mood. I let my thoughts flow, figuring out different scenarios, finally deciding the simplest was the best. I would stick to my original thoughts of her going away. I had her phone. I could send texts to myself and invent enough phone calls, so they would be none the wiser.

Except . . .

My head fell forward. That wasn't what I wanted. I wanted to know where Katy went. I needed to know she was safe. I wanted to talk to her. She was grieving and not thinking straight. She thought she was alone.

I gripped the windowsill, staring out over the city. She was out there, somewhere, and she was on her own. I had to find her. For both our sakes.

I RETURNED TO my building and pulled into my parking spot, letting my head fall back against the headrest. I had driven everywhere I could think of where she might go. I'd been to the airport, the train station, the bus depot, even car rental places. I'd shown her picture to what felt like hundreds of people but had found nothing. She left her cellphone behind, so I couldn't try to call her. I knew she had a credit card of her own, and I tried to get in touch with the issuing bank, to see if it was used recently, but was shut down immediately. If I wanted that information, I would have to hire someone. I hadn't been able to find a clue on my own.

Discouraged, I dragged myself upstairs and flung myself on the sofa, not bothering to turn on the lights. Daylight was fading, the gray of night slowly eating away at the sky.

Where the hell was she?

Anger overtook me, and I grabbed the closest item and flung it at the wall. It exploded, sending shards of glass around the room. I stood, fuming and anxious. I paced around the room, glass crunching under my shoes as I made the circuit. I grabbed a bottle of scotch, twisting off the lid, drinking without a glass. This was why I didn't allow emotion into my life. It was like a donkey, slow and useless, and it would kick you in the face when you least expected it. My parents never gave a fuck about me, and I had learned to rely on myself. I had let my guard down with Katharine and the bitch had fucked me over. She wanted to be gone? Well, good riddance. She could stay gone. When she finally called for her things, I'd send them along with divorce papers.

I froze, the bottle partway to my mouth. The chasm in my chest that had been threatening to crack open all day, broke. I sat down heavily, no longer interested in the bottle.

She wasn't a bitch, and I didn't want her gone. I wanted her here. With me. I wanted her quiet voice asking me questions. Her teasing laughter. The way she would arch an eyebrow at me, and whisper "go fuck yourself, VanRyan." I wanted her to listen to my ideas, and hear her praise. I sighed, the sound low and sad in the empty room. I wanted to wake up beside her and feel her warmth wrapped around me, the way she had enfolded herself around my dead heart and revived it.

I thought back to our argument a couple weeks ago. The way she tried to convince me love wasn't such a terrible thing. *Had she been feeling something for me?* Was it possible? I had dismissed her as being overdramatic—the sadness in her eyes, the weariness of her voice when she told me she was tired of lying, and the guilt that weighed on her. I had insisted we weren't hurting anyone. Graham got a great employee, Penny had a wonderful care home, Katharine would move on to a better life once this was over, and my life would continue. No one would be the wiser, and no one would suffer.

How wrong I was—because we were both suffering.

I wanted my wife back, and this time, I wanted it for real.

I simply didn't know how to get it.

I PACED AND brooded for hours, the bottle of scotch never far from my hands. When my stomach growled around two o'clock in the morning, I realized how long it had been since I had eaten anything. In the kitchen, I yanked open the refrigerator door and grabbed a container with leftover spaghetti. Not even bothering to heat it up, I sat at the table, twirling the cold pasta and chewing. Even cold, it was good. Everything Katharine made was delicious. My mind drifted to the night she had made me filet and asparagus with béarnaise sauce—a meal that rivaled anything I had eaten at Finlay's. My praise had been honest, and her reaction had been one of her rare blushes. With her fair skin, she often had traces of color on her cheeks when she cooked or drank something hot. When she was angry, or nervous, her skin flushed a deep red, like a burning element, but her soft blush was different. It highlighted her face, making her even prettier than usual.

"I like that," I mused.

"Like what?"

"The way you blush. You don't do it often, but when I compliment you, it happens."

"Maybe you don't compliment me enough."

"You're right, I don't."

She laid her hand over her heart in mock shock. "Agreeing with me and a compliment? It's a rare day in the VanRyan household."

I threw back my head in laughter. Picking up my wineglass, I studied her over the rim. "When I was a child, for a while, my favorite dessert was ice cream with strawberry sauce."

"Only for a while?"

"Nana made it for me. After she left, I never got it again."

"Oh, Richard—"

I shook my head, not wanting to hear her sympathetic words.

"She would give it to me, and I loved to mix the sauce into the ice cream. It turned everything pink and soft." I traced the edge of the table with my finger. "Your blush reminds me of that."

She didn't say anything for a moment, then came over to me, bent down, and dropped a kiss onto my head. "Thank you."

I didn't look up. "Yep."

"And if you think your pretty words are getting you out of the dishes, forget it, VanRyan. I made dinner. You clean up."

I chuckled as she left the kitchen.

My fork froze midway to my mouth. I had loved her even at that moment. The easy banter, her teasing, the comfort I found with her presence—it had all been there, but I hadn't recognized it. Love wasn't something I knew or understood.

I dropped my fork and pushed the container away, my appetite gone. I looked around the kitchen seeing her touches everywhere. They were all over the condo. Little pieces of Katharine she'd added, making the place more than somewhere I lived. She made it into a home. Our home.

Without her, it was nothing.

Without her, I was nothing.

"RICHARD? WHAT ARE you doing here?"

I turned and watched as a familiar scenario played out in front of me. My boss, walking into my office, finding me packing it up. In my hand was a picture taken on my wedding day. I had been holding it, staring at it for God knew how long, thinking and remembering.

Graham stepped in, looking confused. "You're supposed to be home with Katy. I told you to take all the time you needed." He spied the small box on my desk. "What's going on?"

"I need to speak with you."

"Where's Katy?"

I met his gaze head on. "I don't know. She left me."

He reared back, shock written on his face. Reaching in his pocket, he withdrew his phone.

"Sarah, cancel my appointments and calls for the day. Yes, all of them. Reschedule as best you can. I'll be out of the office." He hung up.

"I didn't see your car downstairs."

I shook my head. "I took a cab."

"Put the picture back on your desk and come with me. We're going somewhere private where we can talk."

"I'm almost done," I argued. "I didn't have a lot here."

"Are you resigning?"

My sigh was laced with pain. "No. Once you hear what I have to say, though, I won't have a job. It's easier to do it this way."

He frowned, and his voice became firm. "Put down the picture, Richard. Once we talk, I'll decide what happens next."

I looked down at the picture grasped in my shaky hand.

"Now."

I did as he asked. He held out my coat, studying my face. "You look terrible."

I shrugged my coat on and nodded. "I feel it, too."

"Let's go."

WE DIDN'T SPEAK in the car. I stared out the window at the city I loved but would possibly be leaving. Without Katharine or the job I wanted, there would be nothing left for me in Victoria. Once I had settled things with Graham and Katharine, I would move on to Toronto. It was a huge, impersonal city. I could lose myself there.

"Richard."

I startled, looking at Graham.

"We're here."

I had been so deep in thought I hadn't realized where we were headed. He had brought us to his house. I frowned, looking at him.

"We'll have complete privacy. Laura is home, but she won't interfere."

I swallowed. "She deserves to hear this, too."

"Maybe in a while. We'll talk first."

I pushed open the car door, too weary to argue. "Okay."

Twenty-Seven

RICHARD

I STARED OUT the window overlooking the vast property. Memories of bringing Katharine here the first day flitted through my head. How nervous and anxious we both had been. How well she played her part. My gaze swept over to the deck. Remembering our wedding dinner, my chest became tight. She had looked so pretty, felt so right in my arms when we danced. The day, which should have been nothing but another piece of my plan, had been a joyful one.

Had I loved her then?

"Richard."

I turned to face Graham. He held out a steaming cup of coffee. "I thought you could use this."

I took the mug with a silent nod and turned back to the window. My thoughts were jumbled and confused. I had no idea how to start this conversation, but I knew I had to have it. I needed to wipe the slate clean, then figure out my next move.

Taking in a deep lungful of air, I turned back to Graham. He was leaning on his desk, feet crossed, sipping his coffee. He was his normal, calm self, yet the look on his face was intense.

"I don't know where to start," I admitted.

"The beginning is usually the best."

I wasn't certain what the beginning was in this instance. The real reason I left Anderson Inc.? The arrangement I made with Katharine? The hundreds of lies and deceptions that followed?

"Why did Katy leave you, Richard?"

I shrugged, feeling helpless. "I don't know. Maybe because she didn't know how I really felt about her?"

"Which is how, exactly?"

"I love her."

"Your wife didn't know you loved her?"

"No."

"I think you've found your beginning."

I nodded grimly, knowing he was correct.

"I lied to you."

"Which part?"

I sat down, putting my coffee mug on the table. If I held it, I would either smash it in between my tightly clenched fists or throw the whole thing, contents and all, at the wall. Neither boded well for a civilized conversation—not that this was going to be.

"All of it. It was all a lie."

Graham sat across from me, crossing his legs. He ran his fingers down the crease of his trousers, then looked up.

"You lied to me to get the job at The Gavin Group?"

"Yes."

"Tell me why."

"I was passed up for partner, and I wanted to piss David off. I wanted out, but I wanted to stay here, in Victoria. I like it here. I heard about the opening at Gavin and I wanted in."

Aside from the small tilt of his chin, he said nothing.

"I knew you would never hire me. I had heard of the tight-knit way you ran your business. My reputation was less than stellar, on a personal level." I barked a laugh. "It didn't matter what I could bring to the table, business-wise, because my lifestyle and personality would stop you from even considering me."

"That's true."

"It occurred to me, if you thought I wasn't *that* person, maybe I would have a shot."

"And you came up with this plan."

"Yes."

"How did Katy come into this scheme of yours?"

"Not willingly. With the rules at Anderson, I knew she was the most obvious choice. Aside from the fact she was different from any other woman I had dated, that she was my assistant was the perfect set up." I shrugged my shoulders in resignation. "I didn't even like her. She wasn't crazy about me, either."

"You both played it well."

"We had to. It was important to both of us." I leaned forward, earnest. "She did this for one reason, and one reason alone, Graham."

"Penny."

"Yes. I paid her to pretend to be my fiancée. I practically coerced her into marrying me to continue the charade. She hated the lying and the deception." I rubbed the back of my neck, my fingers digging into my skin hard. "She was, *is*, so fond of all of you that it became too much for her, I think. She couldn't do it anymore."

"How much of this deception was Brian Maxwell privy to?"

I had already decided not to let anyone else suffer because of me. I refused to jeopardize either Brian or Amy. "None. I told him the same story I told you. If he suspected anything, he kept it to himself. I think he truly thought I had changed, or he wouldn't have been part of this. Amy," I added, "knew nothing. Nothing."

He regarded me for a moment, tapping his chin. "I'm not sure he was as innocent as you say. However, I'm going to let it pass. Amy is a trusted employee, so I do believe she knew nothing."

"She didn't."

"So you came on board. What was your plan?"

Putting my head down, I clasped my hands behind my head, pulling my neck. I felt tight and anxious, as if I would jump out of my skin any second.

"Richard, you need to calm down. Try to relax."

With a huge exhale, I released my neck and looked up at him. "I don't know where my wife is, Graham. I can't relax. My life is in turmoil, and the one person who can make it better is out there somewhere"—I waved my hand toward the window—"thinking I don't care."

"When did you fall in love with her?"

"I have no idea. It was supposed to be an act. I needed her to make me more likable. I thought if I could get my foot in the door, prove my worth to you and your company, show you what I could offer to your campaigns, maybe my personal life wouldn't matter as much. Eventually, I would divorce her, and we'd go our separate ways. I'd keep working; she'd be in a far better place financially than she had been. No one would be any the wiser."

"But?" His question hung in the air, simple and heavy.

"Things changed. *I changed.* What was supposed to be an act became real. We became friends. Allies. Then we became more. I never saw it, though. I never saw how important she was becoming to me. I never thought I was capable of having feelings like that for anyone."

"Where does Penny fit into this situation? I think she was a huge part of it all."

"Katharine never wanted me to meet her or have anything to do with her life. She didn't want to confuse Penny's already muddled mind. The night you had the get-together when I joined the firm, and I had too much to drink—we argued. Or rather, I was an ass and I pushed her. She told me about her parents' accident and how Penny came into her life. She informed me, in no uncertain terms, exactly what she thought of me." Even with my worry and the seriousness of the conversation, my lips curled into a smile. "I saw a side of Katharine that night I never imagined she possessed. She wasn't an insignificant weakling as I'd originally thought. She was, *is*, fierce and strong. Loyal." My smile fell. "And she opened my eyes to what a bastard I truly was—to her, to everyone around me. The next day, I went and met Penny."

"I assumed she impressed you?"

"She reminded me of someone from my past. One of the few good people I had in my younger life." I tugged at my cowlick and stopped talking, knowing I had to regroup my thoughts. I didn't want to dig that far into my past with Graham. "Despite everything, Katharine married me that day because we had a deal and she kept her word."

"And you fell in love with your wife."

"Yes, I did. But it was too late."

"Why do you say that?"

"She left me. She left everything I gave her behind. Her phone, the money, even the car. I have no idea how to find her or where she might have gone."

"What about Penny's things? Did she take them?"

"No, those are at the condo, along with a few of her personal things. I assume she'll contact me as to where to send them."

"You don't want to wait until then."

I stood up, going back to the window. "I don't think there is anything to wait for, but no, I need to find her."

"Are you willing to fight to change that—do you want to fight, Richard?"

I spun around. "Yes. I want to fight for all of it. Her. My job. Everything."

He stood up, crossing his arms. "I suspected you were lying the first time I met you."

I gaped at him. "What?"

"I was fairly certain. I found your thought process intriguing, though. *You* intrigued me. Talking to you, I had a sense there was more to you than you allowed people to see. There was a spark, for lack of a better word, I could see. For the first time ever, I wanted to hire someone I wasn't entirely sure about. Laura felt the same way about you—even stronger, to be honest. She felt you needed to be given a chance."

"You said as much one other time."

He nodded. "Katy—she was the deciding factor. She was open and real. Whether you realized it or not, you *were* different with her." He smiled. "It was actually enjoyable watching you fall in love, Richard. We could both see it. We saw the changes in you." He studied me, his head cocked to the side. "At the office, you were a wonder to behold. The way your mind works, spinning ideas, concepts. Your enthusiasm even got me going again. It was quite the spectacle to witness."

My throat tightened. I could hear the finality of his words. *Were.* *Was.* My career at The Gavin Group was over. Even though I knew it would happen, hearing it was still a blow—a small flicker of hope had burned, and now, it was gone.

"Your company, Graham. My time there has been, without a doubt, the most positive, creative environment I have ever been part of in my career. The way you allow your people to work, the cohesive energy that permeates the environment you created. It was an honor to work for you. I can't even begin to express my apologies for deceiving you. I won't ask for your forgiveness, since I know I don't deserve it. All I ask is that you forgive Katharine. I made her do it. I backed her into a corner until she had no choice." I paused, unsure what else to say. "She's so fond of Jenna and Laura. Once she comes back, it would give me great comfort knowing she had a friend she could rely on."

"Where will you be?"

I shrugged. "Toronto, maybe? I don't know. I won't leave town until she returns and we settle everything."

He raised his eyebrows. "This is your idea of fighting? It sounds as if you've already given up."

"I can't work for some obscure online advertising company, Graham. I'll never go back to Anderson Inc., so I have no other choice really, except to move to another city and start again."

"Have I fired you?"

"I assume it's coming any minute."

"And when it does?"

"I'll shake your hand, thank you for being someone I'll respect the rest of my life—someone who believed enough in me to take a chance. Very few people have ever believed in me." I swallowed the thick emotion in my throat—Katharine had been one of those people.

"Why are you telling me all this, Richard?" he asked, confused as to my motives. "You could have stayed silent and ridden this out. Katy may come back and all this will have been for nothing. My suspicions would have remained simply that—suspicions."

I met his stare. "Katharine isn't the only one tired of living a lie. I want to move forward on a clean slate, whether it's here with you or elsewhere. I didn't expect this plan to deviate. I hadn't planned to fall in love with my wife, and I never expected your opinion of me would mean as much as it does. I didn't"—I cleared my throat—"expect to feel this close to your family. I've never experienced anything like it—I never had a family, not a real one like yours. It was as if I had come to my own crossroad, and I had no choice *except* to tell you the truth. I'm sorry I let you down, Graham. I regret that more than I can express."

He stepped forward and I held out my hand, surprised to see it was shaking. He looked down, ignoring my outstretched palm. His hand was heavy as he clapped my shoulder and met my gaze. "I'm not firing you, Richard."

"You . . . you're not?"

"No. Not now. You have work to do. You need to find your wife and get her back. Then we'll discuss your future with the company and in general."

"I don't understand."

"There is more to all of this than meets the eye. Your past has dictated the person you became as an adult—which frankly wasn't the nicest of people, until Katy."

"What do you want, Graham?"

"I want you to find your wife. Find out what she's thinking—how she's feeling. Be honest—lay your cards on the table."

"Then?"

"Bring her home or finish it. One way or another, get your life on track. You and I are going to sit down and talk—really talk. I think you have a lot to offer my company." He stopped and gave a nod as if he had reached a decision in his head. "I think my family and I have something to offer you."

"And what do I have to do to get it?"

"Be honest. Real. I want to know about your life. The Richard you were and the Richard you are now. As well, I will expect apologies to my family. If you stay on board, you are going to have to earn our trust all over again."

"Back to square one?"

"I'd say right now you're a negative five."

"I understand." I really did. His offer surprised me—it also terrified me. The thought of telling him my past life—the person I was growing up and before working for him—was daunting. However, I had something else I needed to do first.

"I don't know how to find Katy."

"I suggest you do the same thing as you did with me today. Start at the beginning."

"What?"

"She and I talked a lot the day of Penny's memorial. I think I know where she may be. If you look hard enough, you'll find the answer in your home."

"Tell me," I urged. "Please."

"No. You need to figure this out. Get to know your wife without help. If you *try*, if you think, you can do this, Richard." He squeezed my shoulder. "I have confidence."

"What if I can't?"

"Then you don't want it badly enough. If you love her, if you *really* love her, you'll figure it out." He paused and regarded me thoughtfully. "I'm going to ask you a question. I want you to answer me without thinking. I want your first thought."

I straightened my shoulders. I was good at that. "Shoot."

"Why do you love Katy?"

"Because she makes me look at the world in a different way. She grounds me." I lifted a shoulder in frustration of how to explain. "She makes life brighter. She showed me what real love meant."

He nodded. "I'll drive you home now."

Twenty-Eight

RICHARD

IN THE HALLWAY, Laura stopped us. She looked up at me, a frown on her face.

"I was listening by the door, Richard."

"Okay."

"I heard almost everything."

I dropped my gaze, hers too intense to meet any longer.

"You lied to me. To my family."

"Yes."

"So did Katy."

My head shot up. "Because I made her, Laura. She hated it. She hated the fact she had to lie in the first place, but once she got to know you, she loathed it." I stepped forward. "She did this to make sure Penny was looked after and had a safe home. She . . . she became so fond of you, of all of you, this ruse ate her up inside." I gripped the back of my neck, wrenching on the tense muscles. "I think it was the main reason she left. She couldn't take the lies anymore."

She stretched up, tugging on my arm. I released the grip on my neck and allowed her to clasp my hand.

"Was it still a lie when she left?"

"No," I admitted. "I love her. I'm lost without Katy." I swung my gaze to Graham and back to her. "That's why I had to tell you. I needed a clean slate, no matter what else happens. I needed you to understand this was all on me. Not her. If I leave town, and she comes back, I hope you'll forgive her. She's going to be all alone."

Laura smiled. "You've grown, Richard. Your first thought now is Katy and her well-being."

"It should have always been."

She squeezed my hand. "Find your wife. Tell her the truth. I think you'll find you aren't the only one who's lost."

My chest constricted. I wanted to believe—to believe she loved me, too. That she ran because she needed to figure out her next step. I needed to find her so she understood she didn't have to make it alone.

"I want that."

Graham spoke up. "Then work for it. Earn it. Figure out your personal life. Once you do, we'll discuss your professional one. As of this moment, you're on leave until we talk again. You aren't fired, but your future isn't set in stone, either."

"I understand."

I had expected to be fired instantly. Thrown out of his house. No matter the outcome, or how difficult it would be, a future discussion was more than I deserved.

"Thank you," I stated sincerely.

"I'll take you home now."

I followed him to the car reflecting that without Katy there, it wasn't my home. It was the place where I lived. Wherever she was right now, *that* was my home. Beside her. I had to find her and bring her back. Then I could call it home again.

AFTER GRAHAM DROPPED me off, I wandered the condo, unsure where to start. On the coffee table was the file holding all Katy's color swatches and ideas for the place. She had added to the list for my bedroom, her little sketches included rearrangement of the furniture and color on the walls. She was talented. I had noticed but had never told her that, though I should have. There were many thoughts I should have shared.

I tossed the file back onto the coffee table. When I got her back, we could discuss whatever changes she wanted to make to *our* room. She could do whatever she pleased to the entire place, as long as she was there, it was fine.

First, I had to find my wife.

I went to her room, dragging a small file box off her closet shelf. I knew it contained legal documents for her and Penny. I sat down on the chaise and opened the lid, ignoring the sense of guilt. These were her personal things and I felt as if I shouldn't be looking through them without her permission.

However, I had no choice.

An hour later, I put everything back in the box, my head reeling a little. Katharine was very good at keeping records. For the first time, I understood how close to the edge of poverty she'd been living. How every cent she made went toward Penny and her care. I was able to see how the expenses became greater while her income only increased marginally. She had cut back further and further on her own expenditures—moving to cheaper accommodations, spending as little as she could on everyday necessities. Thinking back to how I treated her at the office, the things she put up with on a daily basis, how I mocked her menial lunches—it all made me squirm. Shame, hot and deep, ran through me as I thought of the things I'd done, the way I'd spoken. How she ever moved past it, and had forgiven me, was a miracle.

I shut the lid. Although I gleaned a bit more insight into her life and her unconditional love of Penny, this box held no clue as to where she might be.

I hauled out the two unopened boxes from the floor of her closet and scoured them for clues. Yet, hours later, I sat back in defeat. They contained various personal items: school projects, report cards, pieces of bric-a-brac, a few family pictures, and mementos from her teenage years. They were memories that would mean a great deal to her but meant nothing to me, nothing to guide me to her whereabouts.

I repacked the boxes and stood up, weary, but determined. I glanced around the room, then did a sweep of the drawers, shelves, bookcase, and bathroom. I pored over the pictures on the shelves, looked over the small knickknacks, and ran my finger over the book spines. I doubted her choice of literature would give me any clues.

I flicked off the light and went downstairs. I poured a scotch, surprised to see how late it was. I looked around the kitchen but had no appetite to eat. I grabbed an apple, chewing it while sitting at the counter. Thoughts of her in the kitchen, cooking a great meal, floated through my head. I remembered her laughter and how she teased me when I growled about dinner taking too long.

"Patience, Richard. All good things come to those who wait," she said with a chuckle.

I shut my eyes. I couldn't be patient when it came to finding Katharine.

I tossed away the half-eaten apple. In the den, I fired up the computer to check for an email from her, not surprised when there wasn't one. I sipped my scotch, staring around the room. I always liked it when she would come in and sit across from me. I would show her what I was working on, and her comments were always positive and helpful.

How had I not noticed how deeply she'd become embedded into my life? When our arrangement first started, the lines were clearly drawn. Bit by bit, they disappeared until they were non-existent. It all became as natural as breathing—me watching her cook, her chatting with me over the desk, sitting beside her while she watched TV, or even the quick kiss she would drop on my head on her way up to bed. It was simply a part of my daily life, just as making sure my door was open so she could hear me snore was something I did without thinking.

I had fallen in love with her by building one small, new positive habit at a time. She had slowly replaced the bad ones, until they were gone, by simply being her.

With a groan, I let my head hit the back of my chair.

I needed her back.

EARLY THE NEXT morning, after another restless night, I carried the boxes from the home up to Katharine's room. I had put them in the storage room, knowing she wasn't ready to deal with the contents so soon after Penny's death. All of her paintings, drawings, and other pieces of artwork were also stored there and would remain so until Katharine decided what to do with them.

The first box contained a lot of knickknacks and mementos that had been scattered around Penny's room. I carefully repacked it and set the box aside. The next box was all pictures and photo albums. I spent some time poring over the albums, where I saw Penny's life laid out in black and white images that slowly bled into colored pictures. The last book I opened began when Katharine came into her life—a thin, frightened teenager, whose eyes looked far too old for her face. As I turned the pages, she changed—growing up, filling in, and discovering life once more. I puzzled over the many pictures of them sitting in restaurants, huge tables of smiling faces with them. I grinned at the pictures taken on a beach, Katharine staring off into the sunset as the waves hit the sand, or digging in the sand for clams, a bucket partially full beside her. The album ended two years ago, and I assumed it was when Penny became ill. I recalled some photo albums in the bookcase and resolved to look through those, as well.

Finally, I opened the third box, digging through some well-read books and a few other items. At the bottom was a pile of black books, the pages dog-eared, and the spines well-worn. The front of the books contained only a label with a set of dates written in Penny's spidery hand. I opened one, scanning the first few pages until I figured out what I was reading.

Penny's journals. There were ten of them, all documenting different spans of her life. I found the one that corresponded with the year she found Katharine and I started to read.

So many things began to take shape in my mind. I knew her husband was a chef, and now the pictures I had seen made sense. She and Katharine would work with one of Burt's chef friends, and after the work was done, they would gather and eat together.

My Katy learned a new recipe from Mario today. Watching her work with him made my heart so happy—hearing her laughter and seeing that sadness disappear as she chopped and stirred. It was her marinara that they served

*at the wedding reception! Mario insisted it was better than his! Tasting it at
dinner afterward, I had to agree.*

*Tonight, my Katy wowed us all with her Beef Wellington. She worked for
hours with Sam, and everything we had after the dinner was her creation. Burt
would have adored her and been proud. I'm so proud.*

A smile pulled at my lips. No wonder she was such a good cook.
Professionals had trained her for years, given her one-on-one instruction
in exchange for help. I flipped forward to another short entry.

*I am taking Katy to the cottage next week! We can stay for free in exchange
for some housekeeping duties at the resort. Her eyes lit up so bright when I told
her!*

Katharine had told me they didn't have much money, and how
Penny always made things that should be work seem fun. That
remarkable woman used every trick she had to give Katharine things
she couldn't afford. She showed Katharine by working hard, there was a
reward. Like a dinner out for waiting tables, or making beds at a resort,
it was a break from the city and memories to share. I looked at the
journals scattered around the floor. I knew they held more stories about
Penny and her life. I wanted to read them all, but they would have to
wait for another time. I had to concentrate on her life with Katharine
and hope they gave me a clue.

*My Katy loves the beach. She sits for hours, sketching, watching, so at
peace. I worry she is alone too much, but she insists this is where she feels
happiest. No sounds of the city, not surrounded by people. I must figure out
how to bring her back.*

*I spoke with Scott and we can come back mid-September. I'll have to take
Katy out of school—but I know she'll catch up fast—she is so smart. The resort
isn't as busy then, the weather is still nice, and he has the cottage free. I will
surprise her with the news on her birthday before we leave.*

So the entries continued. Posts about the cottage, the beach,
Katharine cooking, growing up—a great deal of information, yet not
what I needed. I was tempted to call Graham, tell him I thought she was
at a cottage, and beg him for the name, yet I expected he would tell me

to keep looking.

I shut the book, rubbing my eyes. I had been reading for over eight hours, only moving to flick on the light when clouds began to cover the sun and get some coffee. The one clue I had was the cottage Penny had mentioned going to every year and the owner's first name: Scott. Unfortunately, there was no last name, or even better, the name of the town or resort where the cottage was located. Reaching down, I grabbed the photo albums that held the pictures of Katharine and their life. I scanned the beach pictures, taking them from the album, convinced they were the same beach but taken on different trips. I couldn't find any clue in the pictures, and nothing written on the backs to help me. With a heavy sigh, I sagged back on the chaise, staring around the room. For the first time, I wished for some horrid touristy souvenir with the name of a town emblazoned across the front to be on the shelf with her books. Tilting my head to the side, I noticed something odd on the bottom shelf. The last two books had no wording on the spine. They were tall, slim books. I glanced down at the pile of journals scattered around the floor, then back at the bookcase. They were exactly like the worn journals I'd been reading.

I pushed off the chaise and grabbed the books. Katharine kept a journal, or at least she had. I glanced at the dates, flipping from the front to the last page. She had started about a year after coming to live with Penny and these books had lasted her five years. Her journals weren't as wordy as Penny's. There were random thoughts, some longer passages, even a few postcards taped inside. They also contained sketches, small images of things she must have loved.

I sent up a small prayer as I opened the first book. I needed a clue, a name, something to help me find her.

Time stopped as I scanned her words. I found I wasn't able to stop reading. Her brief passages were filled with her essence; it was as if she was in front of me, telling me one of her stories. The depth of her love for Penny, the gratitude she felt for the home and unconditional love given to her by Penny was blatant. She wrote of their adventures, even made the search for bottles and cans sound fun. She described the dinners with Penny's friends, her love for the different foods, and even jotted recipes on the pages. My breath caught at one passage.

We're going to the beach next week. Penny has a friend who owns a small resort and she made a deal with him. We'll clean the cottages daily, and in exchange, we can stay there rent-free for a week! With the two of us, we can get it done in no time and I'll have most of the day to play! I'm so excited! I haven't been to the beach since my parents died. I can't believe she has done this for me!

My heartbeat sped up. This had to be it. Penny had mentioned cottages, and there were pictures of them from the beach. I kept reading.

Our cottage is so pretty! It's bright blue with white shutters and is right on the end of the row. I can hear the water all day and night! There are only six cottages, and because it's May, they are only half-full, so Penny and I are done by noon every day, and we spend the rest of the time exploring. I love it here!

Then there was another one a few days later.

I don't want to go home, but Penny told me we could come back in September. Scott even promised her the same cottage. Another week to look forward to! I'm so lucky—the best birthday gift ever!

My eyes watered with the last entry. A working holiday. That was all they could afford. The same way they could only afford to eat out with the generosity of friends, and yet she felt lucky. I thought of my life of excess. Anything I wanted I could have—even growing up, I was denied nothing material. Yet, I was never satisfied, because the one thing I wanted most, they never provided.

Love.

Penny gave it to Katharine in spades. It made something like a trip together, even if she had to be a housekeeper for a week, special.

I started flipping through the pages faster, searching for entries about the location of the cottages. Near the end of the second book, I struck gold. One of her sketches was an archway with the name *Scott's Seaside Hideaway*. I grabbed my phone, doing a search on the net for the name.

I found it. The picture on the site was the same archway as in her sketch, and the map indicated it was two hours away. Another picture showed the row of small cottages, the end one hardly visible, except for the blue color.

I looked back at her journal. Under the sketch were the words:

My favorite piece of heaven on earth.

I closed my eyes as relief washed over me.

I had found my wife.

Twenty-Nine

KATHARINE

THE GENTLE SOUNDS of the waves breaking on the shore soothed me. I rested my chin on my knees, trying to lose myself in the beauty of the beach. The gulls flying overhead, the ebb and flow of the moving water, and the utter peace.

Except, I wasn't peaceful. I felt lost, torn. I was grateful Penny was no longer trapped in a never-ending nightmare of forgotten moments, but I missed her terribly. Her voice, her laughter, the tender way she would cup my cheek, kiss my forehead, tweak my nose, and in her rare moments of clarity, provide her wisdom.

If she were here I could talk to her, tell her what I was feeling, and she would explain it to me. She would tell me what to do next.

I was in love with my husband, a man who wasn't in love with me. A man who felt love made you weak and couldn't love himself. He would never be able to see his good traits; the ones he had buried deep inside in order never to be hurt again.

He had changed a lot since that fateful day he asked me to be his pretend fiancée. Gradually, he allowed a gentler, more caring side of himself to emerge. Penny broke through his remaining barriers. She reminded him of a time when he had felt love from another person. Graham Gavin had shown him how to work *with* people, not endlessly compete. He'd proved to him there were good people and he could be part of a positive group. His wife and children showed him a different version of what he believed a family could be. One filled with support and care, not neglect and pain.

I wanted to think I had something to do with his change. That somehow, in some way, I had shown him love was possible. Maybe not with me, but it was an emotion he was capable of giving and receiving. He didn't give himself enough credit, though.

I wasn't sure when I realized I had fallen in love with him. The seed might have been planted on our wedding day and it grew every time he shed a bit more of his caustic, hurtful nature. Every real smile and easy laugh watered the sentiment, making it stronger. Each kind act toward Penny, one of the Gavins, or me, had fed the fledgling emotion until it took hold so tight I knew it would never change.

The day Jenna showed up was the day I *knew* I loved him. The headache that plagued him all day, made him unusually vulnerable. He not only allowed my care, he seemed to enjoy it. His teasing had been sweet and funny, bordering on affectionate. When he came to bed, he had shown a different side to his character. His voice had been a low hum in the dark as he comforted me, his apologies rang sincere as he asked for forgiveness for the way he had treated me in the past. Forgiveness I granted—that I had granted days, maybe weeks, before he had asked for it. Then he drew me close and made me feel safe in a way I hadn't since my parents died. I slept content and warm in his embrace.

The next morning, I had seen yet another side—his sexy, funny side. The way he reacted to waking up entwined together; the amusing way he ordered Jenna out of the room, kissing me until I was breathless. His passion simmered below the surface, his voice low and raspy from sleep. His comment about expanding our boundaries made my heart race, and I knew for the first time in my life, I was falling in love.

Sadly, though, I knew he would never change *enough* to allow my love. That he would never want my love. We had a truce. To his shock, and mine, we became friends. His insults were now teasing, and his dismissive attitude gone. However, I knew that was all I was to him. A friend—a collaborator.

I sighed as I dug my toes deeper into the cooling sand. I would have to go inside soon. Once the sun set, it grew colder, and I was already a little chilled, even with a jacket on. I knew I would pass another night pacing and rambling around the small cottage. Chances were I would end up back on the beach, bundled up, walking to try to exhaust myself so I could fall into a restless, unsatisfying sleep. Even in my slumber, I couldn't escape my thoughts. Asleep or awake, they were filled with him.

Richard.

My eyes burned as I thought of how he had taken care of me when Penny died. How he acted as though I would shatter like glass if he spoke too loud. When he had carried me to his bed, intent on comforting me, I already knew I had to leave him. I couldn't hide the love I felt much longer. I couldn't stand the thought of watching his face morph into that cold, haughty mask he used to cover his true self as he dismissed my confession—because he would.

Until he could love himself, he could never love anyone. Not even me.

Impatiently, I brushed the tears away, hugging my knees tight to my chest.

I had given him the one gift I had left—myself. It was all I had, and in truth, I was being selfish. I wanted to feel him. To have him possess my body and be able to keep that memory as the one I held the tightest. It was still painful to think of, but I knew as time passed, eventually the edges would soften and wilt, and I would be able to smile thinking of the passion. Remembering how his mouth felt on mine. The way our bodies joined perfectly, the warmth of his form surrounding mine, and the way his voice sounded as he groaned out my name.

Unable to take the barrage of memories, I stifled a sob and stood up, brushing off my jeans. Turning, I stopped, frozen. Standing in the waning light, tall and stern, hands buried in his coat pockets, staring at me, with an unfathomable expression, was Richard.

RICHARD

SHE WAS TOO thin again. Even with a jacket on, it was evident. Her appetite had been non-existent after Penny passed, and in the few days we'd been apart, I knew she wasn't eating. She was suffering as much as me.

When I arrived at the small cluster of cottages, I parked far enough away I wouldn't alert her to my presence if she was, indeed, there. Walking onto the beach, I spied her right away, a small, huddled mass on the sand, staring into the horizon. She looked lost and tiny, and the need to go to her, lift her into my arms and refuse to let her go, was strong. I had never felt anything that intense until today. However, I resisted, knowing I needed to approach her cautiously. She had run once, and I didn't want her running again.

We stood, staring at each other. I began to head toward her—slow, wary steps, until I was in front of her, inches away. Up close, she looked as ravaged as I felt. Her blue eyes were bloodshot and weary, her skin paler than ever, her hair limp and dull.

"You left me."

"There was no need to stay."

I frowned. "No need?"

"Graham had already waved your probationary period. Penny died. You didn't need the cover of our marriage anymore."

"What did you think I was going to tell people, Katharine? How did you expect me to explain your sudden disappearance?"

She waved her hand dismissively. "You always tell me how good you think on your feet, Richard. I assumed you'd tell them I was overwhelmed with losing Penny and went away to clear my head. You could string it along for a while, then tell them we'd been having problems, and I decided not to come back."

"So you expected me to blame you. Lay it all at *your* feet."

She swayed slightly. "What would it matter? I wouldn't contest it."

"Of course not. Because you weren't there."

"Exactly."

"But it did matter. It *does* matter to me."

Her brow furrowed as she watched me.

I took a step forward, wanting to be near her. Needing to touch her, worried at how fragile she seemed to be.

"You left things behind. Things I would think were important to you."

"I was going to contact you and ask you to send them—wherever I ended up settling."

"You didn't take your car or bankcard. How were you planning on accessing the rest of your money?"

She stuck out her stubborn chin. "I took what I earned."

"No, you earned so much more, Katharine."

Her lips trembled. "Why are you here? H–How did you find me?"

"I came here for you. A friend suggested I start at the beginning."

"I don't understand."

"Graham told me where to find you."

"Graham?" She frowned, looking confused. "How . . . how did he know?"

"He had a suspicion, and because he listened better than I ever did, he knew the answer was in our home. He told me to look. He refused to tell me. He said I had to figure all this out on my own."

"I–I don't understand."

"After you left, I did a lot of thinking. I wallowed some, drank too much, and ran around looking for you. Finally, I realized I couldn't do it anymore."

"Couldn't do what?"

"I finally understood what you were feeling. My life had become one lie after another. I couldn't tell where reality ended and the lies began anymore. Even at my worst, when I was a complete bastard, I was honest about it. I had been hiding for so long and I didn't want to hide anymore. I told Graham you left me."

A tear ran down her face.

"Then I told him everything. Every single, fucking lie."

She gasped. "No! Richard—why did you do that? You had it all. Everything you wanted! Everything you worked so hard for! Why did you throw it away?"

I grasped her arms, shaking her a little. "Don't you get it, Katharine? Don't you see?"

"See what?" she cried.

"I didn't have everything! Not without you! I had nothing, and without you, it all *meant* nothing! The one real thing I had, the one honest, real thing was you!"

Her eyes grew round and she shook her head. "You don't mean that."

"I do. I came here for you."

"Why? You don't need me."

I ran my hands up her arms, over her shoulders and neck, cupping her face—her tired, beautiful face—between my palms. "I do need you." I met her weary gaze with my determined one, speaking the words I had only ever spoken once in my lifetime. Back then, I spoke them with a childish mindset, and the words really had no meaning. Now though—they meant everything.

"I love you, Katharine."

Her hands wrapped around my wrists, the doubt plain on her panicked face. "No," she breathed.

I leaned my forehead to hers. "I do. I need you so much. I miss my friend, my *wife*. I miss you."

A wild sob broke from her throat. I gathered her in my arms, refusing to allow her to escape. She pushed at my chest, fighting against the comfort I needed to give her.

"You can't run. I'll follow you, sweetheart. I'll follow you anywhere." I pressed a kiss to her head. "Don't leave me alone again, my Katy. I couldn't bear it."

She broke. Flinging her arms around my neck, she buried her face in my chest as hot tears soaked my shirt. I lifted her into my arms, and carried her across the hard sand toward the bright blue cottage at the end. It was the one with the white shutters she wrote about in her journal.

I held her tight, dropping light kisses on her head. I wasn't letting her go.

THE RUSTIC COTTAGE was exactly how I pictured it in my head from the description in her journal. A well-worn sofa and chair were in front of a fireplace. To the left was a rudimentary kitchen with a table and two chairs. An open door led to a small bedroom, and beside it, a bathroom. That was the entire cottage. I sat Katy on the sofa and turned to the fireplace. Soot and smoke from years of use had settled into the stone and brick, turning the entire mantle a dull gray. I added some logs and kindling, wanting a fire to warm up the cool interior.

"The flue sticks." Katy kneeled beside me, reaching past me to tug on the duct.

I struck a match, making sure the kindling caught, then stood, replacing the small screen. Bending down, I brought her to her feet, tugging her damp jacket off her shoulders, tossing it to the side. Wrapping my arms around her, I held her tight, the sense of relief saturating my body. She shivered, a long, low breath escaping her mouth. I cradled her head in my hands, dropping a kiss to her crown. She tilted her head back, the firelight dancing over her features, highlighting the delicate contours of her face.

"I can't believe you're here."

"Did you really think I wouldn't try to find you, Katy?"

"I don't know. I wasn't thinking. I only knew I had to go."

I pulled her to the sofa, gathering her hands into mine. "Why, sweetheart? Why did you run?"

"Because I fell in love with you, and I didn't think you could love me back. I couldn't hide it any longer, and I knew when you realized how I felt you'd—"

My heart clenched at her words. She loved me. I squeezed her hands, prompting her. "I'd what?"

"You'd turn back into the Richard I hated and laugh at me. You didn't need me anymore and you would tell me to go. I thought it would be easier if I went."

"Were you planning on coming back at all?"

"Only to find out what you wanted to do and get my things. I assumed you wouldn't want me around anymore."

"You thought wrong. About all of it. I need you. I want you back. I . . ." I faltered. "I love you."

She looked down at our joined hands, then back up. Bewilderment was evident in her expression; blatant disbelief was in her eyes. I couldn't blame her, but I wanted to eradicate both.

"You don't believe me."

"I don't know what to believe," she admitted.

I slid closer, knowing I needed to find a way to convince her I was sincere. My gaze swept the small cottage as I mulled over my words, landing on the small urn sitting on the fireplace mantle.

"Did you bring Penny's ashes with you to scatter them?" I asked.

"Yes. We had many happy memories here. She worked hard to make sure I could come here every year. She and Burt used to come here, too. She scattered his ashes on the beach." She swallowed, voice quivering. "I thought maybe, somehow, they'd meet up and be together again in the sand and water." Her gaze lifted to mine. "I guess that seems silly."

I lifted her hand to my mouth, kissing the knuckles. "Silly? No. It sounds like a sweet gesture. Something a gentle soul like you would think of."

"A gentle soul?"

"You are one, Katy. I realized it a few weeks ago, when I stopped being such a bastard. I watched you, the way you were with Penny. The interactions you had with the Gavin family. The kindness you showed to the staff at the home." I traced the back of my fingers down her cheek, the skin like silk under my touch. "The way you treated me. You give. You constantly give. I had never experienced that until you came into my life. I didn't think there was anyone like you on this earth."

I bent closer, needing her to see the sincerity in my eyes. "I didn't think anyone like you could ever be a part of my life."

"Because you didn't deserve it?"

"Because I didn't believe in love."

Her reply was a whisper. "And now?"

"I know now I *can* love someone. I do love someone. I love you." I held up my hand when she started to speak. "I know you might not believe me, Katy. It's true, though. You taught me to love. You showed me everything you said was true. What I feel for you makes me stronger. It makes me want to be a good man for you. Be honest and real. That's why I came clean with Graham. I knew the only way I had a chance to get you back, and keep you, was to be honest. Make you proud."

"When?"

"Pardon?"

"When did you start to change? When did you stop disliking me?"

I shrugged. "I think maybe the day you told me to go fuck myself. That was the first time I saw the real Katharine. You'd been hiding that fire."

"I had to. I needed my job. Penny was far more important than you or your nasty attitude."

"I know. My behavior was horrendous. How you managed to get past any of it and agree to be with me—even for Penny—is still a mystery. That night you told me your story and let me know exactly what you thought of me was an eye-opener. I don't think I've ever sobered up as fast in my life. And once again, you forgave me—you married me."

"I had given you my word."

"Which you could have backed out of easily. I expected you to, but once more, you surprised me. You surprised me at every turn." Smiling, I tucked a lock of her hair behind her ear. "Not much surprises me, yet you do—constantly. I like it."

She smiled back, her expression not as wary as it had been.

"The most amazing thing to me was, and is, the way you were with me."

"What do you mean?"

"All I asked, all I expected, was for you to put on an act when we were out together. I fully expected you to ignore me when we were in the privacy of the condo. I know I planned to ignore you. But . . ."

"But, what?"

"I couldn't ignore you. You were everywhere. Without even trying, you were in my head—it was as natural as breathing. The condo became a home with you there. You teased and laughed with me. You took care of me—no one has done that my entire life. Your opinion became paramount. Everything I did, I wanted to share with you. Instead of ignoring you, I wanted more time with you. I wanted to know everything about you."

She gazed at me, her eyes wide.

"And Penny. I loved spending time with her. Hearing the stories she shared about you. I got to know more of you each time I saw her, and the more I knew, the more I fell, until the moment I realized how deeply I was in love with you."

I gathered her hands in mine, holding them tight. "None of my cruelness changed you. Instead, your sweetness changed me, Katy. You and Penny brought out that little boy who could still love."

"What if he forgets again?"

I shook my head. "He won't. He can't—not as long as I have you." I lifted her hand. "You left your wedding rings behind, yet you're wearing this ring." I tapped the diamond band on her finger. "You moved it to your left hand. Why?"

"Because you gave it to me. It was the first thing you'd given me that you didn't have to." Her voice caught. "I–I put it there because it was closer to my heart."

I shut my eyes, hoping I understood the meaning behind her words. Pressing her hand to my face, I opened my eyes to look into hers. Tears swam in the depths of her expressive blue gaze. "I gave you my heart, too, Katy. Will you keep it, as well?"

She drew in a breath that stuttered and shook her small frame.

"You gave me your body. I want your heart. I want your love. I need it. I need *you*."

"Say it, Richard." A tear slipped down her cheek.

"I love you, Katharine VanRyan. I want you to come home with me. Make my life complete. I'll do whatever it takes to get you to believe me. To make you believe in me."

"I already do."

I cupped her face, my thumbs tracing frantic circles on her skin as my heartbeat sped up. "And?"

"I love you, Richard. I love you so much, it scares me."

"Why are you scared?"

"You could break me."

I shook my head. "It's you who's broken me, Katy. I'm yours."

"I'm yours, too."

That was all I needed. Pulling her to me, I covered her mouth with mine, groaning at the sensation of having her close. Our lips moved, tongues stroked and caressed as we reacquainted ourselves with each other. Her arms wound around my neck, holding me tight as I folded mine around her like a steel cage.

One I didn't plan to release her from—ever.

Thirty

RICHARD

I LIFTED MY head, squinting in the silent darkness. We had been sitting, holding each other, needing the closeness. I didn't know for how long, but enough for night to have descended. "I need to add some more logs," I murmured. "The fire is going to die."

"I like it right here. I'm warm enough."

I chuckled and pressed a kiss to her head. "We have to move eventually."

"I should make us something to eat."

"I need to find a place to stay."

She froze. "You aren't staying here?"

Tenderly, I cupped her face, brushing a kiss to her lips. "I want to. But I don't want to push."

"It's a queen-size bed."

I quirked my eyebrow at her. "Small for us. I suppose I'll have to snuggle with you. I guess if it's the sacrifice I have to make—"

Her lips curled into a smile. "I suppose so."

"I've missed snuggling with you. I've missed your warmth and your smell."

"Well then, I guess you better stay."

"I guess so." I paused, needing to ask her the question that had been simmering in the back of my mind for days. "I need to ask you something, Katy."

She drifted her finger over my stubble. "I like hearing you call me that."

I tweaked her nose. "Good. I like saying it."

Her expression changed to serious. "Now, what did you want to ask me?"

I shifted, acutely uncomfortable. "The night before you left. The night we made love."

"Is that what it was?"

"Yes," I said firmly. "It was."

"What about it?"

I got straight to the point. "I didn't wear a condom. Is there any chance you're pregnant?"

She shook her head, looking embarrassed. "When I was young, I had a lot of trouble with, ah, my periods. They put me on birth control pills to regulate them. I still have trouble, so I'm still on them."

"Oh." I sighed in relief.

"Don't worry, Richard." She looked away. "I know how you feel about children."

The sadness in her voice hurt me, and I slipped my hand under her chin, forcing her to look at me.

"You told me once you thought if I loved the mother, I would love the child. I think, perhaps, you were right."

"So you want children?"

I fidgeted on the sofa, unsure how to answer. "This is all very new to me. I never thought I could love anyone. I've barely come to terms with the fact I'm so deeply in love with you, I can't function without you. You knocked down every idea I held as the truth. I need you. I love you." I shook my head with a wry smile. "I suppose it's only natural to assume my thoughts on children could change as well."

"It's something we could talk about—later on?"

"Yes. I would ask for a little time, however. I want to have you to myself for a while. I want to know you—all of you—and you to know me."

"I think that's smart."

"You'll have to help me, sweetheart. I know nothing about kids. Nothing. The thought of screwing one up the way my parents did terrifies the fuck out of me, if I'm being honest."

She tilted her head, studying me. "Richard VanRyan. You surpass every goal you have ever set for yourself. Do you really think I'd let you fail as a father?"

A grin tugged at my lips. "I suppose not, no."

"It won't happen. Knowing you're willing to discuss it is a huge step."

"You're sure you're not pregnant now?"

"Yep. Sure."

"Okay, then. I guess we'll discuss this again—in the future."

She nodded. "The future."

I slipped my hand into my pocket and held up her rings. "In the meantime, I want you to have these back. I want them on your finger." I took her hand. "I know you think they meant nothing, Katy, but they mean everything. They mean you're mine." I indicated her finger. "May I?"

She nodded. I tugged the small diamond band off and transferred it to her right hand, sliding her wedding band and the larger diamond back on her left hand. Bending low, I pressed a kiss to the rings.

"That's where they belong."

"Yes."

I grabbed my coat from the chair and withdrew the folded papers from the inside pocket.

"What are those?"

"Our contract—both our copies."

"Oh."

"It doesn't mean anything anymore, Katy. It hasn't for a long time. It's time to get rid of it."

I held them up, tearing them in half. I carried them to the fireplace and dropped them into the flames. I watched as the edges turned black and curled, the flames licking at the pages until they were nothing but ash. Katy stood beside me, watching in silence.

I wrapped my arm around her waist. "The one document between us now is our marriage license. From today onward, it's what holds us together."

She looked up, a tender expression on her face. "I like that."

"Maybe, once things have settled, you'd marry me again?"

Her eyes glowed. "Really?"

"Yes. Maybe somewhere prettier than city hall. I'd like you to have the wedding you deserve."

"I kind of liked our wedding. I liked dancing with you."

"Yeah?"

She nodded. "You were nice."

"I promise to be far nicer from now on. I want to be the man I should be for you."

"You are."

"Be patient with me, Katy. I'm gonna fuck this up sometimes."

She laughed low, stroking my cheek. "Everyone does. No one is perfect."

"But you'll stick with me?"

"Like glue."

I dropped a kiss to her full mouth. "Then we're good."

I PEERED AROUND her shoulder at the contents of the small refrigerator. The old wire shelves held a small amount of food. Tugging her aside, I picked up the carton of eggs, opening the lid. Only two were missing. The loaf of bread was barely touched, the package of cheese unopened, and the cream was almost full. There were two apples, some unopened yogurt, and on the counter, a few bananas. That was it. My suspicions about her lack of appetite were confirmed.

I shut the door, turning to face her. "This is all the food you have? Have you been eating at all?"

"Not much," she admitted. "I wasn't hungry."

I recalled the small town I drove through on my way to the cottages. There was a little grocery store and I was sure I'd passed a restaurant. "I'll take you into town for supper. You need to eat."

She shook her head. "Nothing is open this time of night, Richard. It's off-season. We'd have to drive farther to get to a bigger town. It's a good hour away."

"That's fine."

"I can make us some scrambled eggs."

I relented easily, not really wanting to go anywhere. "All right. I'll make toast."

"You can make toast?" She gasped, laying her hand on her heart.

I yanked her close, kissing her teasing mouth. "Yes. My wife taught me. She's a smart woman."

Her cheek folded in, and I knew she was chewing on it. I tapped the rounded flesh. "Stop it."

"I like it when you call me your wife," she admitted.

"It's funny how often I found myself thinking of you as such. Never Katharine or Katy, but my wife. I liked the way it sounded, although I never questioned why." I snorted. "Too stupid to realize how I felt about you, even in my own head."

"Or too scared."

The air caught in my throat. As usual, she hit the nail on the head. I had been too scared to admit what I was feeling. To admit an idea I had my entire life was wrong.

"I'm not scared of loving you anymore, Katy. I'm only scared of losing you."

She curled herself into me, resting her head on my shoulder. I cradled her close, stroking through her hair in long passes.

"I'm here," she whispered. "You found me."

"Thank God."

I SET DOWN my plate on the old coffee table, my gaze on Katy. The firelight played over her face, the flames casting a red glow around her head. She pulled her legs to her chest, chin resting on them as she stared into space. She hadn't eaten much, but she did finish the toast. I polished off all the eggs and ate both her apples. We'd replace them, and more, in the morning. For now, though, I needed to find out how she wanted to proceed together on the road ahead of us.

"What would you like to do, Katy?"

She turned her face toward me. "Hmmm?"

I ran my knuckles down her cheek. "Tomorrow. The next day. The one after. Tell me what you're thinking."

"I don't know."

"How long did you want to stay here? Or do you want to go home?" A sudden tightness enveloped my torso, making me breathless. "Are you coming home?"

She slipped her hand into mine, one word easing my worry. "Yes."

"Okay. Good. When?"

"Can we stay here for a few days? Or if you have to get back, I'll follow you then?"

I shook my head. "I'm not leaving here without you. If you want to stay, we can. I'll bring you back in the summer, too."

"The cottages won't be here in the summer."

"Why?"

"Scott passed away last year. His son, Bill, is selling the land. After speaking with him, I gathered whoever buys it will tear down all the cottages and develop something new and modern." She looked around the room, her eyes drinking in memories. "He told me business has been poor, but it's a good time to sell because of the location. The land is worth a lot of money. It's a good opportunity for his family."

"I'm sorry, sweetheart. I know this place is special to you."

She smiled, rubbing her cheek on my hand. "I have my memories. I'm grateful Bill let me come back one last time." She sighed, the sound low and sad. "I have one more good memory to add."

"We can make our own memories, together. New ones."

She nodded.

"Do you want me to buy this place for you?" I searched her eyes. "I can afford it," I added. "If you want me to, I will."

"*No!* No, Richard. You don't have to buy an entire resort for me. What on earth would I do with it?"

"If it made you happy, I would. We'd figure something out. It's probably a good investment. We could rebuild it, including a bright blue cottage with white shutters just for you."

She leaned forward, teary-eyed and kissed the corner of my mouth. "Thank you, my darling, but no. The fact you would offer means more than I can say."

"Okay. If you change your mind, let me know."

"I'll do that."

I reclined back on the sofa, looking around the room, an idea forming in my head. I would have to see if I could arrange it. I tugged on Katy's legs, bringing them onto my lap.

"We're going to have a lot of questions to answer when we get back."

"I know." She drew in a deep breath. "Do you think they'll ever forgive us?"

I was honest. "I don't know."

Graham had been more than fair after our talk. However, I knew it wasn't over. Once I had figured out her whereabouts, I wasted no time throwing a few things into a bag and heading for the car to arrive before dark. I had called him prior to leaving, telling him I knew where Katy was and I was going to find her. He had been encouraging and wished me luck.

"I hope you find your happiness, Richard. Believe you deserve it and hold on to it."

"Thank you."

"Call me when you get back. We'll talk."

"I will. Thank you, Graham."

No other words had been spoken and no reminder of a job waiting. I had no idea what the future held for my career. All I knew right now was that Katy was my future. That was enough.

"I may not have a job, Katy."

"What will you do?"

"We"—I stressed the word—"we may have to move. I can put out feelers in Toronto or Calgary, maybe Vancouver."

She nodded, playing with my fingers. She kept turning my wedding band around, twisting it nervously.

"Will you go with me?"

Her head shot up and she met my gaze. "I'll go anywhere with you, Richard."

"Okay, then. We'll figure it out, together."

"What if we don't have to?"

"I'd be ecstatic. I like working for Graham. I enjoy the positive energy and the teamwork." I barked out a laugh. "I'm even fond of that dynamo they call Jenna."

"I think you're fond of them all."

"I am. It's what I want, and I'm willing to do whatever it takes to earn Graham's trust back. As long as he gives me the chance to do so, we'll stay. If not, we'll have to move on."

"Okay."

"It's as simple as that for you? After everything, you'll pack up and follow me?"

She rested her head on the sofa. "I love you, Richard. If you have to leave, then so do I. The past is just that now—the past. Like the contract you burned, it's gone. I don't want to dwell on it or keep throwing it in your face. That's not how love works. It's not how I work."

In a second, I had yanked her on my lap and was kissing her with all the emotion I felt. Every thought and new sensation went into my kiss. Love, want, desire, relief of having found her—and an emotion I had never known—joy. Joy she was here, joy she returned my love, and joy for the future, because the future contained my Katy.

I tilted her head, needing her closer, wanting more of her in every way. My arms locked around her, molding her softness to my hard body. I slipped my hands up her shirt, pressing against the smooth expanse of her back, groaning with desire.

"Please, baby," I begged, needing more.

"Bed," she whispered against my mouth. "Take me to bed, Richard."

I stood up, holding her. I didn't need to be told twice.

THE BED WAS old and it creaked. The headboard ricocheted off the wall repeatedly as I took her, the sheets bunching around our bodies from our frenzied coupling. None of it mattered.

Before we hit the mattress, I tore off her shirt, yanking her pants away, leaving her bare to my thirsty gaze. I ran my hands over her warm skin, wanting to feel the silkiness under my fingers. She tugged at my sweatshirt, and I fell on top of her, needing her mouth back. She proved adept at using her small feet to push down my sweats so we were skin to skin, my aching cock trapped between us. I memorized her all over again with my hands and mouth. Her rosy nipples begged for my attention, growing to hard peaks under my tongue. The sweet indent of her waist on the right side was ticklish, and I reveled in her giggles as I feathered it with light kisses, and teased her skin. The swell of her hips fit perfectly in my hands as I pressed down gently, opening her up to me. I kissed her belly button, dipping my tongue in to taste the saltiness of her skin. I rained small kisses down to her thighs; her tiny gasps ramping up my desire. Slipping my fingers into her wet heat, I hissed at the sensation. "God, Katy, I want you, baby."

She sat up, wrapping me tight in her arms, drawing me back down. "Take me," she pleaded.

She wound her legs around my hips, urging me to the place where I was desperate to be buried. I stilled as I slid inside, inch-by-inch, until our bodies were flush. Our eyes locked, and I lowered my mouth to hers as I began to move. Slow, even thrusts that built until we were both lost in the heat of us. She clung to me, fingers digging into my back, grabbing my ass, yanking on my hair, as she keened and whimpered my name. I clutched her tight, taking her now with powerful thrusts, our sweat-soaked skin sliding together, our bodies moving as one. With a guttural cry, I buried my face into her neck as she stiffened, her body tightening around me. My orgasm washed over me, cresting hard, every nerve on fire as I released deep inside her, groaning out her name.

"Katy! My Katy."

Sliding my arms around her back, I rolled to the side, holding her close, pressing kisses to her face, hair, and neck. She hummed, contented and warm, into my chest.

"Love you," she whispered.

"I love you," I breathed into her skin. I felt around on the floor, finding a blanket, which I drew up over her bare skin, tucking it around her neck. She curled into my side, fingers tracing a slow pattern over my heart.

"Tomorrow," I vowed. "Tomorrow we start fresh. Real. Us."

"Us," she repeated. "Yes."

I waited until she fell asleep before I allowed myself to drift off. I shut my eyes, knowing when I awoke she would be beside me.

Secure in that knowledge, I slept.

Thirty-One

RICHARD

I SHOOK BILL'S hand and walked across the beach. Katy was sitting on the sand, a sketchbook on her knees, pencil in hand, but she was motionless. The breeze picked up the strands of her hair, blowing them back like ribbons of dark silk. I sank down behind her, pulling her back into my embrace.

"Hey."

She tilted her head back, observing me upside down. "Hi. What were you talking to Bill about for so long?" A frown crossed her face. "Please tell me you didn't ask about buying the resort."

I snickered at the expression on her face and dropped a kiss on her forehead. "No. I think he has a buyer. I was thanking him for letting you come back, and we were talking about other things. Where he is moving to, stuff like that."

She pursed her lips and shrugged, turning back to face the water.

"What are you sketching?"

She held up the book. "Nothing. I'm enjoying the view."

I wrapped my arms around her waist, holding her tight. "It's a great view."

"Penny and I used to build bonfires, cook our supper over them, and watch the sunset."

"We can do that."

"You'd eat a hotdog skewered on a stick?"

"Only if there's mustard. And marshmallows after."

"Huh."

Leaning down, I nipped the skin at the juncture of her neck. "You don't think I've ever done any outdoor activities, Katy? I built the fire last night."

"I wondered where you'd learned to build a fire," she admitted.

"It's a man thing. It's in our genes."

Twisting around, she rolled her eyes. "Uh-huh."

Laughing, I pushed the hair from her face. "We did camping trips at school. They taught us how to build a fire, pitch a tent, that sort of thing."

"You did that at school?"

I rested my chin on her shoulder. "When I was a teenager and stayed at school over spring break, they offered different activities. Camping was one of them. I liked it. And yes, I even liked the hotdogs. I'm not a total snob."

I expected one of her quick comebacks; instead, she pivoted, reached up, and cupped my cheek. "You stayed at school rather than go to your parents'?"

"If given the choice, yes. They could get away with me not coming home if they told people I was on a school trip or something. I avoided an entire summer when I was fourteen. I did go on a school trip, then I went to camp for a month. It was the best summer of my life."

"I'm sorry, my darling."

"Don't feel sorry for me," I snapped.

"We had this discussion already. I do feel bad for the child who was abandoned." She pushed up to her feet. "And, you, Mr. VanRyan, are being rude again."

She stomped away, her sketchbook under her arm. I scrambled to my feet, catching up to her in a few strides. Those short legs of hers couldn't cover the ground the way mine could, thank goodness. I grabbed her around the waist, spinning her, and holding her to me.

"I'm being a dick again. Let me apologize."

She stared at my chest.

"Katy."

She looked up, meeting my gaze.

"I'm sorry. I strike out without thinking. I'm not used to talking about my past or having someone care about how I felt then, or now."

"I do care."

I lifted her up, bringing her face level with mine. "I know. I'm trying to get used to it, okay? Cut me a little slack." I kissed the corner of her mouth. "I'm new at this trying to be a good guy thing."

Her eyes softened, and I kissed her again.

"Was that our first fight?"

"Not sure I'd call it a first or a fight." She smirked.

"Still, I think make-up sex is needed, yeah?"

She tried to look stern, but an impish grin broke out on her face.

I swung her up into my arms, bridal style, striding toward the cottage. "Come on, Mrs. VanRyan. Let me make it up to you. After, we'll go back into town for hotdogs and marshmallows."

"And mustard."

I tossed her on the bed, yanking my shirt over my head. "And mustard."

I THREW ANOTHER piece of wood on the bonfire and crossed my legs. Katy curled up beside me, her head on my shoulder. I patted her knee. "Warm enough?"

She nodded, bringing the blanket tighter around her shoulders. "It gets cold when it's dark now."

"It is fall."

"I know."

"How much longer do you want to stay?"

She sighed, her fingers fiddling with the blanket. "I suppose we should get back."

It had been three days since I arrived. It was the first time in my adult life I had no place to be—no office to head to, no meetings planned, no agenda. The one thing I had to concentrate on was Katy. Aside from the couple trips into town for supplies, we hadn't left the resort. We walked the beach, made use of the small game room where I tried to teach her the game of checkers and failed miserably, and used the time to know each other better. We talked, often for hours at a time. She knew more about me than anyone in my life. She had a way of asking questions that made me want to tell her things I'd never shared with another person. She shared more stories of her life prior to and after she met Penny. Some of the stories she told, about the time she was alone and on the streets, made me hold her tight and thank whatever deity was listening for keeping her safe.

We made love, often. I couldn't get enough of her. The body I once found unappealing was now my version of perfection. She fit me so well, and the passion I felt for her was paramount. Her lack of experience made her response to me even more erotic. I loved watching her discover the passionate side of her nature.

She was right, however. We did have to go back to our life, or what was left of it, and figure out what our future held.

"Why don't we stay another couple days, then we'll head back? I heard on the radio the weather is changing, so we'd be stuck in the cottage anyway. Not"—I grinned, leaning forward and kissing her— "that I'd object being stuck inside with nothing to do except stay in bed with you."

"All right," she agreed with a soft laugh, then turned serious. "I still have to scatter Penny's ashes."

"Are you ready to do that, sweetheart?"

Her eyes had a far-away look in them when she spoke. "The fall was her favorite time of year. She didn't like the heat of the summer. She looked forward to coming here as much as I did. I think she'd like to stay here."

"As long as you're sure."

"Tomorrow," she whispered.

I lifted her over to my lap, pressing a kiss to her head. "Tomorrow."

I WOKE UP, the fluttering of panic fast in my chest when the spot beside me was empty. I sat up, throwing the blanket back and striding out of the bedroom. I relaxed when I spotted Katy on the beach. She stood, facing the water, holding something to her chest. I glanced over, confirming the fact Penny's urn was gone from the mantle.

My wife was saying goodbye.

Returning to the bedroom, I grabbed my pants, tugging them on. I picked up my T-shirt and yanked it over my head as I hurried outside, crossing the beach. The weather system they had predicted was already making its presence known. The waves were higher, hitting the sand with loud slaps. The wind was picking up, and I knew, soon, the rain would follow, and the storm would make my wife nervous.

I reached her side, enveloping her in my arms.

"I was waiting for you."

"You should have woken me up."

"I wanted a little time. I knew you wouldn't be far behind me."

"Are you sure?"

She smiled up at me, the glimmer of tears in her eyes telling me the whole story. "Yes."

"Okay, sweetheart." I reached for the urn. "Do you want me to open it?"

"Please."

I held the simple green container in my hand, running my fingers over the wildflowers that decorated its smooth surface.

"Thank you." I murmured to Penny. "You won't regret trusting me."

Carefully, I opened the urn and handed Katy the small bag. She walked away from me toward the edge of the water. I let her go alone, knowing what a personal, emotional moment this was for her.

She was motionless. I could see her lips moving, and I knew she was saying her final farewell. She crouched down, opening the bag and letting the contents drain to the sand at her feet. She stood up, shaking the bag, the final remains caught and taken by the wind. Her head bowed, and she wrapped her arms around her waist, a solitary figure against the backdrop of the heavy skies.

I wanted to go to her, comfort her, but I was still unsure how to handle all the emotions I had when dealing with Katy. Should I leave her alone? Wrap her in my arms?

She solved my dilemma, turning and holding out her hand wordlessly. I grasped it and brought her close.

"Are you all right?"

She looked up, her eyes damp. "I will be."

"Can I do something?"

"You already are."

"I want to do more."

"Take me home, Richard. I'm ready."

"Okay, sweetheart."

AFTER WE LEFT the beach, it hadn't taken us long to gather the few things she had brought to the cottage. I packed up the remaining food and threw it all in the trunk. I waited, giving her some privacy in the cottage for yet another goodbye.

The drive home was in direct contrast to the frantic pace I had set getting to the resort. Katy was beside me, her hand clasped in mine as we made our way back to the city. I drove leisurely, giving her a chance to relax. I stole glances at her frequently.

"I know you're looking at me."

"I like looking at you."

"I'm fine, Richard. Really, I am."

"Are you nervous about coming back with me? The difference in our relationship?"

She leaned her head back, looking at me. "Nervous?"

"It's all changed now, Katy. We're going home as a real married couple. For starters, as soon as we get home, your things are coming to my room. *Our room.* For good."

"I know. You get to snuggle me every night."

"And you get to listen to me snore." Then I became serious. "We have a lot to face together."

"And we'll do it." She hesitated. "Are *you* nervous?"

"In some ways, yes."

"Why?"

I pulled over to the side of the road, draping my arm over the back of her seat. "I'm still me, Katy. Deep inside I'm still the same asshole. I have a temper. I'm not perfect—not by a long shot."

"I don't expect you to be perfect, Richard. But I don't think the asshole inside is the same as the one you used to be."

"You have a great deal of faith in me."

"I've seen the change in you." She smiled. "Plus the fact, I love you."

"I'm worried I'll let you down."

"What about when I get mad at you and I act like an asshole?"

That made me chuckle. "Since I'm sure it will be justified, when it happens, we'll deal with it."

"We'll deal with it all together, Richard. Asshole behavior included."

"I swear I'll try to be better."

"I know you'll try, and even more, I know you'll succeed."

"Why are you so sure?"

"Because you love me."

Running my knuckles down her cheek, I nodded. "I do, sweetheart. Very much."

She covered my hand and kissed the palm. "We all have our moments, you know. Even me."

"Is that right?"

"I used to get angry at the way you'd talk to me when you were being more . . . *dickish* than usual."

"You hid it well."

"I got even, in my own way."

"Now you've piqued my curiosity. Do tell me, how did you get even with me?"

The ghost of a smile played her lips.

"Katy?"

"On the days you were extra pissy, I would swap out your low-fat cheese and mayo for the full-fat version on your sandwiches. I never cut the fat out of your foam in your lattes—ever actually. I just let you think I did."

"What?"

"I forgot to ask one day when I was getting your sandwich and you never noticed. It was my own silent revenge."

"*That* was your way of getting even?"

"I figured if your pants got tighter, you might have to work out a little harder. Maybe sweat the asshole out of you."

I started to chuckle. That turned into laughter. Deep, belly laughs that made my eyes water.

"Such a vindictive bitch you are, sweetheart. I'm glad you're on my side now. My treadmill trembles over your immense wrath."

"Go fuck yourself, VanRyan."

Leaning over the console, I kissed her. She had no idea how incredibly endearing she was in this moment, or how much my love for her increased every time she uttered those words. Once spoken in anger, and now in jest, they were a reminder of how far we had come together.

"Take me home, Richard."

"Okay, sweetheart."

I pulled back onto the road, my nerves gone and a smile on my face.

Thirty-Two

RICHARD

THE CONDO WAS silent when we arrived. I set down our bags and looked at the mess I had left behind.

"I should have cleaned up. I was anxious to get to you."

She walked around, picking up a couple bottles. "You need to stop drinking so much scotch."

The words were out before I could stop them. "You need to stop leaving me."

Her eyes widened.

I tugged on my cowlick. "*Shit*. Home five minutes and the asshole comes out."

"I'm going to give you that one. I shouldn't have run. I should have stayed and talked it out with you."

Reaching out, I brought her into my arms. "You had no reason to trust me, then. I'll make sure you won't have that excuse next time. Not," I added, "that there is going to be a next time."

She nuzzled close. "No."

"Then we're good?"

"Yep."

Glass crunched under my feet when I moved, and I looked down with a grimace. "Careful."

"Another asshole moment?"

"A big one," I acknowledged. "I was angry at you—but it passed quickly."

"I think you were allowed."

"I'll get someone in to clean up."

She shook her head with a grin. "It's not bad. We can get it done fast." Bending, she picked up her bag. "But you're ordering dinner and doing the dishes."

I grabbed my bag, following her through the condo. "There you go—issuing orders."

"Get used to it." She turned her head and winked.

I swatted her ass, causing her to yelp and try to hurry ahead of me. She tripped, almost falling on the steps, except I lunged, catching her around the waist. "Sorry, sweetheart. I forgot about your leg. Are you okay?"

She wrapped her arms around my neck. "I'm fine. You can carry me the rest of the way, though."

Lifting her, I captured her mouth with mine and kept it there all the way to our room. Inside the doorway, I set her on her feet, releasing her lips. "Welcome home, Mrs. VanRyan."

She smiled up at me, running her fingers along my jaw. "You're scruffier than normal."

"I'll shave later."

"I kinda like it."

"Then I'll leave it."

Rising on the balls of her feet, she pressed a kiss to my cheek. "Okay." She glanced around. "Where do you want to start?"

I sat down on the mattress, pulling her beside me. "I didn't change the sheets. They smelled like you—like *us*, and I couldn't . . ." My voice trailed off. "I couldn't."

"I'm here now."

"I know." I stood up. "I'll get your things. I want them back in here. They never should have left."

"We weren't ready. We are now."

"Yep."

"All right, then. Let's get started."

I STEPPED OUT of the shower, toweling my hair. Entering the bedroom, I looked around with a low sigh. Katy had moved in. Her clothes were in the closet and dresser, her lotions and girly things in the bathroom. Her bedside table held her books, and her scent was already in the air. She'd been a little shocked when she saw the mess I had made in her room, but she had it straightened while I carried things back and forth.

I dragged on some sweats and a T-shirt and jogged downstairs. The bottles, papers, and broken glass were cleared away, the kitchen already back in order. She sat at the counter, a bottle of wine open, and a glass waiting for me. I took a sip, appreciating the bold flavor of the red wine.

"Dinner?"

She looked up from her book. "Pizza is in the oven, waiting."

I grabbed some plates and set down the box between us. We ate in silence, and although it wasn't an uncomfortable one, I wanted to know what she was thinking. She seemed contemplative.

I covered her hand with mine. "Where did you go, Katy? What are you thinking about over there?"

She smiled, flipping her hand so our palms pressed together. "I was remembering my first dinner with you. We had pizza and wine that night, too."

"We did."

"I was incredibly nervous. I didn't know what you wanted to discuss with me. You never spoke to me in the office unless it was to bark out an order or tell me what I was doing wrong. Sitting beside you, I had no idea what to expect. I couldn't believe what you had to say."

I smirked. "I couldn't believe I was asking you—Miss Elliott—the bane of my existence, to live with me and pretend to be my fiancée." I shook my head. "I was a rat bastard to you, wasn't I?"

"Yes, you were."

"I'm not sure I can ever apologize enough."

"Stop trying. That was then, this is now." She laced our fingers together and squeezed. "I like now."

I lifted our joined hands, kissing her knuckles. "So do I."

"We still have to face the Gavin family."

Releasing her hand, I reached for my wine. "I know. I'll call Graham in the morning. I'm sure we'll be summoned to their house in due course."

"What do you think will happen?"

"I don't know. I expected him to fire me on the spot. When he told me he already suspected I was lying, I was certain of it." I huffed out a laugh. "Of course, nothing is what I expect anymore, so I'm not the best judge of the situation."

"Are you prepared for him to fire you?"

"I dread it, to be honest, but if it happens, then we move and start again. I certainly won't get a reference from him or David. I can only hope my work speaks for itself. Brian can help me with his contacts and I have some of my own. Clients I've worked with in the past and such."

"And if he doesn't?"

"Then we stay. I want to stay. I want to work for Graham. It'll take some time, but I'll show him he can trust me. I'll work my ass off for him and his company."

"I know you will." She met my eyes, smiling sadly. "I hope Laura and Jenna can forgive me."

"Out of all of this, I regret that the most," I admitted. "You already lost Penny, and I know how fond you are of both of them. I don't want you to lose that as well."

"I guess we'll know soon enough."

I nodded. "We will."

RUNNING A WEARY hand over my face, I flipped through the documents I had printed from Brian.

The day after we came home, I texted Graham to let him know I was back and Katy was with me. I didn't receive a response. Katy also texted Jenna and asked if they could meet for coffee, but she was only met with silence. I knew she was upset, though neither of us was surprised.

By the end of the second day, I contacted Brian for some leads in other cities. He seemed surprised by my request but sent along a few for me to look over. Two were in Toronto, one was in the States, and the last one in Calgary. It was by far the most tempting, even if it was the least dynamic of all the companies. At least we'd be surrounded by mountains and close to lakes and amazing scenery.

Although I didn't want any of them, I was sure the writing was on the wall, in regards to my place at The Gavin Group. It was time to look at my, *our*, options. I wanted Katy to be happy, and I knew she wouldn't be in a large, crowded city like Toronto. Also, I had no desire to start commuting hours to get into the office. I had to put away my pride and choose what would be best for us.

I stood up, heading to the kitchen. I needed coffee and to show Katy what Brian had sent over. She looked up from the huge cookbook she was studying and smiled at me.

"What are those?"

I tossed the pile of sheets on the counter and reached for the coffee pot. "Job leads."

"Oh." She tugged the papers closer. "Okay. Anything good?"

I tapped the top page. "This is interesting."

She looked it over, frowning. "It's pretty small compared to what you're used to."

I sat down, sipping my coffee. "I'm going to have to make some concessions."

"Do you have to jump right away?"

"No," I acknowledged. "I don't want to be out too long, though. Financially, we're fine; it's more the staying on top of my game."

"Well, in case," she drawled, "I have some money I can loan you, if you need it."

I quirked my lips. "Is that so?"

"Uh-huh. I did a job for this asshole who paid me well. It's just kicking around if you need it."

I wound my arm around her waist, tucking her close. "Are you still working for this asshole?"

"No. The asshole disappeared."

"Is that right? Did a prince on a white steed replace him?"

"No, a complex, demanding, but very sexy and sweet real man did."

"Sweet?" I snickered. That was a new one for me.

She nodded. "You are, at times, very sweet."

"Maybe with you. I don't think anyone else would ever call me sweet."

"I'm okay with that."

I rubbed my nose to hers affectionately. "Good."

Our eyes met, the warmth of her gaze distracting me. Heat bubbled around us, the way it did every time I was close to her now. Lowering my head, I brushed my lips over hers.

"Now, about that sexy part . . ."

The intercom buzzing startled us both.

"Damn it." I growled.

"Rain check," she whispered against my lips.

I wrapped my hand around her neck, holding her close, kissing her hard. "Not a long one. I'll deal with whatever they want, and then you're mine."

I hit the speaker button. "VanRyan."

"You have visitors, Mr. VanRyan. Mr. and Mrs. Gavin are here to see you."

I met Katy's shocked gaze, reaching for her hand.

"Send them up."

I PAUSED PRIOR to opening the door, still holding tight to Katy's hand. "No matter what, we're okay, all right?" I said quietly.

"Yes."

Steeling myself, I swung open the door and was met with Graham's serious countenance. Laura was beside him, her expression somber, as well. The real kicker was the box Graham held. The last time I'd seen it, I had been packing up my desk.

Even though I wasn't shocked, and I had suspected this would happen, the rush of disappointment in my chest was crushing. I inhaled sharply, tightening my grip on Katy's hand. Beside me, she uttered a muffled gasp, her eyes on the box Graham held. I leaned down, pressing a kiss to her head.

"We're okay," I reassured her. "Remember?"

"Okay," she repeated.

I stepped back, not wanting this to happen in the hallway outside our home. "Come in," I managed.

Graham set down the box on the floor beside the sofa. I was grateful when Katy spoke up, giving me a few extra seconds to gather myself.

"Can I get you coffee?"

Laura smiled and sat down. "I would appreciate a cup."

Graham nodded. "As would I."

I followed her to the kitchen and watched numbly as she set out cups and napkins on a tray, pouring the coffee. "Should I add cookies?" she whispered.

I shrugged. "I, uh, have no idea what the protocol is when your boss comes to fire you, Katy. Cookies seem too nice for the occasion, though."

She worried at her cheek, and I tapped the side of her face.

"Joke. That was a joke, albeit a bad one. Put out some cookies, sweetheart. We might as well be civilized about this. It's not as though we weren't expecting it."

"Are you going to yell?"

I shook my head. "No. To be honest, I'm too sad to yell."

She flung her arms around my neck, tugging my head down to her shoulder. "Thank you for telling me. I love you."

I lifted her, the warmth of her body needed to calm my racing heart. Her feet dangled high above the floor, and I held her close. "That makes this all bearable." Setting her down on her feet, I picked up the tray. "Let's go get fired."

I PASSED OUT the mugs of coffee with hands that were not as steady as usual. Laura directed a few comments to Katy, inquiring how she was coping in regards to losing Penny. I wrapped my arm around her shoulder when Katy's voice quivered talking about scattering Penny's ashes.

Graham watched us closely, setting down his mug.

"I assume the two of you have reached an understanding?"

"There is no understanding, Graham. I'm in love with Katy, and thankfully, she feels the same about me. We're going forward on equal ground."

"So this is no longer a marriage-for-show?"

I resisted the urge to tug on the back of my neck. "It ceased being that a long time ago. I was just too obstinate to see or admit it."

He turned his gaze to Katy. "And you?"

She lifted her chin, the stubborn cleft prominent. "I love him. I have for a while. I was too afraid to tell him, in case he didn't return my feelings." She threaded her fingers through mine. "But he does, and we're ready to face the future together."

"Good." Graham bent down and picked up the box, setting it on the coffee table. From his pocket, he withdrew my contract, tearing it in half, and placing it on top of the box.

"Well, then," I muttered. "That hurt more than I thought it would." I held up my hand as Graham started to speak. "Let me finish. It hurts, but I understand. I came into your business on false pretenses, so I recognize you have to let me go. I want you to know how much I enjoyed working for you. With you. You showed me how a person *should* run their company." I swallowed the thickness in my throat. "You and your family came to mean a great deal to both of us. I hope one day you can forgive us."

"Why did you want to work for me?"

I decided to be honest. "At first it was revenge—to get back at David. He disliked you so much, I knew that if I had the chance to work for you, he might very well offer me a partnership to stay. All I wanted was the offer. Then . . ."

"Then?" Graham prompted.

"Then I met you, spoke with you, and it changed. You listened to me, encouraged my ideas. I hadn't felt that level of excitement or positive reinforcement in years. The revenge became a back seat to wanting to be part of the whole atmosphere you had in the office. I wanted the chance to work with you." I paused in embarrassment, lowering my voice. "I wanted to make you proud."

For a moment, the room was silent. Graham spoke up. "I see."

I cleared my throat. "Again, I apologize. Katy and I wish you well, both personally and professionally."

Graham's fingers tapped out an irregular beat on the top of the box. "David hates me because of the way I chose to live my life. We went to school together, did you know that?"

I shook my head.

"We were friends, once. We even discussed going into business together. As usual with David, it was all or nothing. He expected dedication to the point that you couldn't possibly maintain a life both inside and outside a business. I met Laura, and I knew I wanted more than just work. When I told him I wasn't interested, well, we exchanged some heated words. We parted ways; he opened his business and I opened mine. We're both successful, except his was achieved in an entirely different manner. It's all tied up in money and business. I've lost count of the number of staff he has had through the years. The questionable campaigns associated with his company. The number of women connected to his name. I think he's been married and divorced four times."

"Five," I corrected.

He grinned a little, the corners of his eyes crinkling. "I guess I missed one along the way. The point is, to him nothing is more important than money. He hates me because I chose to have a life outside of work, and I still became a success. He knows, as well as anyone who knows me does, to me the most successful thing I have, the thing I hold the dearest, is my family. I would give it all up as long as I had them—without even blinking an eye."

Graham met my gaze steadily. "He has no solid reason in his life to give it up for. That's why he hates me."

"I was fast becoming like him until Katy entered my life."

He nodded. "I'm glad it changed." He rapped the top of the box with his knuckles. "Which is why I had to end your contract, Richard. It was signed under false pretenses."

"I appreciate your honesty and bringing my things, Graham."

"I'm not done yet."

"Oh?" I asked, confused.

He sat back, an almost amused expression crossing his face. "I find myself down a very talented staff member. I've seen your work, Mr. VanRyan, and thought, perhaps, you may fit in with my company."

I frowned, certain I had heard him incorrectly.

"I'm sorry?"

"I think you are, *now*, exactly the sort of person I would like on my team."

"I don't . . . I don't understand."

"I am offering you a job, Richard. With a clean slate." He reached in his pocket, bringing out a new contract. "We'll start fresh."

I swallowed, hardly believing this was happening.

"Why?" I managed through tight lips.

"Because, like Katy, I believe in second chances." He took Laura's hand. "We both do."

Laura nodded at me, tears in her eyes. "You could have kept silent about your relationship with Katy, Richard. You could have continued to deceive us. We may have suspected, but we would never have known if you hadn't been honest. We both saw how deeply you cared for Penny. We know how kind you were to Jenna. *That* is the Richard we want in our company. The one who wants to grow with it—be part of it." She smiled. "Be part of our family. Because that is the way we think of the two of you."

Katy made an odd noise in the back of her throat. Angling, I saw the tears sliding down her face and the way her body shook, trying to keep her reaction in check. I slid closer, drawing her head to my shoulder. "Shh, sweetheart, it's okay."

I turned back to Graham. "You believe me? After everything, all the lies, you believe me?" I asked, dumbfounded.

"We do, because of *that*." Graham indicated the way I was holding Katy. "You can't fake that, Richard. We can feel the love you have for your wife."

"Give him a pen!" Katy burst out. "He'll sign! We want to stay—we both want to stay!"

Graham and Laura both grinned at her words and I had to bite my lip to stop my laughter. She would make a lousy poker player, but she was right. We did want to stay.

Keeping my arm around her, I extended my hand. "I would be honored to work for you, Graham. I won't let you down again. I promise, I will make you proud."

He took my hand, shaking it firmly. "You already have."

I had to look away to make sure Katy was okay. It had nothing to do with the way my vision blurred or the sting of tears behind my eyes.

Nothing at all.

Thirty-Three

RICHARD

I CARRIED THE tray to the kitchen, leaving Laura and Katy talking. Graham followed me, carrying the box and waited so we could go into the den and talk more. He glanced at the papers on the counter, picking up the job listing for Calgary.

"Really, Richard?" He smirked. "You would have died of boredom there."

"I couldn't take Katy to Toronto. She'd be miserable."

He studied me for a moment, a smile crossing his face. "How you've changed."

"Grown up, you mean."

He nodded, clapping me on the shoulder. "It's good to see."

I glanced over his shoulder to where Katy was standing, hugging Laura. "It feels good," I admitted. "I never thought it was something I would experience."

"The right person can open our eyes to many things, Richard."

He was right.

He held out my new contract. "Let's go sign some papers."

"Why did you bring my things if you planned on rehiring me?"

A strange look crossed his face, and he flipped open the lid. "The box is empty, Richard."

I gaped at him. "What? Why then?"

"The same reason we showed up unannounced. I wanted to see how you would act if you thought it was over. I wanted to see your real, gut reaction. Not one you had planned in advance."

"And?"

"You looked shattered."

"I was. I wanted to keep working for you. When I saw the box, I knew I'd fucked it beyond repair. I wasn't surprised, but it hit me right then, *how much* I wanted it. I knew there was nothing I could do to fix it. I had done it to myself after all."

"Your reaction told me everything I needed to know. You were upset, yet you immediately reached out to comfort Katy. I knew you *had* really changed." He grinned. "Sorry for the subterfuge."

I stuck out my hand, which he took, shaking it hard. "I understand."

He flipped the lid shut. "Use it and bring a few more things into the office. Make it yours, Richard."

"Does anyone know?"

"Outside the family, no. The staff thinks you've been off with Katy. You come in on Monday and start again. No one else is the wiser."

"Thank you. I won't let you down this time."

"I know," he said and nodded emphatically. *"I know."*

A SHORT WHILE later, Graham shook my hand goodbye. "I'll see you Monday."

Laura gave Katy one last hug, then turned to me. "We expect great things of you, Richard."

"I'll deliver."

She patted my cheek. "I know you will."

"I have a lot to make up for, and I'll do my best."

"We're starting fresh. You come in on Monday with a clean slate with Graham and me." She smiled ruefully. "You can work through your relationships with Adam, Jenna, and Adrian on your own. They had equal say in keeping you on, and they all were for it." She arched an eyebrow at me knowingly. "Although, I think one of my children may have more to say on the subject than the other."

I snickered. "Of that I have no doubt, and I'll take whatever anger

Jenna wants to direct my way. I'll make sure to talk to all of them in private next week."

"Welcome back on board, Richard."

"Thank you."

I walked them to the elevator, returning a few moments later. Katy wasn't inside the door, or in the living room. I hurried up the stairs, surprised when I found her sitting on the chaise in her old room.

"Sweetheart?"

She looked up, a somber look on her face.

"What is it? Why are you in here?"

She shrugged. "I was thinking."

I sat down in front of her, cupping her face. "About?"

"How nervous and scared I was the first night I spent here."

"About being here—with me?"

"That and the future. In one move, you had changed my entire life. I wasn't in that horrid little apartment, I was leaving my job, and I had no idea how we were going to pull off such an elaborate charade. All I could think was how bad it was going to fail, and I didn't know how I was going to pick up the pieces when it did." She paused, her finger tracing the pattern on the cushion. "My thoughts were chaotic and I was so uncertain."

"I wasn't any help either, was I?"

She tilted her head, studying me. "No, actually, your calmness, the way you took control of everything was a help. You were so certain, so intent on your goal; I had only to follow your lead."

"Would it help to know I was in awe of you even then, Katy? You showed me so much bravery." I smirked as I remembered our earlier conversations. "The first time you told me to go fuck myself—I saw a spark you kept hidden. You stopped being the doormat I mistakenly thought you were and became a force." I pushed her hair away from her shoulder, caressing the silky strands. "You became my force. My light."

"You became my everything," she whispered.

I bent low, brushing my mouth over hers. "How far we've come."

"Today was a good day."

"It was. I've signed a new contract; I get to go back to work on

Monday to a place where I really want to be. We can stay in Victoria, and the best part of all, is that I have you. We can make a life together."

"I think I want to go back to work."

I was somewhat surprised. "Why? You don't have to."

"I know, but what am I going to do all day, Richard? Wander around an empty condo? Paint and repaint rooms? I want to be useful." She sighed. "I don't have Penny to fill my days anymore."

The sadness of her words made my heart tighten.

"What about some volunteer work besides the shelter? You know so many of the residents at Golden Oaks—maybe you could spend some time there. I'm sure they'd appreciate the help."

"I thought of that."

I shifted forward, pulling her close. "Katy, I want you to do whatever you want to do. Volunteer, work, whatever makes you happy. But, listen to me, sweetheart. The past few months have been one thing after another for you. Everything you said earlier about how I changed your life is true." I stroked the softness of her cheek with my knuckles. "And although it's turned out well, I know how stressful it all was on you. Everything changed in your life, and you lost Penny. I know, at times, it must overwhelm you, so I'm going to ask you to think about it. Don't rush into anything. Please."

Her eyes were fathomless as our gazes locked. I didn't know how to express how important this was to me.

"I want . . ." I swallowed and breathed deep. "For the first time in my life, I *want* to take care of someone. Let me do that. I'll support you in whatever you decide, but let me look after you for a little while. I need to make sure you're okay."

"I'm fine," she insisted.

"Please," I repeated. "Just a little time. I want you to relax. Decorate our room. Read. Sleep. Make me some of your incredible dinners. Bake me cookies." I pressed her hand to my chest. "Look after me. I need you, sweetheart. I need to know you need me, too."

She cupped my face, her thumbs rubbing small circles on my cheeks. "I do need you, Richard."

"For me," I pleaded, leaning my forehead to hers. "All I'm asking for is a little time."

"All right."

"Thank you."

She met my lips with hers, and I captured them hard. I slid my arm under her legs and lifted us from the chaise. Striding from the room, I carried her to our bed. I laid her on the mattress, smiling down at her stretched out for me.

"I think we were interrupted earlier, and someone promised me a rain check. I'm collecting now."

She tugged me back to her mouth. "Good."

I brushed her lips with mine, already filled with desire. It was a mystery to me how I had denied my attraction to her for so long. All I needed from her was a shy glance or one of her teasing smiles, and I wanted her. Everything about her was alluring and beautiful. The way she supported—loved me—was the strongest aphrodisiac I had ever known.

My eyes fluttered open, meeting her vivid, blue gaze. In an instant, the rampant desire dimmed into a simmering pool of emotion. Everything that occurred today—every good thing in my life—was because of her.

My Katy.

The love and ache I would only ever have for *her,* consumed my body. Hovering over her, I dropped my mouth back to hers, my kiss tender and filled with the depth of my affection. She wrapped her arms around my neck, her fingers sliding up my head in a caress so light, I shivered. Her touch conveyed so much tenderness. Her love saturated into my skin every time we were together, grounding me, bringing me focus when I needed it the most. I soaked up her essence, her soul becoming one with mine.

I pulled off our clothes with gentle hands, my mouth rarely leaving her body. I stroked her warm skin, adoring every curve and imperfection with my touch. I smiled as she became impatient, pulling me down with arms that clutched me tight, her voice pleading for more. Sliding into her welcoming body, I stilled, reveling at the utter perfection of being joined with her in the most intimate of ways.

I had planned to fuck her—hard. Tease her until she begged for release, but it all changed in one second. All I wanted now was to make love to her, claim her, leave her sated, content and secure in the knowledge she was mine.

And equally secure in the fact I belonged to her completely.

I began to move—long, slow strokes. I worshipped her with my hands and mouth, leaving no inch untouched, praising her the whole time. "Your skin, baby, I love how it tastes."

She wound her fingers in my hair, tugging at the short strands, moaning my name.

I thrust faster, needing more. "My cock feels so good buried inside you."

She wrapped her legs tighter, holding me close, as she clutched my shoulders, her blunt nails burrowing into my skin.

My movements became frantic as my orgasm began to gather strength, overtaking my being. "Mine, Katy. *You're mine.*"

She shattered, her muscles clenched, crying out in her release. Burying my face into the fragrant skin of her neck, I let the waves of pleasure roll over me, intense and deep, my mind blank as I drifted, my body humming in contentment.

Lifting my head, I met Katy's tender, sleepy gaze. I captured her lips, nuzzling the softness.

"Love you," I breathed out.

Her smile was sweet. "I know."

MONDAY, I WAS nervous when I walked through the door of The Gavin Group. I wasn't surprised to find Graham waiting for me. He shook my hand, inviting me to sit down with him in his office, and he went over everything that had occurred while I was gone. He piqued my interest with a new campaign and we were deep in conversation about it when Adam, Jenna, and Adrian walked in. I stood up, extending my hand. Both Adam and Adrian shook it, however, Jenna stood back, gazing at me coolly. Understanding her anger, I nodded and sat back down. She was slow to join in the discussion, but soon was arguing with me as she always did over concepts and ideas. I was grateful for the normalcy of the moment, knowing we'd be having a far more personal discussion later.

I was right.

I was in my office, going through messages, catching up on emails and the files Amy had left for me, when Jenna walked in, shutting the door.

She stood in front of my desk hand on her hip, glaring at me.

"Just say it," I encouraged her, even though I knew she wanted to scowl at me a while longer.

"You lied to me, you bastard. To all of us."

"Yes, I did."

"Katy lied to me."

I was out of my chair instantly, rounding my desk. "She didn't want to, Jenna. She hated lying to you—to all of you. This was all me. My fault."

"I trusted her. I thought she was my friend."

"She is—at least she wants to be. She misses talking to you."

Her eyes misted over. "I miss her."

I leaned back against my desk. "I did this for selfish reasons. *She* did this to ensure Penny was safe and looked after. If you want to be mad, be mad at me. Forgive *her*, though." I grasped the back of my neck. "She's lost enough already. Don't take away your friendship."

She bit her lip, tilting her head, studying me. "That was spoken like a man who is in love with his wife."

"I do love her. I don't deserve her, but I love her." Dropping my arms to my side, I drummed my fingers on the hard wooden surface. "I'm not a man prone to gestures or romance, but I'm trying. For her. I want to be the husband she deserves—the man she's placed her trust in."

She kept staring at me.

"Listen, Jenna. I know you want to yell and berate me. That's fine. I'll take it. I deserve it. I know I need to earn your trust, and I will. Somehow, I will. Just don't"—I waved my hand, not sure how to ask—"just don't punish Katy."

She tapped her foot. "I like the idea about the cruise ship you had earlier."

I blinked in confusion over the fast change of subject.

"Ah, good."

"Maybe we can discuss it more this afternoon."

"Sure."

She turned on her heel, pausing at the door. "When I'm ready to talk about the rest, I'll let you know."

"All right."

"Until then, I'm glad you're back." She pursed her lips, her hand back on her hip. "I've missed your surly ass around here."

I couldn't help my laughter. "Thanks. I've missed our chats." I winked since usually she was the one chatting and I was the one listening.

"Don't let it go to your head." She huffed. "We aren't friends again."

"Of course."

"Not yet, anyway," she added and left.

I sat back down at my desk.

It was a start. At least she was speaking to me. A little.

BY THURSDAY, I felt like I got my groove back. The days were filled with meetings, strategy sessions, and a lot of work. It was much like my time before, although now, I had somewhere I wanted to be at day's end.

Home with Katy.

I loved arriving home, knowing she would be there. I enjoyed our nights together, sitting, talking, and sharing our day. I craved the feel of her mouth beneath mine, and the way our bodies moved when we came together at the end of the evening—or earlier, as the mood dictated. We used various surfaces in the condo—the kitchen counter, the sofa, even the wall inside the door. My desk in the den was still one of my favorite places to take Katy. Dinner was often an afterthought—I couldn't get enough of my wife.

Tonight, I stopped and bought flowers for no reason except I wanted to show her I loved her. It was still an odd sensation for me to want to express an unfamiliar emotion like love, but I kept trying. I found Adrian a good sounding board for advice at times.

Entering the condo, I heard voices. I stepped into the main room, stopping when I saw Jenna sitting with Katy at the high counter separating the kitchen. An empty bottle of wine was between them, their glasses half-full. Jenna had left the office around two, and I suspected she'd been here since leaving. I bit back my grin as I strode across the room, handing Katy her flowers, kissing her hard. She beamed, eyes wide with happiness. I knew what it meant, Jenna being here. The silence from her had weighed heavy on Katy's heart, and it frustrated me I could do nothing to make it better. It was something they had to deal with between them—and the ball was squarely in Jenna's court.

"Shall I order some Chinese for dinner?" I asked, bending low, stroking her pink cheek. She always flushed when drinking. I liked kissing her skin when it was warm. So, I did—I trailed my lips over her cheek to the edge of her mouth, pressing against her full lips.

"Yes, please. And thank you for the flowers."

I placed another kiss to her tempting mouth and stood up.

"Two spring rolls"—I looked at Jenna—"or three?"

"Four," Jenna replied. "Adrian will be here in a while. I'm sure he'll be hungry, too."

"I'll get another bottle of wine."

Jenna shrugged. "Or two."

Chuckling, I squeezed her shoulders as I went past. "Good to see you, Jenna."

She dismissed me with a wave of her hand. "Whatever."

I caught her sly wink to Katy, however.

They started chatting again. I stopped in the hallway listening. Katy's laughter was low and happy. Jenna's voice was its usual excited tone as she told Katy about a new art exhibit we all had to attend together. I drew in a surprisingly shaky breath and smiled. My wife had her friend back.

Katy was slowly picking up the pieces of her life, which meant mine was aligning with hers. We were creating a new life.

Together.

Thirty-Four

RICHARD

J ENNA BENT FORWARD, tapping a mock-up. "I like this one."

I shook my head. "No, it's flat." I shifted through a pile of heavy stock, grabbing one near the bottom. "This one gets your attention."

"It's too in your face."

"It *needs* to be in your face, Jenna. We're selling fun here. It has to *grab* you."

She pursed her lips, and I took the chance to take a sip of my coffee. I'd been "back" for almost three months. My relationship with all the Gavins was on solid footing, both professionally and personally. My career had never been as fulfilling as it was now.

My life with my wife was amazing. Katy brought a peace to my world I never realized I was missing or needed. She was my nucleus, and everything I did revolved around her in some way. She spent her time volunteering, and two days a week, she worked at The Gavin Group—but not for me. She assisted Laura, and the two of them made a great team. It was a win-win situation for me since I could see her in the office and still have her at home.

Jenna pushed away the mock-up with an angry snort. "I still hate it when you're right."

I chuckled at her indignation. Before I could speak, her phone rang. She answered, another low groan made me grin at her level of frustration.

"Fine. No, I'll make other arrangements." She hung up, tossing her cell phone on the table.

"Problem?"

"My car is in the shop. The part is back-ordered and won't be here until tomorrow. Adrian is away and I need a lift home. I have to see if I can catch Dad."

"He left for a meeting right after lunch. He said something about heading home after he was done."

"Shit."

"I'll run you home."

"You sure?"

"Yep. I can swing by and pick you up tomorrow, too."

"Dad will drive me in. You don't have plans with Katy tonight?"

"No. In fact, she has her computer course tonight, so I'm free as a bird."

"Great. Thanks."

"Sure. Now, let's finish this, then I'll take you."

THE DRIVE WAS pleasant and quick. Having been there many times, I didn't need directions. Jenna, as usual, found lots to chat about, filling the time in the car with stories of looking for a new sofa.

She and Adrian lived on the edge of town in a new subdivision. It was close to the water, the homes large and set well apart. I liked the quiet, affluent look to the area.

After dropping Jenna off, I took a drive around the surrounding streets, admiring the houses and the peacefulness of the neighborhood. I slowed down, pulling to the curb in front of a house that caught my eye. The deep gray of the brick and the vivid blue trim stuck out in the area of more subdued colors. Two-storied with a huge wrap-around porch and large windows, it looked homey. What caught my eye, though, was the man pounding the *For Sale* sign into the ground. There was also a cylinder attached with a place to keep information sheets about the house. Without thinking, I was out of my car, walking toward him. He grinned at me when I asked for a copy.

"Those are still in the house. I need to grab them," he replied in answer to my query. "The owners aren't home, but I'm sure they wouldn't mind. Did you want a quick look?"

I looked back at the house, not at all certain why I was interested. Katy and I had never broached the subject of a house, or moving.

Except, I liked it.

"Yes, I would."

An hour later, I was back in my car, the information sheet clutched in my hand, another appointment booked for the morning. I wanted Katy to see this place.

SHE LOOKED OVER the sheet, confused. "A house? You want a house?"

I tapped the paper. "I want this house."

"Why? You don't like the condo anymore?"

I had been thinking about it all evening, while I waited for her to get home. "It's fine. I've always liked it. I was thinking, though, it's not a good place in which"—I nervously scratched the back of my neck—"to bring up children."

Her eyes widened.

"They need a yard to play in, yes? A place to run?"

She grinned, patting my hand. "Well, they aren't dogs, but yes, a yard for children is a good thing." She ran her tongue over her bottom lip, a mischievous smile curling her mouth. "Are you . . . are you pregnant, Richard?"

"No," I scoffed. "I was thinking one day, you would be."

She laughed, then turned serious. "One day in the near future?"

I inhaled a calming breath before replying. "If you wanted to be."

"*Richard*," she breathed out. "Are you sure?"

"I'm not saying tomorrow, or even next month. Eventually, yes, I want a family with you, Katy. However, I don't want to bring them up in a high rise. I used to wish for a yard instead of only being allowed to play at the park for a set amount of time. I want that for my children." I paused, clearing my throat. "Our children."

"Then I would love to go see this house with you."

"It's close to Jenna," I added.

"Is that a plus for you or a drawback?"

I smirked. "Depends on the day."

"You really liked this place?"

I nodded. "It's only two years old—the owner built it himself, so it's solid. His wife's been transferred which is why it's up for sale. It's open and light. Four good-sized bedrooms and a great office for me. It's got a well-equipped kitchen I think you'll love."

"Sounds great."

"The backyard is huge. Plenty of space for a pool, which I've always wanted. We'd have to fence it off, of course, but it's doable."

"It sounds as though you're ready to move in."

I wrapped an arm around her waist, pulling her close. "As long as you like it, I am. If you're happier here for the time being, then this is where we'll stay. If you want to look at other places, that's fine, too." I looked down at the picture. "There was something about this place I liked."

"I can't wait to see it myself."

KATY LOVED IT even more than I did. She went from room to room, opening closets and looking at fixtures. In the master bedroom, she gazed in silence at the view from the private balcony. We were close enough you could see the ocean. To the left and right of us, tall, thick trees surrounded the property. It was spectacular.

"You like it?"

"It's amazing," she murmured. "It's so peaceful."

I pointed to the break in the trees in the middle of the yard. "There's a path that leads right to the edge of the property. It's all open at the end. You can see the ocean for miles. It's like at your cottage. Your own little piece of paradise."

"Oh, Richard."

"I want to give you that."

She turned in my arms, her eyes luminous. Cupping her face, I drew her into me, kissing her full mouth.

"Let's go see some more, okay?"

"Okay."

The en suite was luxurious. The deep corner tub made me think of relaxing in the warm water with a glass of wine, and my wife nestled in my arms.

I drew her into my embrace, resting my chin on her shoulder. "I want you in that tub, Katy," I whispered, dragging my lips up her neck to her ear and nibbling on the lobe. "I want to make a huge puddle on the floor and hear the way my name echoes off these walls as you scream it."

She shivered, and I placed another kiss on her neck. I stepped back with a grin, holding out my hand. "Shall we keep looking?"

She narrowed her eyes at me, making me chuckle. I loved making her flustered.

The kitchen got the biggest response. I crossed my ankles, relaxing against the counter, watching her as she walked around. I always loved observing her reactions. She traced her hand over the richness of the wood cupboards, the cold of the quartz countertop and the sleek appliances.

"I could cook so many things here!" she exclaimed as she peeked in the double ovens, and sighed over the huge sub-zero refrigerator. "I'm not sure I'd ever leave this room!"

Meeting her eyes, I knew we'd found the next step in our journey together. I wanted to do this for her—for us. I wanted to give this to her. A home of her own, where she would feel safe. A place we could create memories that belonged to us and build a life.

I raised my eyebrows in a silent question. There was no hesitation in her nod. I knew we could look at other places; in fact, we probably should, but this one felt right. It felt like us.

Turning, I smirked at the agent, who was watching us with eager eyes.

"We'd like to make an offer."

I WAS CERTAIN my ears were going to burst when we shared our news with the Gavins a few days later. We invited them all for dinner and, after we ate, told them we purchased a house, and we would be living only a few blocks away from Jenna.

"The gray one?" She squealed. "With the bright blue trim? I love that house!" She threw her arms around Katy. "We're going to be neighbors!"

Katy beamed, her intense blue gaze finding mine. She had been smiling all day—joyful and laughing. Her eyes were peaceful, her happiness evident. I felt a sense of pride that was different from the kind I was used to experiencing. This had nothing to do with a job well-done, or praise for a campaign I had put hours into. This was personal pride based on the fact I had made another human being happy. A human being I loved more than I thought was possible.

I had done that.

Graham caught my eye, tilted his head toward Katy, and raised his glass in a silent toast.

I lifted mine, accepting his unspoken approval, knowing that for the first time, ever, I had earned it.

Thirty-Five

RICHARD

THE FAMILIAR ACHE formed by degrees in my head, my eyes became heavy, my shoulders and neck sore. I stared out the window at the gathering storm, wondering if I would make it home before it and the massive headache hit.

The three raps that Amy always used sounded like gunshots to my aching head. I slouched back against the cool leather of my chair, shutting my eyes.

"Come," I called as loudly as I dared.

"Do you need anything, Richard?"

I didn't bother to lift my head. "Can you cancel Board Tech?"

"I already did."

"Great. You might as well take off the rest of the afternoon, Amy. I'm going to be useless."

"Can I do anything else?"

I sighed, keeping my eyes closed. "If it wouldn't offend you, a cup of coffee and a couple of pain relievers would be appreciated. If you can get my wife on the phone, it would be great."

Her chuckle was low. "I think I can handle it, Richard."

"Thank you."

She left, and I rubbed my temples. I knew when I spoke with Katy, she would tell me to leave my car and grab a cab home. I also knew, when I got there, she would have cold compresses, much stronger pain pills, and her soothing touch to make the headache ease. I only had to get to her. The coffee and Tylenol Amy brought me would help until then.

I heard footsteps, felt pills pressed into my hand, and the smell of coffee hit my nose.

It wasn't Amy's voice that met my ears, however. "Drink."

I swallowed the pills gratefully and reached out blindly for my wife's hand.

"What are you doing here? You aren't scheduled to be in today."

"Amy called and said you were off this morning. She thought you had one of your headaches coming on, so I came to take you home. I intercepted her on her way back from the lounge."

With a groan, I bent forward, burying my head into Katy's stomach. The icy temperature of the compress felt good as she draped it across my neck and ran her fingers through my hair.

"We'll give the pills a bit to kick in, then I'll take you home."

"Okay."

"You should have called earlier," she scolded gently. "You know how these low-pressure storms affect you."

"I had work to do," I protested, tightening my arms around her waist, wanting her closer.

"And how much did you accomplish?"

"Not a lot."

"Good plan, then," she teased.

"Go fuck yourself, VanRyan," I muttered, using her favorite phrase.

She shook with suppressed laughter, never stopping her tender caresses.

"Thank you for coming to get me."

I felt the press of her lips to the back of my head. "You're welcome."

"Our boy unwell, Katy?" Graham's voice was low in the hush of the office.

"Bad headache."

"I wondered. He wasn't himself in the meeting this morning."

"Everyone knows me so well," I snipped, not lifting my head. "Can't a guy have a headache without everyone noticing around here?"

They both ignored me, as if I hadn't spoken.

"You're taking him home?"

"As soon as he feels up to it."

I waved my hand. *"He's* right here."

Katy patted my head. "He's always grumpy when he isn't well."

"I've noticed."

Laura's voice suddenly became part of the discussion. "Oh no, a headache? Poor Richard!"

I groaned. This was getting out of hand.

"I'm fine," I mumbled.

"He's grumpy," Graham stated. "Rather argumentative."

"He always is when the headaches hit him," Laura mused. "Good thing you're here, Katy."

"Do you need any help?" Jenna asked, the click of her heels announcing her arrival. "Maybe we could carry him to the car or something?"

I was done. Nobody was carrying me anywhere. They all needed to back off.

I lifted my head slowly, peeling open my eyes, fully intent on telling them all to leave. I met Katy's concerned gaze. She smiled, cupping my cheek, arching her eyebrow. I shifted my gaze to the people behind her, and nothing but worried and caring expressions met my stare. Graham leaned against the wall, looking amused, knowing how I hated being fussed over. All the anger drained away when I realized the people surrounding me were there for one reason only: they cared.

"I don't need to be carried anywhere," I grumped, dropping my head back to Katy's warmth. "Katy and I can manage fine."

"Make sure you wait long enough, so you don't blow chunks in her car," Jenna advised.

Her frankness made me chuckle.

"Good point."

"Call if you need anything, Katy."

"I will. Thank you, Graham."

"I'll assume you aren't coming for yoga tonight," Jenna mused.

"I'll let you know."

There was shuffling of feet and the quiet closing of my door.

"Are they gone?"

Katy lifted my chin, stroking my hair back from my forehead. "Yes." Bending low, she pressed a kiss to my skin. "They worry, my darling, that's all."

I smiled at her endearment. "I know. I'm still getting used to it."

"You're getting better. You didn't even curse at them."

I snickered. "That's because you were here."

This time it was her turn to snicker.

"You can go to yoga. I'll probably sleep."

"I'll decide later. Do you think you're up to the ride home?"

I cracked an eye open and nodded. "The pills are working."

"Okay, let's get you home."

I stood up, not surprised to see her already holding my briefcase. She was always a step ahead of me.

We made our way to the elevator, the hall deserted. I kept my arm around her, not only for the support she provided, but because I liked her close. In the car, I leaned my head back, shutting my eyes again, letting the cool seep back into my skin from the compress she tucked around my neck.

I slipped my hand over hers. "Thank you."

Her lips brushed mine. "Always."

I DREW IN a deep, bracing lungful of air. I loved living this close to the water. Katy had gone to yoga, and after I woke up, I came outside, grateful the storm had passed, taking with it the worst of my headache. I glanced around the backyard, thinking of the changes that had occurred in the months since we moved in.

A pool had been the first order of business, and it now sat to the one side, glistening and serene in the early evening light. Beside it was the pool house—Katy's favorite part of the backyard. It was the cottage she shared with Penny on their brief holidays; bright blue, with white shutters, her memories still intact. I had arranged with Bill to purchase it and have it transported here for her. Inside, it was remodeled and useful, but still held the same rustic appeal. Her reaction to seeing it had been emotional and deep.

"Come with me, Katy." I pulled at her hand, dragging her through the house. "I have something to show you."

She grinned. "Is the pool done already?"

"Almost."

I led her onto the deck, suddenly nervous. I had never done anything so sentimental in my life. I threw out my arm. "I got you a pool house."

She froze, staring at the hut I had bought, refurbished, and had installed on a cement foundation by the pool. The porch was rebuilt, the paint fresh to match the shutters of the house, but it was her cottage.

"Richard!" She gasped. "What . . . how?"

"It was important to you. I wanted you to have it."

She flung her arms around my neck, her tears hot and wet on my neck.

"Tell me these are good tears," I demanded quietly. I still hated when she cried. I never knew what to do when she did, or how to make things better.

"The best kind." She sniffed.

"I still don't like them. Stop, please."

"Thank you, Richard. I can't even tell you what this means to me." She gazed up at me, the love blazing from her eyes. "I love you."

I blinked at the sting behind my eyes.

"I love you."

Just the thought of her reaction still made me smile and brought warmth to my chest. The one only she could create.

The door opened behind me, and Katy's scent enveloped me as she came close, pressing a kiss to my head.

"Feeling better?"

"Much. Especially now you're home."

"Good."

"How was yoga? Take anyone out tonight?"

She laughed. "No, people know to stay clear of me now. I always thought yoga would help with my balance, but I seem resistant to that benefit."

I cast my eye over her as she moved in front of me. Her body was perfect: tight and toned. "I dunno, sweetheart. I sort of like the benefits." I patted my knee. "You could come over here and I can show you how much I like them, if you want."

She slid on, draping her arms around my neck. "You've been showing me how much you like the benefits a lot lately."

I skimmed my hand down her leg, curling it around her calf. "Just showing my appreciation."

She played with the ends of my hair, a nervous look crossing her face. I frowned. It reminded me too much of how she looked when we started.

"What's wrong?"

"Nothing's wrong, but I have something to tell you. I'm not sure how you're going to react."

"Just tell me."

She drew a deep breath. "I'm pregnant, Richard."

The air stilled around me. The breath caught in my throat, constricting and thick. Her words echoed in my head.

We'd had the discussions, agreed she should stop taking the pill, and I would wear condoms, then when we were ready, start a family.

"Uh . . ." *Were we ready?* "When?" I breathed out.

She cupped my face. "It's early. Really early. I think after the award dinner when we couldn't wait, and we celebrated in the car? We didn't use protection, my darling. It was only one time, but that's all it takes."

I managed to nod, remembering that night. My campaign for the Kenner Footwear company had won the highest award for the year. Graham had been thrilled and so proud—and so had I. I had celebrated hard with my wife.

Apparently too hard.

"Richard," she whispered. "Talk to me."

I waited for the panic. The anger. Except, when I gazed into the eyes of my wife, there was only one emotion I felt . . .

Elation.

I spread my hand over her still-flat stomach and grinned.

"I knocked you up."

"You did."

"Just the one time, eh? My boys are determined."

She arched her eyebrow.

"I'm going to be a father."

"You're going to be a *dad*. You're going to be a great dad."

I mulled over those words in my head. Not a father—a dad. I wouldn't be an absent figure from my child's life. I refused to allow that to happen.

"With you helping me, I will be."

"I won't let you fail."

"I know." Wrapping my hand around her neck, I drew her face to mine, kissing her reverently. "Are you all right?"

She nodded. "I'm fine. I see the doctor again in a few weeks."

"I'm coming with you."

"Okay."

"Maybe no more yoga. You may be even more off balance than usual."

She rolled her eyes, pushing on my shoulder. "Go fuck yourself, VanRyan."

I burst out laughing, pulling her close. That was my wife.

"I love you, my Katy," I murmured.

"I love you, too."

She curled up, and I held her close, returning my hand to her stomach. Looking down, I realized I now held my entire family within my embrace.

Everything, every moment of my life, had brought me to this point. The past was behind me, the darkness banished because of the woman I was holding, and the gift she had bestowed upon me.

The future was bright, and because of her and this one moment in time, it was filled with promise and light.

It was, as Penny once said, one of the great moments in time.

In fact, it was the greatest moment of them all.

About the Author

MELANIE MORELAND LIVES a happy and content life in a quiet area of Ontario with her beloved husband of twenty-six-plus years. Nothing means more to her than her friends and family, and she cherishes every moment spent with them.

Known as the quiet one with the big laugh, Melanie works at a local university and for its football team. Her job, while demanding, is rewarding as she cheers on her team to victory.

While seriously addicted to coffee, and highly challenged with all things computer-related and technical, she relishes baking, cooking, and trying new recipes for people to sample. She loves to throw dinner parties, and also enjoys travelling, here and abroad, but finds coming home is always the best part of any trip.

Melanie delights in a good romance story with some bumps along the way, but is a true believer in happily ever after. When her head isn't buried in a book, it is bent over a keyboard, furiously typing away as her characters dictate their creative storylines to her, often with a large glass of wine keeping her company.

Acknowledgements

A FEW WORDS of thanks.

To Meredith, Pamela, Sally, Beth, and Shelly
Thank you for your eyes, your support, and being such wonderful cheerleaders.
Hugs and snuggles to you.

Ayden, Carrie, Trina, and Suzanne, having you in my life is a blessing.
Your friendships mean more than I can express, and your unwavering belief in me keeps me going.
Much love to you all.

To my street team, Melanie's Minions—love you all!

To my ladies at Enchanted Publications—you rock. Thank you for the support.

Caroline, your help and support for this book is greatly appreciated.
Thank you is not enough, but it is all I have—well, that, and lots of love!

Jeannie McDonald—there are those rare instances when someone comes into your life for one reason, then becomes so much more than you expected. You, my girl, are one of those people. I am proud to call you friend, and thrilled you are in my life.
Thank you doesn't cover it. No words can. Love you.

To my editor and friend, Deborah Beck.

This book wouldn't have happened without your insistence that I allow Richard his voice. Thank you for pushing me. Your thoughts, red pen, and amusing comments have made my rambling words into a book I am proud of.

Mark another one complete, my friend.

And, as always, to my Matthew

Thank you for your patience as I bent my head over the keyboard and you lost me for hours while I typed away.

Your love and support is what keeps me strong.